BROKEN KING

RESTLESS KINGS BOOK 2

BELLA MATTHEWS

ASIN: B09DDH7NZB

Editor: Jessica Snyder, Jessica Snyder Edits

Copy Editor: Dena Mastrogiovanni, Red Pen Editing

Cover Designer: Jena Brignla

Photographer: Michelle Lancaster, Lane Photography

Model: Tommy Fierce

Interior Formatting: Savannah Richey, Peachy Keen Author Services

On my 16th birthday, I met my very own Scarlet. She was intelligent and beautiful, funny and totally badass. At 26, she had her life together in a way I hoped I one day would, and I decided then and there I wanted to be her when I grew up.

Deana – You are everything I've spent the last twenty years trying to be. An amazing wife and mother. A caring, compassionate, and loyal friend. And a successful businesswoman. Thank you for taking me under your wing all those years ago and for never letting me doubt myself.
I will be forever grateful for you.

Have enough courage to trust love one more time and always one more time.

— *MAYA ANGELOU*

PLAYLIST

- Demons – Live London Sessions - Imagine Dragons
- Try - Tyler Ward
- I still Love You - Josh Jenkins
- Story of My Life - One Direction
- When You Were Young - Benjamin Francis Leftwich
- With Or Without You - U2
- Love Again - Dua Lipa
- Still Falling For You - Ellie Goulding
- In The End - Linkin Park
- In My Veins - Andrew Belle
- I'm Gonna Be - Sleeping At Last
- You And Me - Lifehouse
- God's Gonna Cut You Down - Johnny Cash
- Make You Feel My Love - JJ Heller

https://spoti.fi/3gCmAMN

SENSITIVE CONTENT

This book contains sensitive content that could be triggering involving loss and grief.

SCARLET

"Amelia, I've got to go. I'm in the parking lot and need to go inside before I'm late." I love my sister. Although we only officially met her a year and a half ago, she turned out to be the missing piece of our fucked up family. But since my nephew was born a few months ago, she's so thrilled to talk to someone who isn't babbling nonsensically back at her, she's pretty hard to get off the phone.

"Okay. Are you still coming over after?" Maddox, my nephew, begins whining in the background, causing Amelia to jostle the phone.

It's been a long Friday. But I cut out of work early for this appointment and am definitely looking forward to drinks with my sisters. "Wouldn't miss it. See you then."

Amelia helps our sister Lenny and I even out the estrogen to testosterone ratio in our family.

It will never be even.

There are five guys to three women and one five-year-old diva.

But at least now, we're a little closer to a balance.

I enter my doctor's office, sign in, take a seat to wait, and pull out my tablet to scroll through the emails that have come through since I left the office. As the vice president of Public Relations and Marketing for the Philadelphia Kings, there's no such thing as time off, not even for a doctor's appointment.

It doesn't take long for me to clear out my inbox,

1

responding to those that were urgent and forwarding the rest to my assistant, Connor. However, in that short amount of time, the already crowded waiting room appears to have hit maximum capacity. The sea of pregnant women surrounding me seems to be closing in. When I switched from the pill to the shot a few months ago, I was looking for something a little more user-friendly. I'd tried a few different birth control pills over the last few years, and the side effects weren't for me.

The shot has been great.

Less migraines to deal with, and I'm a much happier woman.

It would be even better if I didn't have to come back in every few months.

But for now, it'll do.

When a woman, who looks to be about a hundred years pregnant, sits down next to me with a toddler covered in peanut butter and jelly by her side, I hug the opposite side of my chair and pray the nurse calls me quickly.

Don't get me wrong, kids are great. I love my nephew and my little sister.

But I love when I get to give them back too.

I'm not a woman who gushes over other people's kids.

Most babies look more like small aliens than perfect little angels.

This . . . I take stock of the waiting room around me and grimace.

This madhouse surrounding me today is just not for me.

Thirty minutes later, I'm sitting on the exam table in a stiff, pale-pink paper robe when my doctor finally walks in. "How are we doing today, Scarlet? I was expecting to see you two weeks ago for your follow-up." She pulls up my chart on her tablet, then sits down on her little stool on wheels.

"Sorry about the delay. I had to reschedule my appointment. Something came up with work. But I'm feeling fine, Doctor Esher. No complaints. Just ready to get this exam over with and get on with my night." Unless you count how damn cold it is in this room. I could easily complain about that. It's not like they don't know their patients are going to get naked in here. Would it kill them to turn the heat up just a tad?

Doctor Esher scrolls through what I'm guessing is my chart before rolling over toward the table. The smile that was on her face moments ago is gone, replaced by a purposefully blank expression. "Scarlet, have you had any issues since the last time you were here?"

"No issues. Not so much as a cough. Why? Is something wrong with my bloodwork? I wasn't supposed to be fasting, was I? Because I had coffee before I had it done the other day. I thought you said it didn't matter and we just needed to make sure the hormones from the shot didn't throw off anything else." I get migraines. Bad migraines. Sometimes debilitating ones. They started when I was in high school. I've tried every pill out there, and they all exacerbated the crippling headaches. The shot was my next best option. And as far as I'm concerned, so far, so good.

Doctor Esher clears her throat. "Scarlet, according to your bloodwork, you're pregnant."

I tilt my head to the side and study her. I don't think she'd kid about something so serious, but . . . "Is this a bad joke? I mean honestly, that really isn't funny."

Her face stays unmoving.

No reaction.

She's not laughing.

"Scarlet." Her tone has dropped an octave, no longer light

and airy like it was when she greeted me. "This isn't a joke. I wouldn't do that to you. According to your bloodwork from last week, you're pregnant. Judging by your hCG levels, I'd guess you're about thirteen to fourteen weeks along."

"I don't know what to tell you, Doc. But the draft was last month. I've barely had time to sleep, let alone sleep with anyone . . ." I trail off as I run through my mental calendar.

The draft was last month, yes. And the month before that was nonstop, go, go, go. It always is leading up to the draft, leaving no time for any extracurriculars. I was supposed to meet up with a friend of mine in March. He flies into Philadelphia for business every few months, but his trip was cancelled. And we never rescheduled.

I count back fourteen weeks.

But . . . *Oh, hell no.*

Hudson's title fight in Las Vegas was fourteen weeks ago.

Son of a bitch.

I wasn't concerned with a broken condom.

I was covered with the shot.

What are the odds that both forms of birth control would fail?

Apparently, higher than I knew.

"I can't be pregnant." I meet Doctor Esher's knowing brown eyes and cringe. "I would have known by now. Wouldn't I?"

I want to scream at her warm smile. "Not necessarily. At this point in a pregnancy, the telltale sign for most women is a missing period. But you already weren't having a monthly period to miss because of your birth control. It's still too early to feel the baby move for a few more weeks yet. And not everyone experiences morning sickness."

You've got to be kidding me. My chest tightens as the room begins to spin around me.

I am Scarlet fucking Kingston.

I am stronger than this.

I do not panic in public.

"Could you please run the test again? I have to believe there was a mistake." There. I sounded in control. Inside, I might be hyperventilating, but she doesn't need to know that.

Slow deep breaths.

That's better.

A mistake.

This has to be a mistake.

But even as I say it to myself, I think back to that night in Las Vegas and know there's no mistake. If ever there was a man whose sperm could leap tall buildings and blow their way past all hormones in one bound, it would be his.

By the time I knock on the front door of my sister Amelia's house, reality has begun to set in, but I'm having a hard time wrapping my head around it. My sister Lenny opens the door with our nephew, Maddox, in her arms and a slightly tense look on her face. "What the hell, Scarlet? Why are you so damn late? We were starting to get worried."

I push past her into the foyer and run my palm over the black peach fuzz covering Maddox's little head before we both walk into the kitchen. Amelia is slicing a loaf of warm, homemade bread, and the table is covered with enough meat, cheese, and fruit to feed all nine siblings, not just the three of us. I drop my purse on the chair and turn to face my sisters. "My doctor's appointment ran a little late because they wanted to do an ultrasound and confirm that I'm pregnant."

Lenny, who's been swaying with a sleepy Maddox on her hip, stops abruptly, upsetting the baby. "I'm sorry, but you're going to have to repeat that," she all but yells at me.

"You asked me why I'm late, and I'm telling you why." I pop a green grape into my mouth and point across the table between Lenny and Amelia, whose mouths both appear to be unhinged at the moment as they stand, staring at me in shock. "That's pretty much what I looked like when I was finally alone in my car for the proper fucking freak-out that was building the entire time I was in the doctor's office."

Lenny is younger than me by six years.

We weren't close growing up. My little sister never met a problem she couldn't run away from. We couldn't possibly have been more different. She had a luxury most of my siblings never knew. She grew up with two parents who loved each other and adored Jace and her. She was never a bargaining chip for more alimony like the rest of us were.

She was never part of a transaction.

But once she came back to Philadelphia, we worked through some of our differences.

After she finished her master's degree, Lenny moved home and started working for the professional football team our family owns, right around the same time she met her fiancé, Sebastian. Who happens to be Amelia's brother-in-law. Go fucking figure. "Holy shit, Scar. What are you going to do?" Len's voice is loud and carries throughout the kitchen.

She knows I've never wanted kids.

I love my life.

I love my career.

I love my family.

I never felt like anything was missing.

"You don't need to yell, Len. I'm freaking out enough right now. And I'd say you both know me well enough to know . . . I. Don't. Freak. The. Fuck. Out." The words may come out a little harsher than I intended, but I'm holding on by a thin string right now, and it's fraying quickly.

Lenny losing her cool is not going to help me stay calm.

"Umm. You don't get to play the ice queen over something this big, Scarlet." Len's also always been insanely dramatic. "Holy shit. The family is going to lose their minds."

Yeah. I've thought of that, and I'm already exhausted at what it's going to take dealing with all my siblings' reactions to this news.

Lenny drops down in a chair across from me while Amelia takes a sleeping Maddox from her and places him in his swing. In a soft voice, Amelia asks, "Do you know when it happened, Scar?"

"Forget when." Lenny reaches for a bottle of wine, then glances at me sheepishly and places it back on the table. "Who's the father, and are you going to keep it?"

One night.

I let myself have one night with him.

I've avoided him for years.

But apparently, one night was all it took for history to repeat itself.

Damnit.

SCARLET

"I LOVE YOU TOO, SWEETHEART. CAN YOU GIVE THE PHONE back to Aunt Rylie?" Cade St. James runs his hand through his unruly blonde hair while he stands off to the side of the small crowd. We're gathered in a room attached to where my brother Hudson is warming up for his big fight.

From the sounds of it, he's talking to his daughter.

I'm not at all surprised to see he turned out to be a good father.

I always knew he would be.

Even on a night like tonight, when half the world is watching, while he makes sure my younger brother Hudson is ready for his first title fight, he's making time for his little girl.

Damn him.

"Hey, Scar." Lenny's best friend, Jules, slides up next to me and hands me one of the two drinks she has in her hand.

I down the rocks glass, glad it was a Jack and Coke, and refuse to admit even to myself that being this close to that man is having any effect on me.

"Tell me who that fine man is standing next to Becket. Then please, please, please tell me he's single." Jules flew in this morning with Lenny, Sebastian, Becks, Max, and me on the Kings' jet.

Lenny and I run the Philadelphia Kings football organization with two of our brothers, Becks and Max. The four of us have been prepping for the draft that's happening in a few weeks, so we couldn't get out here yesterday for weigh-ins when the rest of the family flew in.

I did send my assistant, Connor, to be here in my place for the pre-fight conference and weigh-in. Thank God, they went smoothly. But I was on FaceTime, watching, ready to give instructions if they were needed. Public relations can get tricky.

They weren't this time.

Hudson was perfect.

Jules flips her hair, stunning as ever. Lenny and she modeled together for a hot minute in high school. Len hated it and never did it again. Jules has turned it into an enviable career and now, ten years later, is one of the top models in the industry. She's twenty-four and already has the ability to be choosy about the jobs she takes. However, none of that stops me from having to tamp down the desire to knock her skinny ass over when she asks about Cade.

"That man is Cade St. James. He's Hudson's trainer. He owns Crucible." When Jules tilts her head as if she has no idea what I'm talking about, I point out the sea of t-shirts Hudson's team is wearing with the words "Crucible Mixed Martial Arts" emblazoned across the front of them. "The gym where Hud trains," I add.

This seems to peak Jules's interest even more. "Ohhh. He looks like that, and he's successful? Yes, please."

Lenny joins Jules and me, wrapping an arm around Jules's waist. "Who are we stalking, ladies? You look like you're on the prowl."

"Not stalking. Scarlet was just filling me in on Hudson's trainer."

He's not mine.

He hasn't been in years.

He wasn't even a man then.

We were both kids.

I was fifteen the first time he kissed me and seventeen when I ended it. He'd just graduated from high school with my older brother Becket and Amelia's husband, Sam. Cade wanted to stop hiding our relationship, and I didn't. So I ended it. Two weeks later, he was gone. He'd enlisted in the marines.

I knew he was leaving. I knew we'd never have made it anyway.

I ended it before he could and didn't see him for nearly seven years after that.

Seven years we both spent growing up and into the adults we are now.

And even then, I only ever saw him from afar.

Cade bought Crucible from his father and, in what felt like a blink of an eye, was the MMA heavyweight champion.

All that was before his daughter, Brynlee, was born. I've heard rumors of the gossip surrounding Cade and his daughter, but I don't know the real story. I'm sure Hudson or Becket know, but I've never wanted to ask.

None of my siblings have any idea that there was ever anything between Cade and me, and I'd like to keep it that way.

All that to say, after all these years, you'd think the idea of Jules being interested in him wouldn't make me irrationally angry . . . But you'd be wrong.

Lucky for me, I'm saved by the bell when someone comes in, alerting everyone that it's nearly time for Hudson to head out to the octagon so we should all go find our seats. Hudson is on the other side of the closed door separating the rooms I just saw Cade walk through.

"Come on, Scarlet. It's time to go." Lenny tugs on my arm as her fiancé wraps his around her waist.

"I'll meet you there, Len. I've got to go speak with Imogen for a minute." She nods and walks away as I knock on the door and am let through.

When I enter the room, Hudson is sitting on the floor.

His long legs are spread out in front of him.

A set of noise-canceling headphones cover his ears.

Eyes closed. His head leaning back against the wall.

Imogen isn't too far away. She's Cade's younger sister, and she runs Crucible. Generally, they keep all the marketing and PR for the gym and their fighters in-house. But most of their fighters don't have a PR queen like me in their corner. Not only do I run the Marketing and Public Relations Department for the Philadelphia Kings football team, but I oversee the marketing and PR for King Corporation as well. I've got more connections in the professional sports world than most publicists could ever dream of.

And I refuse to leave my little brother's career to anyone else.

Imogen wasn't thrilled by that.

I didn't care.

"Gen." I tap Imogen on the shoulder and interrupt the conversation she's having with one of the guys in a Crucible t-shirt. "I don't want any interviews. No questions. Nothing until after we've all had time to regroup. The only questions he's allowed to answer are those asked by the announcer in the ring, which he's contractually obligated to do. Got it?"

Imogen rolls her pretty green eyes. "I got it, Scarlet. I had it when you told me earlier today. I had it when you emailed me earlier in the week. I even had it when Connor repeated it two hours ago. No interviews." She may continue speaking, but I tune her out. Hudson has stood and is warming up. He's going through the motions with Cade. Hud doesn't look at all like that little boy who used to secretly hide in the closet, hoping for the chance to jump out and scare me.

He's a grown man now.

And God help his opponent tonight.

"Scarlet . . ." Imogen says my name as if waiting impatiently for an answer.

Shit. "Sorry, what was that?"

Another eye roll.

Jesus, someone needs to teach this woman how to school her features. Every thought she has is plastered across her face. "Was that everything, Scarlet?"

Once I pull my eyes away from my brother again, I nod and turn to walk out of the room but hear my name called out by Hudson. "Scarlet . . . No good luck?"

Every eye in the room is on me now as I walk slowly toward Hudson. Even standing in front of my brother in four-inch heels, he still towers over me. "Got any words of wisdom, Scar?" He leans in and kisses my cheek, then puts his taped hands in front of me.

I tap knuckles with Hud, then look over at Cade as he takes a step closer to us. "Of course, little brother." I lean in and whisper in his ear, "Fucking eviscerate him," then stand tall and add, "You've got this. I'll see you afterward. And Hud . . ."

"Yeah, I know. No interviews until you're with me."

I smile and turn to leave, but I'm stopped by Cade. "You walking out there alone, Scarlet?"

"I'm a big girl, Saint. I think I can manage."

A muscle in Cade's jaw flexes before he yells over to his cousin, "Jax. Escort Scarlet to her seat. Make sure she gets there safely." As if dismissing me, he turns back to Hudson, and they go back to what looks like a dance of sorts to continue warming up his muscles.

By the time I take the last open spot, next to my oldest

brother, Max, in the front of the cage that's set up for tonight's spectacle, the lights are beginning to lower, and the music has changed.

A tremor of anticipation runs down my spine.

Showtime.

CADE

Standing in the velvet-roped-off section of the VIP area of the club where we're celebrating Hudson Kingston's KO tonight really brings home the fact that I'm getting fucking old.

The lights in the club are flashing. The music is too fucking loud, and there are way too many goddamn people in here for me to relax. This isn't my scene anymore.

Who the fuck am I kidding?

This hasn't been my scene in a long time.

Not in the three years since my daughter was born.

More accurately, since she was deposited on my doorstep by her waste-of-space mother, who thought, since I didn't want a relationship with her, that she'd get back at me by keeping her pregnancy a secret. That worked for the duration of the pregnancy, but once Brynlee was born, her mother decided she was more work than she wanted to handle. She marched into Crucible one night and handed me the car seat with my baby girl inside and an envelope with her birth certificate, listing me as the father, tucked neatly up against a blanket.

The rest is history.

"Saint . . ." Becket Kingston calls out over the loud music as he makes his way to my side of the roped-off space and hands me another beer. "Good job, man. Hudson was a beast out there. What a fight."

"That was all Hud." I tap my beer to his. "He earned it." I

take a pull from my bottle as my eyes stray to watch Becks and Hud's sisters out on the dance floor with Lenny's friend.

Not sisters. More like *one* of their sisters.

I don't care who she's dancing with.

Scarlet fucking Kingston is all I can see.

Becks would kill me if he knew we'd dated in high school. She begged me to keep it quiet, so I never said a word. Her mother refused to let her date, so I agreed to keep us on the down-low. It's not what I wanted. But it was what she needed, so I went along with it. Once I was out of school, I tried to convince her to let me tell her brother. I wanted her to wait for me to get out of the marines. But Scarlet wasn't interested in doing the long-distance thing or outing us to her family.

I guess I wasn't as important to her as she was to me.

I can't blame her. We were too young.

By the time my enlistment was up, we'd both moved on.

I should know. I looked her up when I got home.

She was seeing some corporate douche from the stock exchange.

Life goes on.

"So where's your woman tonight, Becks? I figured she'd be here with you." Beckett turns around and leans against the railing behind us. His eyes track mine, and I hesitate momentarily.

"You eyeing up Jules, Saint? She's got the soul of a hippie and the ambition of a president," Becks says with a bit of awe in his voice.

Jules may be gorgeous, but she's not the woman who's caught my eye. No. It's easier to let Becks think that though. But it's hard to take my eyes off the beautiful woman dancing with her. Long, dark-brown hair with flecks of deep red cascades in waves down her back. Her tight, black dress dips low in the front and hugs every sinful curve.

Curves that weren't there the last time my hands skimmed up her body.

"Nice dodge there, King. Your woman? Where is she?" Becks has been seeing a woman for over a year. Problem is, none of his family like her. I've met her a few times, and I don't like her either. But she seems to make the dumb fuck happy, so we go along with it.

"She's prepping for a big trial that starts Monday."

Sawyer Kingston walks over to the two of us, having caught the tail end of our conversation. "Thank fuck for that. She sucks, Becks. Kendall sucks. She's sucking the life out of you. She's sucking the fun out of you. I think she may be a closeted vampire. Why are you still with her?"

No way am I getting involved in this fight. Instead, I walk away and check my phone.

My older sister, Rylie, and her wife, Jillian, are watching Brynlee for me for a few nights. She's been sending me pictures. When I make my way out of the club and into the hall of the casino, the noise buzzing in my head begins to quiet as I stand there, scrolling through the images she sent tonight. Looks like they made homemade pizzas. Brynlee's smile stretches across her cherubic face. Content with her aunts. Completely covered in red sauce.

Once I've seen them all, I contemplate calling it a night when a whiff of familiar perfume transports me back in time.

Vanilla and spice. I didn't realize at the time the spice was bourbon.

As a teen, I just knew it smelled like Scarlet.

As an adult, it's haunted me every time I've sipped a glass of my favorite whiskey.

Scarlet leans next to me against the wall, looking over my shoulder. A gorgeous sparkle in her dark-blue eyes. "How old is she now, Saint?"

A man could get lost in those eyes.

I should know.

I spent enough time doing it.

"She's three going on thirteen." I offer her a closer look at my phone. Our fingers brush, and a frisson of electricity shoots through them when she takes the phone from my hand and holds it closer to her face.

"She's adorable, Cade." A guarded smile pulls at her perfectly painted red lips. "She looks just like you." Scarlet hands me back my phone, the connection of her hand lingering on mine. "I guess it's hard to be so far away from her."

"This is the first time I've gone further than a car ride away since Brynlee came to live with me," I admit and lean my head back against the wall.

Scarlet closes the small distance between us, her arm resting against mine. Even in those fuck-me, red-soled shoes, she only comes up to my shoulder, where her beautiful head leans momentarily. It's the first time we've touched in thirteen years, and my cock jumps to attention, wanting more. "What are you doing here, duchess? Shouldn't you be in the other room celebrating with your family?"

The nickname falls from my lips before I think better of it.

I made the mistake of calling Scarlet "princess" once.

She was furious with me. Asked me if she looked like a helpless princess.

She didn't.

Even back then, she seemed older and more serious than the other girls in school.

She steps back, turning herself to face me. Her delicate hands straighten my black shirt, scorching my skin as she plays with my top two buttons.

Muscle memory kicks in, and I rest my hands on her hips, wishing there wasn't a layer of silky fabric separating us.

"What if I told you I didn't want to go back into that club with everyone?" She steps into my chest and raises up on her toes. "What if I told you that for one night . . ." Those midnight-blue eyes study my face, begging me for something I don't know if I can give. "Just one night, Cade. I want to be upstairs. I want to be celebrating with you. Let's wind back the clock for one night. Tomorrow, we can turn back into strangers."

"Are you drunk, Scarlet?" I need to know the answer before I say anything else. For my sake and hers. If this wasn't her . . . If it wasn't Scarlet Kingston standing in front of me, I'd turn her down. I don't do one-night stands.

But it is her.

The one that got away.

The one I still think about when I jack myself off in the shower.

"No, Cade. I don't get drunk." Her chin lifts just a bit higher, and I get a brief glimpse into why she's called the "ice queen" now.

This woman can put on as cold of an exterior as she wants, but I've felt her on the inside. She's no ice queen.

"We don't have to turn back into strangers tomorrow, Scarlet." I pull her against me and run my nose up the side of her neck before she takes a small step back.

"Strangers tomorrow is all I'm offering." She turns from me and takes a few steps away. "Take it or leave it, Saint." Scarlet reaches inside her sparkly silver purse and pulls out a hotel key card. Then, holding it down by her side, she slowly sashays away.

And like a moth to the flame, I follow.

SCARLET

THE HAIRS ON THE BACK OF MY NECK ARE STANDING ON EDGE from the crazy electricity bouncing between Cade and me as he follows me to the elevator. But it's not until we're standing in the crowded elevator, traveling up to the thirty-sixth floor, that I give myself permission to study his sculpted face. To explore those green eyes that stare straight ahead instead of at me.

My fingers ache to trace the hard lines of his face and run through his blonde hair.

I stare at him, willing him . . . silently begging him to look at me.

But he doesn't.

Two floors up, a group of rowdy young guys from a bachelor party, judging by their conversation, enter the elevator and take it from crowded to uncomfortable. Cade moves his body behind mine and angles us away from the drunk men. He was always protective. And being this close to him feels more dangerous than those frat boys ever could.

But now, with his breath on my neck, and the masculine, salt-water scent of him enveloping me, I don't feel protected. No. The only thing I feel is need.

The match has been lit, and now he's fanning the flame.

The question is, does he even realize what he's doing?

Could he possibly want this as much as I do?

I step back, closing the distance between us.

The soft silk of my dress pressing up against the front of his pants.

Rubbing up against his undeniably hard dick.

The elevator moves so slowly, stopping every few floors. Yet somehow, not slow enough. I grind back into him and tilt my head slightly so I can see his gorgeous green eyes.

Cade sucks in a breath and grabs my hips with both hands.

One more swish of my hips, and his arm bands tightly around my waist.

Holding me still.

Holding me tightly to his chest.

Out of the corner of my eye, I see one of the younger guys openly staring at us, but I can't bring myself to care. My core pulses with need, and I wrap my arms around Cade's before I shimmy again.

Hot lips graze my ear. "Is this show for me or for him, duchess? Because I don't share."

Those words shouldn't send a thrill down my spine, but they do.

As the elevator empties floor by floor, Cade's hands grow bolder. By the twenty-eighth floor, it's just us and an older couple in front of us. One callused palm slides up my bare leg as the other grazes the curve of my breast, the touch eliciting a small moan. Fortunately, the two people standing close to the elevator doors don't turn around.

Probably scared to see what we're doing back here.

As the last of the people in the elevator step off on the thirty-third floor, I turn into Cade's body. His legs are spread wide. Black pants stretch across thick thighs. Strong hands are on my body. A chunky silver watch is showing on his wrist from where his sleeve is rolled up. His black collared shirt is pulled tight across a broad chest, covering muscles I studied from the safety and solitude of my home every single time one of his fights was televised years ago.

I've wanted this man for years. I've strategically kept my distance until now. I knew my willpower wouldn't be able to stand up to the undeniable pull he's always had on me. It's why I've stayed away. Cade St. James is like a drug.

He promises the highest high.

An addictive high.

I lay my palms flat against the planes of his chest. "Do you think this is a mistake?" Maybe we're better off leaving the past in the past.

There's no doubting the disappointment that flashes in his green eyes before he pushes me up against the elevator wall. "Do you really think that, Scarlet?" His strong hands snake behind my neck. "Do you think this is a mistake? Because I don't. I want you so fucking bad, duchess." I'm not sure who moves first, but our lips crash together in a tangle of teeth and tongues. One knee nudges my legs apart, and I shamelessly grind against his thick thigh as my arms circle his neck.

The ding of the elevator doors opening faintly registers in my mind before he lifts me into the air with my feet dangling beneath me. "What room number?" is mumbled between kisses.

"Two down from here," I pant. "3602." I try to wrap my legs around him, but my dress is too tight.

When he turns his head to see where we're going, I lick a trail from his collar up to his ear, then scrape along the lobe with my teeth. A shiver wracks his body, and I make a mental note to do that again.

Cade takes the key from my hand and easily opens my door before throwing it on the table to our right. He doesn't turn on the lights, just lets the glow of the Vegas strip drifting in from my suite's floor-to-ceiling windows illumi-nate the room.

When the door clicks shut behind us, he sets me on my feet. One callused hand moves back to my face while the other spans the width of my back, fisting my dress. My mind struggles to stay in the present when flashes from over a decade ago play out in my memory.

Him fisting my dress after a prom we both attended with other people.

So much the same, yet so different.

Desperate to feel his skin against mine, I start working on the buttons of his shirt while he sucks on the pulse point of my neck. The heat in my body grows from a small fire to a towering inferno with every press of his tongue and suck of his lips.

"Is this what you wanted, duchess?" His words hold an edge of barely disguised anger. But all my thoughts evaporate when his hands slide back up my body, bringing my dress with them, the cool air teasing my hot skin.

Frenzied, I need more. "Yes. God, yes." I stand there, bared to him, in a red lace bra and thong, my heels still on. Needy. Aching. "Cade . . ."

He gives me a groan of approval before picking me up and sitting me on the table, then dropping to his knees.

My hands grip the edge of the table, fingers biting into the wood.

When his hands skim back up my legs, goosebumps break out over my heated flesh. His fingers play with the strings of my panties before he tears them from my body. Literally snaps the strings of my thong with his bare hands. "Holy shit, that's hot."

Cade doesn't acknowledge my words.

No, he's a man on a mission. And I think I'm the prize.

His nose glides up my thigh, followed by his tongue.

And oh, God. I need more.

Need takes over as he places my leg over his shoulder, leaving me altogether at his mercy when his tongue licks up the length of my pussy before he sucks my clit into his hot mouth.

My head falls back against the wall, and a moan escapes my lips as my hands find purchase in his blonde hair.

Already on the verge of coming apart.

"Right there," I hum my approval as he licks slow and heavy, adding one blunt finger, then another. "Don't stop," I pant breathlessly as I grind without shame against his face. "More. I need more."

As if insulted, Cade pulls back and stands up. "I know what you need."

I'm thrown over his shoulder, and a quick smack comes down hard on my ass as I'm carried through the suite. Once we're in the bedroom, I'm tossed down onto the king-sized bed with a bounce, my stinging ass cheek forgotten.

I don't like being manhandled.

I don't let men do that.

I'm in charge. In my life and especially in the bedroom.

I never give that up.

But it's different with Cade.

It always was.

Before I can dwell on that thought, he shrugs out of his shirt and pants. And I can't help but stare at his cock standing proudly at attention.

Is it possible that it's bigger than I remember?

My mouth waters at the thought.

Cade grabs a string of two condoms from his wallet and throws them down on the bed. "Awfully confident, thinking you're going to need two condoms, Mr. St. James." I sit up and run my fingers through my wet pussy, then lightly circle my peaked nipples. His eyes track my every movement with a beautifully hungry look on his face.

"I don't think two is going to be enough, Ms. Kingston," he answers, in a similarly teasing tone, then prowls closer to me on the bed. Cocky and confident, his eyes dance across my body. "But I'm sure there are other ways I can satisfy you once we've used these."

Cade drags me down the bed by my ankle as his body covers mine. Firm lips close over my nipple, and strong hands wrap around my back as we're flipped over in one smooth move.

My legs straddle his, and his thick cock rests between us.

My core clenches in need. I reach down and take him in my hand. Velvety steel. I pump him once . . . then twice as his lips find mine, feasting on them like I'm the most decadent thing he's ever tasted.

I mewl against his mouth.

Needing more.

Squirming.

Knowing exactly what I'm doing to him as he grows impossibly harder in my hand.

When his large palm cups my breast, bringing it to his mouth, my walls clench in anticipation. I need this man. Right now.

Letting go, I lean back and grab a condom, rip it open, and move from his lap to roll it down his shaft. "I'm drenched, Cade. That's enough foreplay." But of course, I don't miss the chance to lick his dick from root to tip teasingly before sliding the condom on.

Cade's eyes roll into the back of his head when I climb back up onto his lap and position myself over his cock, letting it slide through my soaking wet pussy with ease before I take him inside me. "Jesus Christ, Scarlet," he groans, and I preen, knowing I've done that to him.

He sits up, wraps his arms around my back, and fucks me.

I might be on top, but he's in control.

Moving me with ease.

Pulling me down with each upward thrust of his body.

Reminding me what it's like to be fucked by a real man.

My brain is at war with my body.

Wanting to take back control but loving the feel of being at the mercy of this man.

In an attempt to take back some semblance of power, I lean back in his arms and brace my hands behind me against his thighs, helping myself to a better angle. An angle that offers my breasts up on a silver platter to be devoured by his mouth. His teeth scrape my nipple, and lights flash behind my eyes. But I need more. "Harder, Cade."

When he changes his angle to give me what I want, it causes him to brush up against that delicious spot that has my entire body teetering on the edge. "Oh, yeah. That's it."

"You've gotten more vocal, duchess. Tell me what you want." The deep timbre of his voice is so fucking sexy.

"I want you to make me come. I'm so close. I need to come, Cade."

He grabs my legs and wraps them around his waist, changing our angle again and stealing back that little bit of control I had. He slips a hand between us and circles my clit as he fucks me hard and slow, making sure I feel every inch of him and prolonging every single second of ecstasy.

Sleeping with Cade St. James may be the dumbest thing I've done since I was seventeen, but as my orgasm washes over me, I can't bring myself to care.

We can go back to being strangers tomorrow.

His lips lower to the curve of my neck as he pulls me down over him once more and comes on a sexy groan.

I let my fingers dance through his hair while he continues to hold me close.

I permit myself a few moments to bask in the feeling of being held. It's not something I typically allow. It's intimate, and I don't do intimate. But being in this man's arms stirs up too many emotions. Fucking is one thing. Cuddling is an entirely other level of intimacy that won't be happening.

When I walk over to grab the champagne from the minifridge, Cade sits up to remove the condom.

"Shit," he grunts.

Why are men such babies about condoms? I just don't get it. "Something wrong?"

His dark-green eyes grow concerned as they search mine. "The condom broke."

Yup. Babies. "Don't worry. I've got us covered, and I'm clean."

His shoulders visibly relax. "Yeah. Me too."

"Then you better get back over here." I turn to face him with the bottle in my hand. "The Kings' jet leaves early tomorrow. So I've only got a few hours before I turn into a pumpkin."

"Yes, ma'am." His accompanying grin is so sinfully sexy, I wish we had more time.

Or maybe more condoms.

CAD E

ONE OF THE FIRST THINGS THE MARINES BEAT OUT OF YOU AS A new recruit is your need to sleep. Your first oh-four-hundred wake-up call may come as a shock to the system, but you adjust. I've learned since then that my drill instructor had nothing on my daughter. When Brynlee was an infant, she refused to sleep for longer than two hours at a time. It's a little better now, but she's still a prickly sleeper. So when my phone dings at four-thirty, alerting me to an incoming text, it doesn't surprise me to see a picture of Brynlee and Jillian making pancakes.

Cade: Thanks Ry. Give Brynn a kiss for me.
Cade: I'll be home tonight.
Rylie: Have fun, little brother. She's been a perfect angel.
Rylie: See you soon.

Once my phone is back on the nightstand, I reach for Scarlet and pull her naked body back against mine. Our bodies fit together perfectly, as if we were made for each other, and I relax back into the mattress with her spicy vanilla scent surrounding me. We may have used both condoms last night, but there are other ways I can make her come. I gave her a preview of a few of those ways last night.

She's soft and pliant in my arms as she sleeps. That is, until my lips skim along her shoulder blade, and she groans and pulls away. I guess Scarlet isn't a fan of being woken up.

But of course, we never got to do the waking up together thing when we dated back in high school.

"What time is it?" she groans as she rolls over to face me. One eye squints open. The other is covered by her dark hair.

"It's a little after 4:00 a.m.," I whisper softly as I tuck a lock of hair behind her ear.

I'm waiting for her to melt back into me.

I have enough time to make her come at least twice more before doing the walk of shame back down to the peasant-level rooms a few floors below. But when she sits up, bringing the sheet with her, the soft and pliant body from a moment ago is gone.

In its place is something that looks a lot harsher.

Colder.

She stands slowly from the bed, wrapped in her sheet, and looks down at me like I'm a stick of gum stuck on the bottom of her very expensive shoes. "I think it's time for you to go, Cade."

What the fuck? "Scarlet." I let her name linger in the stale hotel air that still carries the scent of sex. "What are you talking about? We've got plenty of time."

"I'm sorry, Cade." She bends down and starts to gather my clothes. "Last night was fun. You were great. But strangers come morning, remember?"

"Last night was fun? You can't be serious? I'm not some dick you picked up at a club." I stand and pull on my boxers, waiting for an explanation that seems less likely to come with every passing second.

The lights of the Las Vegas strip filter in, catching the glints of red in her hair. I itch to run my fingers through it again . . . until she speaks.

"That's exactly what you were, Cade. It was fun. We both got what we wanted. Don't try to turn it into something it wasn't. I had fun. You had fun. And now we go back to being strangers. We've done a good job of that for a long time. It shouldn't be too hard." She glides over to the door and opens it, looking like a damn sexy Grecian goddess, wrapped in her white sheet.

As if taking a side kick to the chest, I stand in place, staring at this woman I let back in for a few hours and realize that she's still the same person who cut me out of her life with ease once before. Why am I surprised she'd dismiss me now? "Wow, Scar. I guess some things never change. You really are the ice queen everyone says you are."

"You would know, Cade."

The door shuts quietly behind me, and I'm left in the bright light of the empty hall, wondering what the hell happened between last night and now. I look around to make sure I'm not giving anyone a show as I slip my shirt back on and carry my shoes toward the elevator.

During the entire walk back to my room, I'm wondering what happened.

How exactly did we go from lovers to enemies in the two hours since we fell asleep?

And why am I surprised?

SCARLET

JUDGING BY THE LOOKS ON EACH OF MY SISTERS' FACES AS I finish telling them my story, I'm reasonably sure I've just blown their minds.

Or maybe that's just me projecting.

My mind has definitely been blown, and I'm still trying to put it back together so I can wrap it around a baby.

A baby.

It doesn't seem real. And yet, I know it is. I saw her heartbeat. I heard it. She's real, and my world is about to change in ways I never imagined.

Once I grab a piece of the warm bread from the charcuterie board, I start anxiously ripping it up and stuffing it in my mouth before glaring at Amelia. "So, how long do I have before I get fat?"

"Umm . . ." She stares blankly back at me, most likely trying to gauge whether it's safe to tread around the landmine I've just dropped at their feet. "When are you due?"

"October fourteenth," I groan as the throbbing in my temple starts back up. "Because having a baby in the middle of the football season shouldn't be a big deal at all, right?" Sarcasm might be the lowest form of wit, but it's all I've got right now. I think I'm going to be processing this for months before it all makes sense.

Here's hoping I've wrapped my head around it by the time she's here.

Lenny leans toward me, moving the charcuterie board aside. Hesitance is written all over her face. "Ummm, Scarlet? Have you decided to keep it?" She glances from Amelia back to me. "I didn't think you wanted kids. I mean, it's a big decision."

Amelia slides her hand across the table and wraps her fingers around mine. "And we'll stand by you, no matter what."

"I never thought I wanted kids either. But the doctor did this thing where I got to hear the baby's heartbeat, and . . ." I let that thought hang in the air as I try to put words to my warring emotions. She's real, but reality hasn't set in yet. "I don't know. Hearing that tiny little heartbeat . . . I know I have options. My brain knows that. But my heart made the decision for me—as if there was no other option at all. Besides, it's not like I'm a scared teenager with no way to give my daughter a good life or a good home."

Not this time.

With shaking hands, I reach into my purse and pull out the sonogram picture the doctor gave me earlier. Placing it gently on the table, I smile at my sisters. "Now, what kind of voodoo do we have to do to make sure she's a girl?"

Kingston Family Group Text

Max: We need a family meeting. Can you be available tomorrow?

Becks: Dinner at the house?

Jace: Nope. I've got a date tomorrow night.

Becks: Does she know you wet the bed till you were 10?

Jace: Fuck off Becket!

Scarlet: Brunch?

Hudson: Works for me.

Max: Sounds good. Let's do ten at the house.

Sawyer: What's with the meeting? Who fucked up?

Lenny: What did you do Becket?

Becks: Why do you assume it's me?

Hudson: Because it's always you, asshole.

Max: Not this time. It's King Corp. business. Just be at the house at ten.

Max: I'll explain everything then.

I've always loved driving down the winding driveway of Kingston Manor in May. The pink cherry trees are in full bloom, lining either side of the brick driveway while the house looms in the distance, the flowery scent catching on the warm breeze. It's a beautiful sight to behold.

The epitome of spring.

A fresh start.

Pure.

Okay, so obviously, I've spent too much time over-thinking things this weekend. Searching for signs and deeper meanings. Lenny wasn't exactly wrong when she said I never wanted kids. I've spent the last ten years not wanting them. I just never saw myself as a mother.

My life, career, and independence mean everything to me. They're the stick I measure my success by. I love that I have the ability to pick up and do whatever I want, whenever I want. And I know that's going to change when the baby comes. If I hire a nanny, the change could be minimal. But I don't want to have a nanny raise my baby the same way my mother relied on nannies to raise Max, Becket, and me.

Max and Becket are older than me. Sawyer and Hudson are next after me. Amelia is between Hudson and Lenny, with Jace rounding out the semi-adult Kingstons. Our youngest sister, Madeline, is the baby of the family. Everyone should be here for brunch today.

We all share the same father with a mix of five different mothers. I never had any illusions that the late, great John Joseph Kingston was a saint. But it sure shocked the hell out of all of us when we found out that there was a missing Kingston sister out there. It turns out, dear old Dad didn't know she existed either. But once he died, and the search was left to us, we spared no resource in our quest to find our missing sister.

We protect what's ours, and Amelia was ours.

Luckily for us, fate turned out not to be the fickle bitch she usually is. Amelia had started her new life in Kroydon Hills, just minutes away from our late father's estate, where a few of my siblings still live.

I've been trying to convince myself that fate is on my side all weekend. I've spent the last few days closed off from everyone. Ignoring calls and texts, trying to consider all my options. But I realized something late last night. There are no options for me. My brain will not sway me one way or the other because my heart has made the decision for me. It was easy to think I didn't want kids before.

But now . . .

Now that I've heard her heartbeat.

Now that she isn't some hypothetical child, I want her desperately.

And that scares me to death.

Almost as much as the idea that I'll have to tell Cade St. James I'm pregnant with his baby is still rocking me to my core.

Maybe fate is a bitch after all.

I was a mess when Cade left for the marines. I was the one who ended things between us. How could it possibly work with him halfway across the world? I was seventeen, and watching the disintegration of my parents' marriage, followed by my mother man-bashing every chance she got and my father cheating on his second wife too, convinced me there was no hope. I didn't want to end it. I just thought it would be easier.

I was wrong.

Not that I ever told him that.

I was an absolute wreck after he left.

My life changed that summer, and I spent my senior year of high school a shell of myself. It wasn't until I left for college the following year and got into therapy that I started to work through my issues. It's the one and only time in my life I've allowed a man to have the ability to destroy me.

I learned from that mistake and never repeated it again.

I refuse to need anyone. The only person I can rely on is me. With the occasional help of a sibling or two . . . or eight.

When I pull up in front of the oversized garage, I see Amelia and Sam are already here, getting Maddox out of the car. And judging by the cars parked beside them, we're the last to arrive. Just as my heels hit the bricks, my youngest brother, Jace, opens the side door of the house. "Come on, guys. You're the last ones here, and I'm fucking starving."

"Jace," Amelia hates when we curse in front of Maddox. It's kinda funny considering he's not even a year old.

"He can't talk yet, Amelia." His smile vanishes when he looks over our sister's head at her very intimidating husband, then changes his tune. "Sorry, Amelia."

Jace comes down the steps and takes the baby from her arms. "Come on, Mad man. Let's go see what trouble we can get into." Maddox giggles and grabs Jace's hair in his pudgy little fist and tugs.

Sam watches the two of them head into the house with a glare plastered on his chiseled face, then glances over at Amelia and me. "We're going to have to limit how much time Maddox spends with that one."

The three of us make our way to the kitchen, where everyone is gathered and making their plates. Our family has grown over these past few years. Now, when we sit down to a family meeting or meal, there are thirteen of us, including my youngest sister and her mother, as well as Amelia's husband and Lenny's fiancé.

I guess it will be fourteen by this time next year.

Max stands and clears his throat once we all take our plates into the dining room. "Thanks for coming on such short notice today. I know everyone's busy, so I'll try to make this quick. Everyone in this room has a stake in King Corp.," he glances at our sisters' significant others, "in one way or another. I was approached last week by Will Brenner."

"The owner of the Philadelphia Revolution?" Jace is practically foaming at the mouth at the mention of the Cup-winning hockey team he loves. "What did he want?"

Max leans his hands against the table in a power move I recognize from sitting in business meetings with him for years. "He wanted to know if King Corp. would be interested in purchasing the team from him. He's made a few bad business deals, and I believe his last attempt to keep himself above water is to sell off the team."

Amelia's husband, Sam, clears his throat. "I'm pretty sure those bad decisions all revolve around a gambling addiction he's doing a piss-poor job of covering up."

No one asks our brother-in-law, the mob boss, how he knows this.

Our coexistence works, in part, due to a *don't ask, don't tell* policy.

"Can we afford it?" Becket enjoys playing the part of the

joker, but his brain for business rivals some of the best minds in the city.

Max begins passing folders around the table. "I had accounting run the numbers Friday. With a little bit of movement, we can easily afford it. The question is, do we want it? Our legacy is set. The Philadelphia Kings is a profitable franchise. King Corp. is doing better than ever before. Brenner came to us because he'd like to see it stay privately owned, and he was a friend of Dad's, but we don't have to do this."

"When do we have to give him an answer?" I quickly read through the numbers on the page in front of me before I look across the table to Lenny. She's the real numbers girl. "What do you think, Len?"

She lays her black folder on the table and runs her hand over it, smoothing it out. "According to this profit and loss statement, it looks like it's running well." She clears her throat. "I mean, it could run cleaner, but I need some real time to dig in before I could say anything for sure."

"It looks like it could be a good investment for King Corp. if we can get it at the right price. I guess it depends on just how desperate Brenner is to sell it." Becks closes his folder and tosses it on the table. The four of us—Lenny, Becks, Max, and I run the Philadelphia Kings. We're also the four most active family members in King Corp., but each sibling holds shares, including Amelia. We each gifted shares to her last year so she could be an equal partner as well.

"I'll have the lawyers look into everything this week to see what they can dig up. The full findings will be in your hands as soon as possible after that. We can't make the final decision until we have all the information." Max sits back down, and I see Jace out of the corner of my eye, running his hands through his hair, frustration evident in the tightness in his blue eyes.

"We're really gonna buy a hockey team? So if I get

drafted, the whole world can wonder if it's because I have the skill or just the name." Jace is a freshman at Kroydon University. He could have put himself in the draft last year, but Max convinced him he needed a few years of college first. He's one of the top players in the country, and my little brother worked his ass off to get there.

Sebastian, Lenny's fiancé, turns toward Jace. "It's not as bad as it seems. Everyone thought the Kings drafted me last year because of your sister. I just had to work harder to prove them wrong. The same thing happened with Declan Sinclair a few years before me. Just worry about getting drafted first. Then deal with the rest."

"Yeah, you don't even have to bang one of our sisters to get drafted." No sooner have the words left Becks's obnoxious mouth than Lenny's hand moves under the table, causing him to groan.

It's safe to assume Becks just got hit with a nut shot, judging by Lenny's triumphant smile.

Sawyer and Hudson have never shown an interest in working for King Corp. or the Philadelphia Kings. But Sawyer sits across from me with a hesitant look nonetheless.

I kick him with the toe of my shoe. "Spit it out, Sawyer. What are you thinking?"

A muscle in his jaw clenches. "Who's going to run it?"

Max sits down and takes a sip of coffee before asking, "Why? You ready to hand Kingdom over to a manager and come work with us?"

"No." He hesitates. "But if we do this, I think it should stay in the family. That's how we do things, right?"

Max catches my eye and smiles.

Oh shit

"It is. That's why I was thinking if we decide to do this, Scarlet should be the new president." My stomach drops at Max's declaration.

This is it. This is the position. The one I've always wanted but never thought I'd get. Max is the president of the Philadelphia Kings. There can only be one, so I've settled for VP. President of the Revolution is my chance, even if it's with a different team.

As agreements float around the table, Lenny and Amelia both sit, waiting.

Staring.

Silently urging me to make my announcement.

Becks raises his crystal champagne flute into the air, full of a blood orange mimosa. "To a new team, and a much prettier, albeit meaner, organization president than Max."

When everyone lifts their glass but me, Becks's eyes zero in on my lack of a flute in front of |me. "Since when do you pass up champagne, Scarlet?"

Lenny elbows him. "Leave her alone, Becket. She can't have champagne."

Fuck. "Lenny."

Realization dawns on her face. "Shit. Sorry, Scarlet."

"Have you ever kept a secret in your entire life?" I should have known this was coming.

Even with my eyes closed, I can feel everyone's attention on me. I straighten my back and lift a fork full of Belgian waffle to my mouth, ignoring them all.

You can hear a pin drop, the room is so quiet.

Even Maddox and Madelyn are quiet.

"Something you care to share with the rest of us, Scarlet?" The strength of Max's stare demands I meet his eyes.

I swallow my waffle, then wipe my lips with my linen napkin. "Actually, yes." I meet his eyes and steel my spine. "I'm pregnant."

When Amelia announced she was pregnant last year, there was cheering, hugging, and congratulations. That's not what's happening right now. My heart sinks as my siblings continue to stare at me until Hudson wraps his big arm around my shoulders and squeezes. "Are you alright, Scarlet?"

"I'm fine, Hud. I might not have expected this, but that doesn't make it any less incredible." I reach up and squeeze his hand as I force my voice to remain calm and not give way to the disappointment taking hold deep in my soul over everyone's reaction.

The questions start coming at me all at once until Max speaks over everyone else. "Who's the father?"

"I only just found out last week, Max. I was planning on telling the father before I told all of you." I throw a little shade my sister's way as I add, "Apparently, that's no longer an option."

Lenny has the decency to at least grimace, like she feels terrible for outing me to everyone.

Maybe I should make her tell Cade so I don't have to do that either.

CA D E

"BRYNLEE, YOU'VE GOT TO GET OUT OF THE CAR."

My daughter dramatically shakes her head no. Her wild strawberry-blonde curls bounce against her face as her nose scrunches up. "No. Uncle Jax was mean yesterday. I don't want to see him."

I swear my kid can hold a grudge like no one I've ever met. "Brynn, Uncle Jax was just kidding. Now, come inside."

She squeezes her teddy to her chest. "Daddy, he said girls can't fight." She gasps in horror. "And he meant it."

Jesus Christ. She's three years old and has perfected indignation.

"Girls can fight, Daddy. Aunt Immie said so."

I press the unlock button on her five-point harness car seat and hold my arms out for her to jump in. "I told Uncle Jax that girls can fight just as well as boys can, baby. You can do anything a boy can do, and don't you ever let anyone tell you, you can't."

She throws herself into my waiting arms and places her little hands on either side of my face, squishing my cheeks together. "Will you kick his ass for me, Daddy?"

"What did I tell you about repeating things you've heard in the gym, baby?" I grab her pink book bag from the back seat and slam the door shut before we push through the front doors of Crucible.

Brynlee goes to pre-school in the mornings, then comes

to the gym with Imogen or me most afternoons. It's been a long week, made even longer by the temper tantrum she threw on the way to the gym today.

It's Friday. I get it. She's tired.

So am I, kiddo.

So. Am. I.

Once we're through the doors, Brynlee wiggles to be put down and makes a beeline for Imogen, who's sitting behind the front desk. I glance around the main room, making sure everything looks good. Jax is working with Hudson in the cage to my right while a few guys work on the heavy bags.

The area to the left houses all our weights. At the top of the steel stairs in front of me, we've got treadmills, bikes, rowers, and stair climbers. And I've transformed the space in the back of the building into a private room for classes.

Imogen, Rylie, and I grew up in this building.

My father's blood, sweat, and tears built Crucible and the St. James family name, one fight at a time. I trained here for years before I joined the marines and came back as soon as my enlistment ended.

Once I make it over to Imogen, she rips a hot pink sticky note from her pile and slaps it against my chest. "The bi—" she starts but catches herself, attempting to watch what she says in front of my daughter, who loves to repeat all the bad words she hears in the gym. "The big bad female dog called again. Call her back, Cade. Or get a restraining order. But you need to do something. Because I'm tired of her voice."

I pull the note from my chest and see Daria's name and number scratched across it. She's been calling since Hudson won the title a few months ago, probably trying to get more money out of me. After she left Brynlee with me as a newborn, I paid her a lump sum in what she referred to as *maternity fees*. Then she signed away all her parental rights.

Never to be heard from again . . . right?

Wrong.

I didn't hear from her again until she ran out of money a little over a year later. Everybody told me not to give her any. That if I gave in then, she'd never stop.

Guess I should have listened.

"Come on, Hud. You can't go soft on me now. You've got a title to defend. Show me you've got this." I watch him grapple with Dave, one of the navy guys who works for me now. When I came home after the marines, having Crucible as an outlet helped me work through the metric ton of shit I brought home with me.

Before I bought this place from my dad, I worked with him to start a program for vets with PTSD. It's grown since then. Now we're able to offer free classes for vets three times a week. It's not much, but if it can help them feel like they're a part of something while they reacclimate to civilian life, then that's a start.

Dave came to us last year, haunted by ghosts. He shows promise. But he's still working his way back. "Come on, man. Throw your leg over and watch where your hand goes." I grab the metal cage and yell again as my shoulder gets tapped.

Turning, I see my sister behind me, her arms crossed over her green Crucible tank. "You've got company."

"Shit. Daria?" I look around, dreading the inevitable.

"No." Imogen steps to the side and clears my line of sight. "Scarlet Kingston wants to speak to you."

Like a kick to the solar plexus, there she stands.

I haven't seen her since Vegas.

What the hell is Scarlet doing here?

"Okay. Be right there." I turn back to the cage and give the guys instructions before making my way to where Scarlet stands next to the front desk. She's a fucking knock-out in a black pants suit with bright red heels on her feet, giving her a few extra inches. Her long auburn hair is pulled back in a sleek ponytail, and her pouty lips are tight. Unsmiling.

I don't know what the fuck she has to be pissed about.

I'm the one who got thrown out like shit on her shoe the next morning.

I stop closer to her than personal space rules would deem appropriate so she'll have to tilt her head up to look at me. Exposing her slender neck that I have the sudden urge to lick.

Fuck. "Scarlet? Is everything okay? You need me to get Hudson for you?" I've been back in Kroydon Hills for six years, and her brother has been training here with my father, and then me, the entire time. Yet, this is the first time I've seen her set foot in Crucible.

Her gaze travels up the length of me.

So I cross my arms over my chest and flex my biceps when her eyes linger there.

She bites down on her bottom lip before meeting my stare. "Actually, I'm here to see you."

Just as I'm about to ask if she wants to move into my office, Hudson joins us. "Scar, what's up? What are you doing here?"

She quickly glances his way. "I'm here to talk to Cade, Hud. Can you give us a minute?"

Hudson's brow furrows as he looks between his sister and me. "I didn't know you two were friends."

"Hud, the amount of things you don't know could fill every last seat in the Kings stadium. I'll see you later," she dismisses him before turning back to me.

"What the fuck, Scarlet?" Hudson takes a step toward his sister.

When she squares her shoulders like she's preparing for war, I slide in between them. I may be pissed at her, but I don't need these two getting into a fight in the middle of my gym.

Because I'm looking at Scarlet, I don't see the hit coming, but pain radiates in my jaw as Hudson clocks me, knocking me to the fucking ground.

I jump back up and shove him backward. "What's your problem, asshole?" He may be the current heavyweight champion, but I've got him beat by ten pounds and three belts.

"Kick his ass, Daddy."

Fucking seriously? "Could somebody get her out of here?"

When Hudson steps forward again, Jax grabs him from behind. "What the fuck, Hud?"

He looks at me, fury radiating from his face. "You're my problem. You knocked up my goddamn sister."

My arms, which had been tensed in front of me, ready to block Hud again, drop heavily to my sides as I turn slowly back to Scarlet.

Shocked.

Confused.

Furious.

I look over in time to see Scarlet place a business card on the front desk, then move in front of her brother and slap him across the face, leaving a bright red handprint behind. "Fuck you, Hudson. That wasn't your truth to tell. You're the second sibling to take away my choice in discussing this. If you ever speak for me again, it will be the last time you ever speak *to* me." She walks away with Hudson calling after her.

Never looking back.

While I stand there, dumbfounded and staring after her.

Hudson shrugs out of Jax's hold and moves toward the door before Imogen grabs his arm, stopping him in his tracks.

"Cade." My sister turns to me as if I'm the biggest asshole to ever live. "Go after her."

I think it's about time I finally did that.

SCARLET

THE DOOR SWINGS SHUT BEHIND ME, AND I SPEED UP. IF trying to keep my composure instead of killing my brother was one of the most difficult things I've done in my life, walking calmly out of Crucible with my head held high rather than high-tailing it to my car definitely comes in as a close second. But no one is out here to see me fall apart now.

Thank God for small favors.

"Scarlet, stop." My spine straightens at the command yelled across the parking lot.

Damnit.

So close to escape.

And double damnit. Feeling like I have to escape is pissing me off even more than I already was.

Knowing I needed to talk to Cade and actually coming here to do it were two very different things. All week, I knew what had to be done. And I'm far from a procrastinator. I live for the satisfaction I get when I check things off my to-do list. But telling this man, who I thought I loved a lifetime ago, that I'm pregnant with his child, after one single night together in Vegas . . . a night I ended abruptly, lingered on that list all week.

I may like everyone to think that I'm made of ice, but it's an artfully crafted façade.

I had a plan.

Come here.

Get Cade to agree to go somewhere for a cup of coffee.

16

Then tell him, in a somewhat controlled environment, that I was pregnant.

And that he's welcome to be as involved or uninvolved as he wants.

Either way, I'm keeping the baby and prepared to do this on my own.

Hudson and his big fat mouth did not factor into my plan.

"Scarlet . . ." Cade's voice may be softer, but it exudes dominance.

I stare at my car in front of me, not ready to face him. I blame the hormones. *Fuckers.* "Not now, Cade. I can't do this now."

"Not now?" A wild laugh booms into the quiet night. "You came to my gym to drop this in my lap, and now you say *'not now'*? Turn around, Scarlet."

Any lingering softness is gone.

Replaced by anger.

The anger hurts my heart, but I deserve it after the way I treated him.

I hate that he's right but still don't move. "I don't like orders, Cade."

"You like them just fine in bed, duchess." The words are meant to strike, and they hit their mark with precision.

I turn around, purposely tempering my tone, and try a different tactic. "Listen, we're obviously both upset. And I don't want to do this in a parking lot. Let's talk later. Call me when you have time."

"I have time now." He moves closer, crowding me. His face is tight, and his tone is demanding. "Tell me. Are you pregnant?"

My head tilts up toward his hardened face. The boy I knew is long gone, replaced by a man I no longer recognize. Anger shines back at me where I'd hope to find understanding, and I think my heart breaks for a second time in front of this man.

At least this time I'm older and better equipped to disguise the hurt.

"Yes." It was supposed to come out strong. Assured. Powerful.

Instead, it's a whisper in the wind when it gets caught in my throat, and I force back the tears threatening to break free.

Dark-green eyes stare at me in disbelief as Cade takes a step back, looking like he's been hit again.

Mustering every ounce of strength I have, I cross my arms over my chest and smooth my hands over my hair. "I'm sorry that's how you had to find out. You didn't deserve that." Taking a chance, I move forward and trace the bruise forming under his eye. "I'm going to kill Hudson for hitting you."

His hand darts out like a snake and catches my wrist. "Scarlet, I get hit for a living. Your brother didn't hurt me." He holds my palm in place against his cheek. "Talk to me." His words are softer than I deserve.

I pull out of his hold, and take a step away, breaking the electricity humming between us. "Believe it or not, I had a plan. What Hudson did was cruel." Over Cade's shoulder, the door to Crucible opens, and I see Imogen standing just inside. Cade's little girl is still sitting on her hip, both of them watching us. "Seems we have an audience."

Cade reaches for me again, but I angle my body away, not wanting to be touched. "Come home with me, Scarlet. Let's talk about this in private."

After a moment, Imogen peeks her head through the door. "Cade," she yells. "I've got to get going. I'm singing at Kingdom tonight."

Of course, she's singing at my brother's bar tonight.

Because this will provide even more fodder for my family phone tree.

Cade ignores his sister and bends his knees to bring himself eye level with me.

At five-foot-seven, very few men can make me feel small and delicate, but this man does.

He always has.

"Cade . . ."

The door opens again. This time a small, strawberry-blonde head pops out. "I put Hudson in a time-out, Daddy. You can come back in now."

"Come home with me, Scarlet. Let's talk about this." He's trying.

He's still angry, but he's trying.

I'm the one refusing to budge.

"Go home, Cade. Your little girl needs you. Take some time and think about it." What I really want to say is *"Give me some space because the control I thought I'd have tonight was shot to hell with my brother's actions, and I can't possibly stay composed through a meal at your house with you and your daughter."*

Not now.

Not when you're this angry.

Instead, I simply say, "We're both adults, Cade. How involved you are in this child's life is up to you."

He studies my face as his jaw clenches. "What are you trying to say?"

"I'm trying to tell you that it's up to you. I'm fully prepared to raise this child alone. If you'd like to be involved, that's fine. But it's not necessary."

I expect anger.

Resistance.

What I don't expect is the slow smile that spreads across his face.

"Nice try, duchess."

The door creaks open again, and his daughter squeals, "Daddy . . ."

"This isn't over, Scarlet. Give me your phone."

Why I revert back to being a seventeen-year-old girl when I'm with this man is beyond me, but I do it all the same. I've done so many things with him simply because he told me to. Reaching into my purse, I dig out my phone and hand it over.

Cade holds it up to my face, unlocking the home screen. Then his fingers fly across the screen before he hands it back to me. "My number is saved in there, and I texted myself so I'd have yours."

"I left you my card."

"I don't want your work number, Scarlet." He moves behind me to my car door and holds it open. "This isn't over."

I slide behind the wheel and glance up at him. "I know."

"Buckle up." Cade watches me put my seatbelt on, then closes my door and stands sentry as I pull out of the parking lot, wondering what exactly that smile was hiding.

CADE

WHEN I WALK BACK INTO THE GYM, HUDSON HAS HIS BAG slung over his shoulder and is getting his ass handed to him by Imogen while Brynlee sits at the front desk, watching in pure fascination. Most kids would be scared of the yelling. But not Brynlee. When you grow up in a gym, you get used to raised voices.

Imogen looks ready to throw down. "Just because your sister's dumb enough to—"

"Hey," I call out and nod to my daughter, who seems to be captivated by the two of them. "His sister is one of the smartest women I've ever met. This isn't your fight, Gen. Don't you have to get to Kingdom?"

She spins on me. "You're right. It's your goddamn fault too, you moron." She glances back at Brynn, then whispers, "Don't you know how to wrap it up, big brother? Seriously, men!" Imogen grabs her keys from the desk in a fucking huff and storms out of Crucible with the door slamming shut behind her, like she has every right to be mad.

The fuck? I turn my attention on Hudson. "You" I point at Hud. "Don't move." Then I squat down in front of Brynlee. "Sweetie, can you go get your book bag from Daddy's office? It's time to go home."

She hops down from the chair and starts to dash toward my office before changing her direction. Coming to a stop in front of Hudson, Brynn kicks his shin, then points her finger at him. "Don't hit my Daddy again." Satisfied she's said her piece, my princess sticks her tongue out, then runs to my office.

I wait until I see her go through the door before I grab Hudson by the front of the Crucible t-shirt he's thrown on. "Throw a fist outside of that cage again, and I don't give a fuck how many titles you hold, you'll never train another day inside Crucible. Got it?"

"Got it," Hud grunts out through gritted teeth, and I let go.

He holds his ground, staring at me. "How long have you been sleeping with my sister?"

"You need to apologize to your sister. Then ask her your questions." I don't think he'd particularly like my answer.

Not satisfied, he pushes harder. "I'm asking *you*. My coach. My friend. The guy I've trained with for the last six years. The guy whose father trained me for two fucking years before that. The fucking father to my future niece or nephew." To anyone else, Hudson Kingston would be threatening. He's six-foot-four, two hundred and forty-nine pounds of solid muscle. But I've taught him everything he knows. I'm bigger, and I'm better. If we went toe to toe, I'd win. And I know, right now, he's hurt and worried about his sister. So I'll be nicer than he deserves.

"Talk to your sister, man. You already fucked up any chance I had of talking to her about anything tonight." One of us might as well get some answers.

Brynlee comes running back to us with her pink backpack clutched in her arms and a smile on her face. My smile. My daughter has my green eyes and her mother's strawberry-blonde hair.

I wonder briefly who this baby will take after.

Holy shit. A baby.

"Ready, baby girl?" I scoop her up in my arms. "Do you have Teddy? I don't want to have to come back tonight. This pink teddy bear is the only thing Brynlee wants when it's time for bed, and I've had to come back here more than once at the end of a day because Teddy was missing. We tried having an emergency teddy, but Brynlee knew the difference right away.

That wasn't a good night.

She pulls him out of her book bag and squishes him to her chest.

I press a kiss to her forehead, then look over her head at Hudson, who hasn't moved an inch. "Call your sister. Fix this, Hud." I move past him. "Don't come back here until it's done."

"You can't be serious." Hudson's training for his next title fight. And if there's anything a fighter knows, it's that every day counts.

"Try me."

Later that night, once Brynlee is asleep and the house is quiet, I sit at my kitchen table, staring at my open iPad. Debating. It's late. Well, in *my* world, it's late. Anything after nine at night is late to me.

Brynn refuses to sleep past six on most days, and even if I do manage to get her to bed on time, there's still a mountain of things that need to be done.

Sleep is a commodity.

I bought Crucible from my dad a few months before I found out about Brynlee. As soon as my parent's house in Kroydon Hills sold, they bought a place on the beach in the Florida Keys. They fly up a few times a year and FaceTime with us all the time, but they're enjoying their golden years on the gold coast of Key West. It'd be nice to have them closer. But they're loving it.

Imogen wasn't ready to live on her own, so she was staying with our older sister, Rylie, back then. But once I found out about Brynlee, Gen moved in with me to help me out. A month later, I was giving up my condo in Center City Philly for a big place in Kroydon Hills. It's got a huge yard with a pool and a bigger swing set than even the local park has. It's also got privacy, which is something I value. I may have chosen the life of a professional fighter and everything that comes with it. But Brynlee isn't one of those things.

She's everything.

I think back to those early days after Daria dropped Brynlee off.

All those nights of no sleep.

Of a crying baby.

Of not knowing what to do or how to make it better, and I shudder.

I want to say they were awful. But they weren't.

For every sleepless night, there were just as many hours I spent in a rocker, shirtless, with Brynlee lying against my chest in her tiny little diaper. Sleeping soundly, as long as I kept her tucked against me. It was being put down she hated. She'd sleep like a champ if she was on my chest.

Skin on skin.

For every time she cried, I was eventually rewarded with just as many smiles meant only for me.

I love my daughter.

She's my world.

And my world's about to get a little bit bigger.

Deciding it's time, I slide the iPad open.

Cade: You awake?
Scarlet: I am.
Cade: What are you doing?
Scarlet: Reading.

Cade: Oh yeah? Anything good?

Scarlet: Surprisingly, yes.

Scarlet: Lenny's friend just published her first book. It's actually really good.

Scarlet: Want me to write you a book report?

Cade: Can we talk?

Bouncing dots appear then disappear on my messaging app twice before it rings with an incoming FaceTime from Scarlet. "Hey." It's dark where she's sitting. The light of the screen is illuminating her face. Scarlet's hair is wet and hanging down around her shoulders and over a soft-looking pale-blue sweater thing that covers a white V-neck tee. Her face is fresh and bare, without a trace of makeup.

She looks younger. Softer. She reminds me of the Scarlet I once knew.

"You look tired, Scar." Jesus Christ. Because that won't piss her off.

She shakes her head and pinches her lips. "Always the charmer, Cade. I am tired. It's been a long week. I guess you could say I've had a lot on my mind." Her eyebrows go up, as if daring me to push her, and I nod.

Guess we're going to dive right in.

"How are you feeling? Besides tired?" I lean forward on the table, angling the iPad against its case.

Her dark, deep eyes hold me captive. They always did. They're the color of the blue night's sky just after the sun sets. When I was deployed, I used to look at the sky and think about her. "Not bad, I guess. If you don't count caffeine withdrawal."

"Ready to talk about it?" I try to hide the bitter tone of my voice but fail miserably.

Scarlet's shoulders rise and fall with the deep inhale of her breath before she begins to tell me everything. When she found out. When she's due. How she had absolutely no idea she was pregnant until the doctor told her. How her siblings found out. And how she struggled with trying to tell me this week.

I want to stay mad, but she only kept it from me for a week, not the months I had thought earlier.

I want to be mad her siblings already knew. But I'm not. She had little control over that. Truth be told, finding out a little late is still better than the alternative. And I force myself to remember this is Scarlet, not Daria.

"I meant what I said earlier, Cade. You can be as involved or uninvolved as you want. I'm a big girl, and I'm completely prepared to do this on my own."

I hate knowing that this woman thinks so little of me that she'd believe for a single second that I may not want to be involved in my own child's life. When did that happen?

That's the first thing that needs to change.

"Scarlet, you may be the one carrying this baby. But it's *our* baby. He's as much mine as yours. And I'm not a man who would ever be okay being a part-time or nonexistent father."

She bristles and readjusts herself on her bed. "First, this baby is going to be a girl. Second, are you saying you're going to fight me for custody because I'll have my lawyers—"

"That's not what I meant, Scarlet. We'll figure it out as we go. No need to get upset. No need to get lawyers involved. I think the first thing we should do is get to know each other again." A plan begins to take shape.

"I'm fairly sure we know each other, Cade." Her pretty eyes roll.

"No, duchess. We knew each other. But that was a lifetime ago. We were kids. I don't know about you, but I'm a completely different man now from the boy you knew. Pretty sure you are too."

"I guess I am."

As Scarlet runs her teeth over her bottom lip, I flash back to the way she used to do that when she was uncertain or nervous. Not often. But it was her *tell*.

Scarlet Kingston has always been so fucking sure of herself and her place in the world that, even as teenagers, I loved forcing her out of her comfort zone.

Convincing Scarlet to go wild and break out of the perfect little box her family kept her in was one of my favorite things to do.

"Let me take you to dinner, Scarlet." I watch those blue eyes consider it.

"You never were good at asking, were you, Saint?"

I may never have been good at asking, but I always knew when she used my nickname, she was about to say yes. And it was so much fucking fun when she said yes.

"Fine. Let's do dinner Monday night. We've got a lot to figure out."

You can say that again.

SCARLET

"Good morning, Connor." My assistant, Connor, is the only person who ever beats me into the office on Monday mornings. I lucked out when I found him. He'd just graduated from Villanova and was young and hungry. He's worked for me for almost two years and quickly became my right hand.

"Mornin', Scarlet. It was a quiet weekend." His big brown eyes look stricken as he says it before he makes the sign of the cross. "You know what that means." Connor stands from his desk and hands me a binder with information I'd asked for last week.

"Yeah. Slow weekend means it's about to be a crazy week." I hold the binder up. "Thank you for putting this together so quickly." Once I move into my corner office, I shut the door behind me before glancing out of my window at the stadium field below. This view never gets old.

The Philadelphia Kings offices have been my home since I was a little girl.

This team was my grandfather's pride and joy before he died.

He used to say it was our legacy.

Every King needs his legacy.

My siblings and I grew up in these offices.

We ran on this field and played in those stands.

We were privileged in a way we didn't understand at such young ages. But I understand it now. We all do. And every one, in their own way, has tried to make their own path in the world. Whether that included the Kings or not.

We're a family of overachievers. Max and I both got our MBAs from Wharton. Becks got his law degree from Harvard. Lenny came home with an MBA from Cambridge. The four of us knew we'd have jobs waiting for us with King Corp., but we wanted to make sure we earned those positions. That we were worthy of them, not just relying on our name and pedigree to get us there.

As I sit down at my desk and power up my laptop, I try to imagine doing this somewhere else. I've never wanted to work anywhere but here. I love my job. I'm the vice president in charge of public relations, and I'm fucking fantastic at it.

But I've always wanted more.

I've wanted Max's job.

I've always known that one day he'd be general manager, and Dad would be president of Football Operations. There would never be anyone else. What none of us expected was for Dad to die so young and for Max to have to step into both roles.

And now he wants me to assume that role with the Revolution.

It's not the team I love.

But it could be.

Can I do this?

Can I have the career I never dared to dream of because I thought it belonged to someone else?

Can I balance it with motherhood?

This dream may be newer, but it's no less important.

Can I have it all?

I guess it's time to find out.

An hour later, a knock at my door is followed by Becket's head peeking around it. "You got a minute, Scarlet?"

I nod and save the document I was working on. "Sure. What's up?"

Becks closes the door behind him, then leans against it and crosses his arms over his chest with a tortured look on his face. "Is it true?"

"You're going to have to be more specific, Becket. I'm a lot of things, but a mind reader isn't one of them." Of course, what I am is full of shit because I know what he's talking about. The Kingston kids have never been able to keep a secret. Tell one, tell all. No way was Hudson going to keep his big, fat mouth shut after Friday night. I'm just glad I got the weekend as a reprieve before this started.

Hudson tried calling and stopping by. And thanks to voicemail and a good doorman, I didn't have to deal with him or anyone else for that matter. There's something to be said for staying home in your pajamas while you read every pregnancy book ever written.

"Saint." He moves across from my desk and drops into the chair. "Is Cade St. James the father, Scarlet? Did you really sleep with my best friend?"

I sigh as I realize just how clueless my brother really is. What would he say if he knew I started sleeping with his best friend more than a decade ago?

Another thing that's okay to think but not to say.

At least not yet.

Becket's brain is already close to exploding. I don't think he could handle more. Instead, I close my laptop and mirror his annoyed look. "Yes, Becks. Cade is the father, as I'm sure our pig-headed younger brother already informed all of you."

"Jesus, Scarlet. Really? Cade? You could have your pick of the guys in Philadelphia. You had to pick my best fucking friend?"

When the vein bulges above Becks's eye, I wait.

I know my brother well, and that tell right there lets me know he's not done yet.

"We're both fucking adults. And I know what you do with your body is your business. But did you not think you made it my business when you screwed my best fucking friend?"

I sit patiently, waiting to see if he's really finished this time.

Once I'm convinced he is, I take a sip of my water and stare at him.

"Are you done?" When Becket doesn't respond, I continue, "You're right. What I do with my body is my business, Becket. That doesn't change because Cade St. James is your friend." I rise from my desk and move around it to stand in front of him. "Cade's a good man, and a good friend. The fact that I'm pregnant doesn't change that. He didn't do this to me. There were two of us there that night. He didn't take advantage of me." When Becks moves to speak, I cut him off. "Becket Kingston, don't you dare say it. Don't put words to whatever fucked up thought is dancing around in that pretty little brain of yours. We're both adults. We both deserve to be treated like adults, not kids sneaking around behind my brothers' backs."

I haven't been that girl in years.

"Besides, you know Cade. Can't you be glad your niece will have an amazing father?"

I lean against my desk and cross my ankles while I wait for Becks's face to soften. When the tension drains away and he smiles, I relax.

"It's a girl?" Becks's smile deepens, popping the dimple in his cheek that only comes out with his real smile.

"I'm putting positive thoughts into the universe. She has to be a girl."

I'm convinced this is going to work.

61

He stands and leans into me, slinging his arm around my shoulders and squeezing. "I love you, little sister. That is one lucky little girl."

"I love you too, bonehead." I lean my head on his shoulder and close my eyes, then whisper quietly, "You think I'll be a good mom?" It's a fear I've been nursing since the doctor told me the news.

I never even wanted kids.

How could I possibly be a good mom?

"You're going to be the best mom. Take everything Mom did and do the exact opposite, and you'll be amazing." He laughs and kisses the top of my hair. "Seriously, Scar. You'll be great. And you've got all of us to help and spoil the newest King."

We're interrupted by a knock on the door before Max opens it.

My siblings and I tend to do that to each other.

We knock but don't wait for an answer.

If it's important or you want privacy, you lock your office door.

Becks and I don't move as he comes in and closes the door. "Maximus."

"What the hell? Scarlet, are you crying?" Max looks scared to death. He's never been good with a crying woman.

I wipe the tears away from my eyes. "I guess I am. I hadn't realized it." Standing, I straighten my pencil skirt and blouse and run a hand over my ponytail. "Sorry about that." I move back around my desk and look between my brothers. "Did you need something, Max?"

"No . . . Well, yes. I was looking for you." He stands next to Becket and glares. "Does one of you want to tell me what's going on?"

Becks opens his mouth, looking guilty, so I decide to save him. "Hormones, Max. Becket was just being a good brother, and it got me hormonal. Be prepared because according to all of the books I read this weekend, they're going to get worse."

Max runs his fingers through his perfectly styled dirty blonde hair, and I watch the fear from earlier begin to subside. "Okay, Scarlet. Bring Cade to the house for dinner soon then."

"Ahh… that would be a no, Max. You're not Dad, and I'm not a child. We're not even together like that, and you're not going to interrogate him. Let me work through this without any interference from you guys, okay? Give me time." I sit down and wait for them to get the hint, but these two aren't taking it. "I've got work to do, guys."

"That's my cue." Becks leaves the office, and Max sits down and hands me the folder he's holding.

"Can you stay late and meet with Will Brenner and me tonight? He's coming in at six."

Guess I'm cancelling my dinner with Cade.

And now I need to decide if the tightening in my chest is disappointment at that thought or heartburn.

CADE

It's already been a shitty Monday morning when my phone rings. Brynlee didn't want to go to school. Jax called earlier to say he was running late, and there's a leak in the men's locker room from the fucking monsoon that's coming down today.

The phone continues to ring, as I shuffle the papers around my desk.

Searching for the offending object but not finding it.

It takes a minute before I realize it's in the pocket of the Crucible hoodie I threw on this morning. When I pull it out, Scarlet's name flashes with an incoming FaceTime.

"Hey." I run my fingers through my hair, and I'm rewarded with Scarlet's face forcing back a smile. She used to love to torture me over how much time I spent on my hair.

"Your hair looks fine, Cade." She smirks.

She also used to love running her fingers through it while I fucked her.

Her dark hair is pulled back. Her blue eyes are framed with long inky lashes. And a pair of black-rimmed glasses sit perched on her nose. "Sorry to bail at the last minute, but can I get a raincheck on dinner tonight? Max just booked me for a late meeting."

Damn. This woman isn't gonna make this easy. "You've gotta eat, Scarlet. You're eating for two now."

"Hate to break it to you, Saint, but the baby is the size of a passion fruit right now. It doesn't require much sustenance.

A solitary diamond sits on a thin silver chain around her slender neck, with her clavicle peeking out from behind a silky looking white blouse.

I have the sudden urge to drip passion fruit juice all over that neck just so I can lick her clean.

I pull myself back from that thought and adjust my pants. "Seriously? A passion fruit? How big is a passion fruit?" I hold up the orange I brought in this morning. "Bigger or smaller than this?"

"Umm." Scarlet runs her teeth over her ruby red bottom lip. "Is it bad if I admit I have no idea? I spent the weekend reading all the *What to Expect* books I could get my hands on, and that was what I remember from my binge. She's the size of a passion fruit." Scarlet smiles. "Oh, and I should be eternally grateful that I haven't spent the last three months vomiting all day."

"There you go with the *'she'* again. What if you're giving our son a complex?" The words leave my mouth on a joke, but Scarlet's quick intake of breath has me studying her reaction. "You okay?"

She starts nervously playing with the pen in her hand. "You don't really think I could be screwing her up already, do you?"

"Jesus, duchess. No. I was kidding. She'll be perfect." Now she's got me saying *"she."* When Scarlet's shoulders relax, I push a little more. "Either way, you have to eat. Come to my house tonight. Let me cook you dinner." I've gotten over my anger. She wasn't hiding this from me. She's not Daria. I may not trust her completely, but she's going to be the mother of my child, so I've got to try.

"Cade . . ." Her rejection is coming, but I'm not going to give her that chance.

"I cook every night, Scarlet. It's not a big deal. Besides,

won't you be more comfortable at my house than at a restaurant?"

She laughs, and it's light and melodic. Not what you'd expect from this ball-buster of a woman. "Umm . . . I might actually be more comfortable in a restaurant."

"Come on, Scarlet. We've got to start somewhere." When she looks off to the side, I fear I'm losing her. "This baby deserves, at the very least, for its parents to be friends."

"Ohh . . . That's not fair, Cade St. James." Crimson red dots her fair skin. Then I hear a knock in the background and a man's voice in her office. "Cade, I've got to go."

"I'll text you my address. Come any time after your meeting."

She shakes her head. "I didn't agree to come."

"You didn't say no either. See you tonight." I disconnect the call as Imogen enters my office, shaking off her raincoat.

"That was smooth, big brother. Using the baby to get her to agree to a date." She hangs her wet coat on the back of my door. "Am I still watching Brynlee tonight, or do you want me out of the house?"

"It's not a date, Gen. It isn't any different than when we were going out to dinner." But it feels like it could be, and I'm not sure what I think about that.

Scarlet Kingston is the only woman I've ever let myself love, and she threw that away. Can I seriously be considering starting something with her again?

Imogen takes an elastic band from her wrist and throws her fiery red hair up in a messy knot on top of her head. "Whatever you say."

"Hey, have you heard from Hudson today?" I stand with my empty coffee mug and walk toward her.

"No. We didn't talk this weekend. I saw him with Sawyer for a few minutes between sets at Kingdom Saturday night. But it was really crowded." Gen's band, Sinners and Saints, has been the Saturday night band at Kingdom for a while now. One of these days, she's gonna quit Crucible, and I'm gonna be lost without her.

When I grunt, annoyed that no one has heard from Hudson, she clicks her tongue. "You told him not to come back until he'd apologized to Scarlet. Guess he's not ready to do that just yet."

"Fuck." We're only a few months out from his next fight.

I thought I'd be forcing his hand.

It was meant to be my way of making sure he apologized to his sister.

Not keeping him out of the fucking gym where he needs to be getting ready.

Gen grabs a water bottle from my mini-fridge and stares at me. Waiting. "Let me ask you, big brother. You want Hudson to fix things with Scarlet, but have you even told Mom and Dad about the baby? Or Rylie and Jillian, for that matter?"

Her hands move to her hips as she waits for the answer she already knows.

I haven't told anyone yet.

I was hoping to have dinner with Scarlet tonight before calling my parents and older sister. I wanted to at least have some kind of game plan. Not to give them a new version of the *holy shit I'm a dad* call they got when Brynlee was deposited in my arms.

"See, that's what I thought. Hudson fucked up and should fix it. But you aren't exactly handling this like a champ just yet either, are you?" She opens the door and starts backing out but not before adding, "Handle your shit with your own family before you start messing around with your fighters and their families, Cade." Then Gen pulls the door closed, and I watch through the office windows as she takes her place at the front desk.

The phone on my desk vibrates with an incoming call, and my mother's face pops up on the screen, causing me to silently curse my sister.

It's only Monday, and it's already shaping up to be a stellar week.

SCARLET

Max holds the door open for Will Brenner as he walks out of the Kings conference room then turns back and levels me with a frustrated glare. "Fuck . . ." He draws the word out as he crosses the room and pours a tumbler of whiskey from the crystal set on the credenza.

"Yeah." I close the proposal in front of me. "Not so sure this deal is going to go through. He's making an awful lot of demands for someone who came to *us*, asking us to solve *his* problems."

My brother downs his drink in one swallow before leaning onto the conference table, his brows creased. "Tell me what you're thinking, Scarlet? We're talking about you taking over as president. If we agree to these terms, you're the one who'll be tied to them."

"Let's see." I stand and cross the room to look out the windows at the dark stadium below. "We have to keep what seems like all his upper-level management staff in place for a minimum of twelve months. So it'll be a long twelve months of arm wrestling with the old guard to get on board with the new way of doing everything." And that's not mentioning that I'll be dealing with all of this while I'm balancing my dream job with a newborn. "Because you know they're never going to want to change what they're already doing, I mean, I'll definitely get ridiculous pushback. That should be fun, right?"

"Right. Guarantee the GM and the . . ." He picks up the

blue portfolio Will left behind, then flips it open before changing his mind and slamming it back down on the table. "Do we want this headache?"

I turn around and lean back against the cool windowsill and meet Max's gaze. "I'm honestly not sure we do."

I'm not sure I can handle this transition.

And that's a tough pill to swallow.

I'm not sure how many balls I'm capable of keeping in the air.

I know I could handle this if I wasn't expecting a baby. But I have no idea what my life will look like six months from now or how much help I'll need. Add the learning curve of an entirely new organization to that, and I'm worried it might be too much.

Whoever said women can have it all needs to explain to me exactly when those women are supposed to sleep. Because I don't see a lot of that in my future.

By the time I slide into my car after the meeting, I'm still undecided about whether to go to Cade's house or just go home.

I'm tired.

So tired.

But I don't think that's going to change over the next few months. So I guess there's no time like the present to get this over with. Cade's not wrong. We don't know each other anymore. And if he's going to want to co-parent, I guess we need to fix that.

I plug the address he gave me earlier into my navigation system, then tell my Bluetooth to call Lenny.

She answers on the first ring. "Hey. How'd the meeting with Brenner go?"

"Not as good as we'd hoped. I just left the office. Max is still there, going over the official proposal." I pause for a moment before quietly adding, "I'm on my way to Cade's."

There's movement on her end of the phone before she practically whispers, "Holy shit. Seriously? I thought it didn't go well when you went to Crucible on Friday."

"Our brother has such a big mouth." Not that I'm surprised.

"All our brothers have big mouths. Which one are we mad at?"

I appreciate that she automatically jumps in with me. "Don't be dense, Len. If anyone knows Friday didn't go well, it's because Hudson activated the goddamn phone tree. PTA moms have nothing on him."

"Yeah, he kinda made sure we all knew what happened before we went to bed Friday night. But we agreed to give you space over the weekend. And let me tell you, you might owe Max for the way he controlled Becks. It wasn't pretty." Lenny blows out a breath, and I can picture the look on her face.

The two of us catch up as I navigate the streets of Kroydon Hills.

My GPS has me turning right onto Cade's street and pulling down a long, curved driveway until I come to a stop behind a sporty little SUV. When Len mentions the proposal again, I feel my temples throb. "Yeah well, Maximus is going to owe me if we go through with buying the Revolution. My head actually hurts, just thinking about it."

"Well, you're about to walk into a gorgeous man's house. I'm sure he could come up with a few ways to make it feel better." Lenny snickers, and I roll my eyes.

It's not like she can see me.

"That would be a no. Friends, Eleanor. Your niece

deserves for her parents to be friends. Wish me luck." That's what Cade said earlier that got me, and he's right.

My daughter deserves for her parents to be friends.

God knows I spent enough time listening to my own parents fight, and I know that's not what I want. Max, Becks, and I have the same mother—Adaline. Our father, the late John Joseph Kingston, cheated on her with Sawyer and Hudson's mom, Elise. Eventually, he cheated on Elise with Lenny and Jace's mom, Kristin. If he ever cheated on Kristin, he was at least discreet about it and managed not to get caught. It seemed like he finally found the love he was looking for. But Kristin died from cancer during Lenny's senior year in high school.

Adaline never got over her hate for Dad.

She hated that he made a fool out of her publicly with the scandal.

She hated that she could be replaced so easily.

I swear she only stayed in Philly until I graduated from high school just so she could have something to hold over Dad. My father may not have been the most loving father in the world, but he never made me feel like part of a transaction the way Adaline did.

If going inside this house is the first step in giving my daughter a better life than I had, then so be it.

Len gasps into the phone. "Holy hell. Scarlet Leigh, you're nervous."

"I'm glad you're enjoying my pain, Lenny Lou. I'll talk to you tomorrow."

I study the gorgeous house in front of me. It's an elegant Tudor home with high-pitched rooflines and beautiful brick-work, mixed with cream stucco, dark wood, and at least two chimneys stacks in the middle of a large lot surrounded by a black wrought iron fence. I'm not sure what I expected, but it wasn't this.

My stomach churns as I get out of the car and slowly make my way to the front door. Just as I raise my hand to knock, it opens, and Imogen appears. She's dressed in short jean shorts and a long-sleeved white shirt with the Crucible logo stretched across her chest in dark green and a backpack resting over one shoulder.

Forest-green eyes, just like her brother's, scan me from head to toe. But Imogen doesn't say a word as she squeezes past, leaving the front door wide open. For a minute, I think she's going to walk away without acknowledging me. But then she manages to mumble something about Cade and the kitchen before getting in the SUV and driving away.

Okay . . . I step through the door, hesitant to call out because I don't know if Cade's daughter is asleep yet or not.

What time do toddlers go to bed?

Shit.

Another question I need to add to my growing list. I quietly pull the door closed behind me and notice a rubber mat with discarded shoes next to the closet to my left and a large arching doorway to my right. I'm guessing the kitchen is that way.

Should I take my shoes off?

Why is this so awkward?

Deciding I'm more comfortable if I leave them on, I make my way deeper into the house, following the incredible smell wafting from the kitchen. I take in all the rooms I pass by, feeling like I'm trespassing in Cade's personal space. Every inch of this home exudes comfort and love, from the toys scattered throughout to the pictures adorning the walls.

As I move closer to the kitchen, I hear the low notes of a U2 song playing and come to a halt at the sight before me. There's a large breakfast nook with a built-in bench and table perfectly placed in front of the French doors, leading out to what I'm guessing is an oversized backyard.

The table is set for two.

And Cade St. James stands at a large, dark granite island, barefoot, in low-slung jeans and a white t-shirt stretched across his muscular chest, singing the lyrics to "With Or Without You," by U2 while he chops the carrots he's throwing into a salad.

And holy shit, it's the hottest thing I've ever seen.

Until he raises his eyes to meet mine.

Those green eyes sparkle as his entire face transforms with an easy-going smile.

Sending my hormones into overdrive.

Keeping this man in the friend zone may be the hardest part of this pregnancy.

CAD E

"I guess Imogen isn't the only singer in the family, is she?"

Scarlet Kingston is standing in my kitchen in the same black pencil skirt and white blouse from earlier. Her hair is pulled back from her face, and her hot-pink shoes match the bag she has resting in the crook of her arm. She's the epitome of elegance and grace.

Perfection.

So far out of my league.

"Hey, duchess." Her cheeks pink, and a small smile graces her face for a single heartbeat before the ice queen returns and a mask drops into place, concealing her emotions.

Scarlet moves further into the room, laying her purse on the counter. She looks around the kitchen almost nervously, then points over her shoulder. "Imogen let me in on her way out. She didn't seem thrilled with me, but that seems to be going around lately."

"Ignore Gen. She's been in a mood all day." I chose not to add that she's taken it out on me the whole time. "Do you want something to drink?"

Scarlet eyes the bottle of beer sitting in front of me, and a perfectly sculpted dark brow shoots up, as if reminding me she can't have what I'm having. "Water, please. I can get it myself."

"Stay there. I've got it." I reach into the fridge and grab a bottle. When I shut the door, she's already standing on the other side of the refrigerator, examining the pictures hanging by magnets.

She's so close, it would be easy to take her in my arms. The pull is there. And when Scarlet's tongue darts out to wet her lips, I know I'm not the only one thinking this.

We were always good at physical.

That came easy.

Communication . . . not so much.

She takes a step back. "Wow. These are great. She looks like a happy little girl."

My daughter's smiling face covers the majority of the fridge.

Everything, from her baby pictures to the masterpieces she brings home from preschool, adorns the surface.

"She is. I'm a lucky man." It's a little crazy to think I'm going to have another baby.

"I'm not sure how she's going to take it when I tell her she's going to be a big sister though. She's not the best at sharing." I think about the conversation I had with my mother today. She was thrilled with the idea of another grandbaby. But not thrilled that Scarlet and I weren't getting married and concerned about how Brynlee would take the news.

A question I'm not ready to get an answer to just yet.

"Have you thought about when you're going to tell her?" Scarlet moves back to the island

"No. Not yet." I pull the chicken scampi out of the warming drawer and hope she still likes chicken. "I think I'm going to wait until you're a little further along. Maybe we could take her to one of the ultrasounds toward the end." Okay, not a bad idea. That might actually work. Or at the very least, help get her excited.

"Do you think we could wait to decide when? I don't know if I'm ready for that yet." Scarlet's face goes a little pale.

"I'm still kinda wrapping my head around the fact I have a real human inside me. And that she's moving and growing in there."

When my smile grows, she laughs. "No dirty jokes, Saint. You know what I meant."

I wasn't going to make a joke. But I like where her mind went. "You hungry?"

She nods and walks over to the table I'd set for us earlier. "Is this as awkward for you as it is for me?"

Typical Scarlet. I don't think she's ever sugarcoated anything a day in her life. "What do you think we should do to make this less uncomfortable?" I pull her chair out and let her spicy vanilla scent wash over me. Flashes of our night together play out in my mind as my cock grows harder in my pants.

She places her napkin on her lap, and I discreetly adjust myself before taking my seat.

This woman has always had this effect on me.

"Well . . . how about we start with getting to know each other again, like you said. Tell me something about yourself I wouldn't know." She cocks her head to the side, her blue eyes boring into me. "Like why did you leave the marines? You told me you wanted to be a career marine before you graduated. I expected you to stay in for the next twenty years."

I want to ask her if that's why she broke things off or if there was another reason, but that would give her too much power in this balancing act of ours. I'm not ready to let her know that over a decade later, I still haven't gotten over that or her. "Not into throwing softballs, are ya, Scar?"

She ignores my joke and chews her chicken, quietly waiting for my answer.

"Okay, the short version is it's hard watching your brothers die. By the end of my enlistment, I was done. I didn't want to be fighting a war where we didn't even know who the enemy was anymore." I take a pull from my beer and watch her let that sink in. "It wasn't an easy decision."

"Are you happy you did it? Enlisted, I mean."

I think back to the kid I was before I graduated.

I thought I was tough.

I thought I knew what it meant to be a man.

I was so fucking wrong.

"I am. It made me the man I am now. Growing up here with the privilege I had . . . It was easy to be a cocky little shithead who didn't know how good life was. I left, not knowing who I really was. I know now, and I like the man I became in the process. My only real regret is the way we ended things before I left." Those words leave my mouth without any forethought.

I guess I was more ready to talk about this than I realized.

Scarlet straightens in her chair, then looks down at the table before raising her eyes to meet mine. "You mean the way *I* ended things?"

"Well, I certainly didn't want things to end the way they did." I try to keep my tone friendly. I wasn't planning on rehashing this tonight, but I guess it's better to get it out in the open.

Her hand slides across the table and rests on mine. "We were kids, Cade. We spent two years sneaking around behind everyone's backs. There was no way we would have stayed together if we did the long-distance thing."

"Sneaking around was never my choice. It was yours." Might as well put it all out there.

She pulls her hand back quickly and places it in her lap. "It was my choice. And looking back, it probably wasn't the right choice. We were kids, Cade. In my defense, my mother would have never let us date."

"You mean she wouldn't have let you date *me*." My family was well-off. My mom was a nurse practitioner and my dad a former heavyweight boxing champion who trained new champions at his own gym. But we weren't in the same financial stratosphere as the Kingston family. And her mother was all about appearances.

"That's not fair." Her blue eyes blaze with anger. "I never thought that, and neither did my brothers. Don't put my mother's bullshit on me."

Fuck. "You're right. I'm sorry. This isn't how I wanted tonight to go."

"It's fine. We needed to get it out there in the open. You've obviously never forgiven me for the awful way I ended things, and I can't say I blame you. I just didn't see any other way. Could you even imagine the way my brothers would have overreacted if we'd told them?"

I bark out a loud laugh. "Your family . . . No way. They'd never get overly involved in your business. I can't imagine why you'd think that." She spent my entire senior year of high school worried one of her brothers or her mother would find out about us. I tried to get her to just tell them, but she never even considered it.

I didn't care because she was mine.

Until she wasn't.

Scarlet wipes her mouth with her napkin and places it on her barely touched plate. "I wrote you letters."

"I never got them." I say, shocked by her words. Shocked by the idea that maybe she didn't let go as easily as I thought, but she's not looking at me. Her eyes are trained on the napkin in front of her.

"I never sent them. I had things I needed to say, but you weren't here to hear them." Her watery blue eyes finally rise to meet mine, and it's a punch to my gut.

The Scarlet I knew never cried.

And the Scarlet she portrays now wouldn't want anyone to see this.

I'm not sure if I should feel awful for upsetting her or grateful that she's opening up.

"I'm here now. I'm ready to listen to whatever you want to say." Damn, this shouldn't be so hard. "Whatever you want to talk about."

Just when I think we're about to get somewhere, the sound of little feet making their way toward the kitchen catches my attention. Brynlee walks into the kitchen clutching Teddy. A few curls are plastered to her tired face while the rest bounce around her shoulders. "I'm thirsty, Daddy."

She walks right to me and climbs up onto my lap, then realizes I'm not alone. She looks at Scarlet, then around the otherwise empty kitchen. "Where's Aunt Immie?"

"She went out, sweetie. Do you remember Scarlet from the gym?" I stand and place her back down in my vacated seat, then move to fill her sippy cup with milk.

It takes my daughter a minute to place Scarlet. But I see when it clicks in her wide green eyes. "You made Hudson mad."

Scarlet sits straighter and crosses her long legs. "I did. Do you know that Hudson is my little brother?"

A few strawberry-blonde curls bounce in Brynn's face as she shakes her head no.

"Well, he is. I have a lot of brothers and sisters, and we make each other mad all the time. But you know what?" She leans down to Brynlee and waits. "It's okay if we get mad at each other because we love each other. A lot. That means we always get over it."

I can't help but wonder if that's meant as a bit of a dig for me holding onto a grudge for over a decade.

Brynlee's big green eyes open wider. "So he did something bad, and you were mad at him?"

"Yes, I was. But it's okay now."

Watching this woman with my daughter stirs emotions in me I'm not ready to lay claim to just yet. Maybe not ever. Definitely not without trust. And I'm not there yet. Brynlee isn't lacking in female attention. She has three aunts who dote on her as if she were theirs. She has my mother, albeit from a few states away most of the year. But there's something about this moment that's different. Something about this woman that's different. I think I was expecting Scarlet to blow my daughter off, or at the very least, not be quite so open with her, not so interested or tender.

But Scarlet never was one to do what I expected.

Hudson never made it to the gym today, so I don't think he made things right with the woman sitting in front of me who's looking so seriously at my sleepy toddler.

When I bring the sippy cup back to her and open my arms, she slowly climbs up and lays her head on my chest. After kissing her hair, I look down at Scarlet. "I'll be back down in a minute."

She nods, but part of me wonders if she'll still be here when I come back down the stairs. Or if the walls she's lowered as the night went on will be built back up with reinforced steel.

SCARLET

I watch Cade carry his little girl down the hall and have the overwhelming urge to cry. Not something I'm used to. I'm not a crier. Never have been. But there's something about knowing what we could have had and what we're being given the chance to share that makes me so incredibly sad and yet hopeful at the same time.

Once I put our plates in the sink, I grab my bottle of water and move into the den that's attached to the kitchen, kick my shoes off, and sit down on an overstuffed sofa facing a stunning stacked stone fireplace. A pink wooden kitchen set sits in one corner, and a matching wooden toybox is placed neatly into the other. I tuck my feet up underneath myself and lean my head back against the couch, closing my eyes. The dull pulse of a headache is beginning, and I pray it won't turn into a migraine. The light isn't irritating me yet, so there's hope.

I know my migraine triggers, and lack of sleep is one of them. Lord knows I haven't been sleeping well since my doctor dropped this lovely little bomb in my lap. Has it really been only a little over a week since I found out I was going to be a mother?

I open my eyes at the sound of bare feet on hardwood floors coming closer to me. Cade moves into the room a minute later with a sleepy look in his eyes. "Sorry. Sometimes she wants me to lie down with her." He grabs his beer from the kitchen and sits down next to me.

"Did you really not know your ex was pregnant with her until after she was born?" I can't imagine doing that to him. This powerful man, who's capable of beating someone unconscious in the cage, is so sweet and caring with his daughter, it makes me go a little soft and gooey.

And I don't do gooey.

"Yeah. Daria kept it from me the entire time she was pregnant. I found out about Brynlee when she brought her into Crucible and told me she didn't want to be a mom, so it was my turn."

"That had to be hard." I'm scared of what those first few months are going to be like, and I have six more months to prepare.

Cade angles himself toward me. "It was hard. But it's my turn to ask a question. I want to know why there's no Mr. Kingston."

It's hard not to laugh at that. "Well, there are quite a few Mr. Kingstons." I look up at him and catch his sexy, crooked smile. "But if you're asking why I'm not in a relationship, that's easy. I'm just not a relationship kind of woman. I have a demanding job I love, and that comes first. I've never met a man I thought would be worth putting ahead of the Kings. And I wasn't willing to settle for anything less." I roll my neck, trying to get a little relief from the building pressure.

"Come here." Cade twists my shoulders, surprising me when strong hands begin to dig into the muscles in my neck and shoulders. "You still getting migraines, duchess?"

I don't speak. Just let a small hum of satisfaction slip past my lips as skilled, callused hands work my sore muscles, and think back to a time where this was my favorite way to beat back one of these headaches.

"So, is working for the Kings everything you used to think it would be?"

That's an easy one. "It is. I love it. I love being part of my family's legacy. I love my job. I love that every player on the team fears me even more than their coach." Cade laughs, but I'm serious. "I was recently offered the possibility of a new position with the Revolution. And while it's my dream job, I'm a little hesitant about taking on a whole new team."

"Wow. That's crazy. So you'd leave the Kings for a hockey team? Blasphemy." He chuckles, then asks, "What do Max and Becks think of that?"

I let my head drop forward, so he can keep working my muscles while I open up more to him than I have to even my siblings since Max made his announcement last week. "It was actually Max's idea. He and Becks were completely on board with it. King Corp. is looking into buying the team." I cut myself off before I say more. It may be easy to fall back into old routines with Cade, but we're not the same people we were back then, and I need to remember that.

"Holy shit, Scarlet. So this could be happening soon? You could be switching teams and positions? That's a lot of pressure to put on yourself right now."

My head snaps up in annoyance, and Cade's fingers halt. "It is. But you wouldn't be saying that if I wasn't pregnant. You'd never say that to a man. I can't not take the job just because I'm going to be a mom."

"Hey." His hands freeze in front of him. "Not what I was saying. You've always been capable of doing anything you want. It just sounds like a lot on your plate and a ton of pressure. That's all I meant." Strong hands squeeze mine, and I try to relax.

But this is it.

My fear.

How am I going to balance it all?

Am I setting myself up for an epic failure?

Cade and I manage to find the rhythm we lost all those years ago as we go back and forth with questions over the next hour. We're older. We've both grown and matured. But at our core, we're still us, and our rapport becomes less stilted as the hour passes.

Our initial awkwardness transitions to ease.

Ease to awareness.

And before I know it, it's time for me to go because awareness won't be turning into anything else tonight.

When I rise from the couch, Cade stands in front of me. His hands rest on my hips, and his warm breath fans my face. It would be so easy to fall into this man. To fall into what I know would be an incredible night. But that's not why I'm here. That's not what we need.

His lips skim over my forehead, but I take a step back and slide my heels back on. "I had a nice night tonight, Saint."

Cade recovers quickly and follows me into the kitchen while I gather my belongings. "You don't have to leave yet, Scarlet."

I slip my keys from my purse and turn to face him. "I really do. I think this was a good idea. It was a good start to the foundation we want to give our daughter. But I think we're better not complicating an already complicated situation." When he looks like he's going to object, I continue. "Like you said earlier, our daughter deserves for her parents to be friends." I hold out my hand, like a complete idiot.

But Cade wraps his arm around me instead. "When is your next doctor's appointment, duchess?"

"Oh. I still have to schedule it. But I think they want me back in three weeks." I pull out my phone and look at my calendar. "Yes. I'm supposed to go once a month, and I saw them a little over a week ago. So about three more weeks."

"I want to come. I don't want to miss a single appointment, okay?" He hasn't let me go yet, and it feels good.

Too good.

Being wrapped in his arms is the first time I've actually felt like everything was going to be okay.

That pisses me off almost as much as it comforts me.

Maybe being in this together won't be so bad.

Before I start my car to head home that night, I decide it's time for a little family wrangling. And in our family, there's no better way to do it than a group text message.

Kingston Family Group Text:

Scarlet: In case there are any Kingstons that missed what I'm sure was a gossip-filled text message last weekend — let me make this clear . . .

Scarlet: Do I have your attention?

Scarlet: Yes. Cade St. James is the father. He and I are going to be coparenting as FRIENDS. And if any of you have a problem with that, feel free to fuck right off.

Scarlet: Any questions?

Lenny: I've got one. Does he still have an eight-pack? I used to love watching him fight.

Lenny: He's so sexy.

Jace: Gross Len!

Becks: I'm sure Bash would love to hear that.

Lenny: Unlike some of my brothers, Sebastian is secure enough to not be threatened by other men.

Lenny: And he's got his own eight-pack for me to count now.

Jace: I don't want to hear about you and Bash and why he's secure. La La La.

Scarlet: Friends, Lenny Lou. I don't count his abs.

Amelia: I volunteer as tribute.

Max: Can I be the one to tell Sam? I think I'd enjoy that.

Amelia: You're a sick man Maximus.

Max: You're not wrong.

Sawyer: I want the record to show, I told Hudson he was acting like an ass.

Becks: Yeah. And now you're acting like an ass kisser.

Sawyer: I'd rather kiss Scarlet's ass than put my lips where yours have been.

Lenny: Now boys, this is not the time to tell Becks how his girlfriend isn't good enough for him.

Max: Adaline likes her. I'd say that right there is a pretty good reason for us to hate her.

Sawyer: That's because she's a younger version of Adaline.

Jace: It's still weird you call your mom by her first name.

Scarlet: Can we focus on my non-relationship and not on Becket's mommy issues please?

Becks: You're all assholes.

Scarlet: No. We're Kings. Now fucking act like it.

SCARLET

THE HEADACHE THAT FADED THANKS TO CADE'S TALENTED hands comes back full force when I exit the elevator and walk down the hall to my condo in Rittenhouse Square. Why do I suddenly have a cavalcade of drummers using their sticks on my brain? Because my idiot brother is sitting on the floor in front of my door.

Stepping over him, I refuse to make eye contact with Hudson as I unlock my door. "How did you get up here?"

"I may have promised your doorman front row seats to my next fight." He slowly stands. "And I might have to name my first kid Bob."

"You know you're an asshole, right?" I push the door open and let him walk in ahead of me. Once I'm in, I go straight to my kitchen, grab two prescription-strength migraine pills, and swallow them with a glass of water.

I know where this is going.

It may have just been a lingering throb earlier, but this is coming on hard and fast now.

"What do you want, Hud? I'm tired, and I need to go to bed, so make it fast." I finish my glass of water and place it in the sink, then turn, waiting for Hudson to speak. Everyone might think I'm an ice queen. But I'm not good at staying mad at my brothers. My parents may never have really been there for us as kids, but we were always there for each other. And our bonds have only strengthened as we've all grown up.

My six-foot-four brother stands in my kitchen, looking small and guilty with his hands shoved in the pockets of his jeans and his purple Crucible hat shading his blue eyes.

Unfortunately for him, my patience is wearing thin. "Say what you came to say, Hudson."

"I'm an asshole, Scarlet. I'm sorry." His shoulders rise and fall as if this is painful for him, but he manages to raise his stormy blue eyes to meet mine.

"Go on . . ." I goad, not quite ready to forgive him but knowing I need to, to move on.

"I may not be thrilled at the idea of you and Cade together, but it's your business. I shouldn't have gotten involved, not like that."

I take two steps forward and flick his ear. "How about not ever?"

He steps back and hisses. "Ow. That hurt."

"MMA Heavyweight Champion of the World, ladies and gentlemen." I mock him because sarcasm is our love language. It's how we show affection, even when we're mad. It used to drive our father crazy. "Even Becket took it better than you, and Cade's been one of his best friends for years."

"Whatever. Will you at least tell me one thing?" He moves across the kitchen and helps himself to a bottle of vitamin water from my fridge.

"Is he good to you?"

Sensing he's not ready to leave yet, I place my hands behind myself and pull up to sit on my counter. At least this way, I can lean my head against the cabinets and be at Hud's eye level so he can see in my eyes that I'm telling him the truth. "We're not even together."

He leans his hip against the counter next to me as he gulps down the entire bottle, then wipes his lips with the back of his hand like he'd been wandering the desert without water for days.

"Jesus, how long were you sitting out there? I think there's some leftover Chinese food in the fridge if you're hungry too."

Hudson shakes his head no. "Just thirsty, and I was out there for at least an hour. I think your neighbor wanted to call the cops. The old lady just kept cracking the door open and peeking out to see if I'd gone. I told her I was your brother, but she looked skeptical."

"You have a key." We all have keys.

A tight smile appears on Hudson's face, accompanied by a low laugh. "I do have a key, but I also like my balls intact. If I'd let myself in here to wait for you, I'm pretty sure you would have castrated me."

"You're not wrong." The dull throb in my head is getting worse, so I kick my shoes off and let them fall to the floor before I hop back down. "I'm going to bed, Hud. Stay as long as you want."

He stops me with a gentle hand on my shoulder. "Did he do something?"

"No. He didn't do anything. We weren't together. We're friends, and we're going to stay friends. It's what's best for your niece." I fail to mention that there was a time when we were so much more.

Hudson doesn't need to know that.

Not now.

Possibly not ever.

His smile creeps back. "You know you can't will her into being a girl, right Scarlet? I mean, I know you've got your ways to make the universe bend to your will, but even you aren't that good." He bends down and picks up my shoes and offers them to me.

I take them and lean in for a hug. "My head is throbbing, I've got to go to bed, Hud. But seriously, stay if you want." Hudson still lives at Kingston Manor with Max, Jace, our father's final wife, Ashlyn, and the youngest Kingston sibling, Madeline. He's never cared about moving out because the gym might as well be his home. And the manor is close to the gym.

He leans down and kisses my head the way Cade kissed Brynlee earlier. "You really forgive me, Scar?"

The words are soft.

Unsure.

Whether it's because he knows my head hurts or he's just scared of the answer, I couldn't say.

I lean into him. "I do. This one time. Don't do it again, Hudson. Dad's dead. And I may have five brothers and two brothers-in-law, but none of you have the right to father me. Seriously, Dad barely did it, and I refuse to let anyone else step in and try." I pull back and turn toward my room. "Night, Hud. I'm done adulting for the day." When he makes no move to leave, I add, "Make sure you lock the door. I'm not getting back up."

"Love ya, Scar."

"You too, little brother."

The next few weeks go by in a flash of late nights and crazy days in the Kings offices. We've all been doing double duty as we keep everything on track for the Philadelphia Kings upcoming season while discussing options and contingencies versus realities for the possible acquisition of the Revolution.

Football season and hockey season may not start at the same time, but they definitely overlap and have us working overtime.

The deal should be done soon.

And I'm not sure how I feel about it.

When Lenny knocks on my office door Friday and pops

her head in, it's with a big smile on her face. "Hey, you ready to head over to Amelia's for girls' night?"

I almost forgot we were doing this tonight.

Truth be told, it wasn't that we were getting together that I forgot.

I just didn't realize it was Friday. This entire week's been a blur.

I'm not sure what that says about me.

A quick look at the clock tells me it's already past six, and I have another few hours of work to get through, but it can wait until tomorrow. "Yeah. Let me just finish this email, and then I'll be good."

She walks in and shuts my laptop with a groan. "It can wait."

"Eleanor Louise Kingston!" I gasp. "You don't know what I was working on."

"Scarlet Leigh Kingston. I said it, and I'm not wrong. It can wait. You haven't left here before eight o'clock a single night this week. You're going to drive yourself into the ground. You even have dark circles under your eyes."

"What? Take that back." I jump up from my chair and run into my private bathroom to check my reflection in the mirror, only to see she's right.

Lenny walks up behind me and looks at me in the mirror. "You do, Scarlet." She moves my hair off my shoulders. "And you look like you're losing weight. I'm worried about you. When's your next doctor's appointment?"

"Next week."

"Good. Want me to go with you?" The two of us have come a long way in our relationship. We've always been very different people, and with the six-year age gap between us, we never really found ourselves at the same place in life until two years ago.

We didn't really like each other much at that point either.

But once she was home from college, we both made more of an effort.

It's nice but still a little odd for me.

I'm not someone who grew up with female friends.

Most of the girls in school annoyed me.

"I appreciate the offer, but Cade is coming with me. If we're lucky, they might be able to tell us that she's a girl." We both move back into my office while I pack up my laptop and grab my purse.

Lenny grabs her bag from where she dropped it earlier, and we head for the elevator. "What are you going to do if they tell you it's a boy?"

I smile at my sister when the door dings open. "Tell them to look again."

CAD E

"Daddy, are we leaving yet?" Brynlee runs to me late in the day Friday and jumps up into my arms. I'm standing next to the cage Hudson is coming out of, covered in sweat, with a stupid grin on his face.

"Soon, baby. We're leaving soon." I put her back on her feet. "Why don't you go get your things out of my office, and we'll get going."

As she sprints toward my door, Hudson laughs. "She doesn't hate me anymore."

"Oh, yeah? How'd you get out of the doghouse?" We start picking up the discarded equipment and returning them to their places. "Last I checked, she still wasn't talking to you."

"Oh, come on now. I can't give away all my moves, Saint." His smile grows.

"Dick." I shake my head.

"Fucknut," he returns.

"Coach Fucknut." I throw a medicine ball that he catches with an umph.

"What's a fucknut?" This kid is going to have the worst mouth at preschool, and I'm so getting another call from the teacher.

Before I can say anything, Hudson scoops her up in his arms. "It's a word you can't say, Brynnie. But it's your daddy's nickname."

"It is not, Bryn." I grab her from him. "Ignore Hudson."

"But he's my best friend. It's not nice to ignore your best

friend, Daddy." The serious look on her face has me hiding my smile.

"It's not nice, baby. You're right. But what did Hudson do to earn best friend status?" If he won't tell me, she will.

Her big green eyes look from me to Hudson, and then I think she tries to wink, but it's really a blink. Sort of. Whatever the hell it was, it required some serious concentration. "Nope. That's only for best friends to know, Daddy. Just me and Hud."

Hudson's shoulders inflate just like his ego, and he preens like the peacock he is.

"I'm not your best friend, baby?" And that pain there was most definitely my heart cracking in half. I thought I had until she was a teenager before I got replaced by a boy.

I glare at my offending fighter. "You. Go run."

Hudson laughs at me. "No can do. I gotta get cleaned up and head over to Amelia and Sam's. Nonna is feeding us tonight."

"Lucky bastard." Sam's Nonna loves to feed people, and her food is amazing.

Hudson looks between Brynlee and me. "You should come with. And bring your money. We might be playing poker later, after the kids go to bed."

"Nah, man. I appreciate it. But I don't want to invade family time."

"Seriously, you should come. It won't be just family. Declan Sinclair is bringing his family too. I think Sam wanted to plan a poker night, and Amelia wanted a girls' night, so they just called everyone. Check your phone."

"Yeah. Maybe." I put Brynlee down and grab my stuff from my office. Hudson's right. My phone's flashing with a message from Sam, inviting us over for food and poker. According to the text, it's just him, Becks, and Declan. Guess he didn't get the memo.

When I come back out of my office, I laugh at Hud squatting down to Bryn's level, whispering about something. "Daddy, I want to go to Nonna's. Huddy says she makes real good food, and he said he thinks Amelia will have cupcakes."

I glare at Hudson. "Don't use my daughter against me, asshole."

He moves behind Brynn. "I would do no such thing."

"There was a text from Sam. Sounds like Dec's kids are gonna be there too."

"Can we go? Please, Daddy."

I look from Brynn back to Hudson and huff. "Yeah, baby. We can go. But we've got to go home first, so I can change."

My three-year-old shocks me when she cheers, then high-fives Hudson. "Told ya if I asked, he'd say yes."

I pick her up and tell my night-time front desk girl we're leaving.

When I'm locking Brynlee into her car seat, I stare at her. "Who are you? And what have you done with my baby?"

She reaches out and smooshes my cheeks between her hands. "You're silly, Daddy. I'm Brynlee St. James. And you always say yes if I ask nice."

I am so fucked when this kid grows up.

When Brynlee and I pull up to Sam's house, the massive driveway is filled with cars.

Sam, Becks, and I went to school together.

We were tight back then.

We're still tight. It just looks different now.

We all went in different directions in our twenties, but the bonds we formed as overly privileged juvenile delinquents have stayed intact. Becks and Sam both have keys to Crucible and tend to use it after-hours. Well . . . Sam, not as much now that he has a woman he loves in his bed and a baby to keep them both up at night.

But who can blame him?

Poker nights happened more often before Brynlee came into the picture. And they happen even less now that Sam's got Amelia and Maddox. But as I walk into his house, with Brynlee more nervous about all the people than excited like she was earlier, I wonder how long this will last.

I also wonder whether Scarlet's gonna be here and if she'll be happy to see me.

We've been texting with the occasional FaceTime thrown in. I like to check in with her and see how she's feeling. I have a funny feeling she's not taking as good of care of herself as she should be. But whenever I broach the subject, I get shot down. She bailed on getting together for dinner last week. Said she had another meeting at work.

Amelia opens the door and kisses my cheek before taking Brynlee from me. "Hi, sweet girl. You haven't stopped in for cupcakes lately."

Brynlee smiles a hesitant smile back up at Amelia before two loud voices come bounding toward us in the form of identical twin toddler girls, washing away any hesitation Brynn may have had. Gracie and Everly Sinclair are Declan and Annabelle's twin daughters, and as Amelia sets her on her feet, Brynlee looks like she could be the third sister.

The twins are two years old. And the three girls are not only in the same preschool class, but Brynlee takes ballet classes with them at Hart & Soul, their mother's studio. In the next heartbeat, one of the two little blonde heads says something about cookies, and all three of them take off.

Amelia assures me they're heading right for Nonna before I catch Annabelle waving hello as she follows behind the trio, hopefully making sure they don't break anything. Amelia guides me further into the house, that seems to be overflowing with Kingstons, until I finally see Sam. The man born to mafia royalty holds his seven-month-old son against his shoulder, bouncing his body to calm him. And I swear to God, it's not a sight I ever thought I'd see.

"Saint, you made it." His son, Maddox, pops his wobbly head up at the intrusion of the loud voice, and looks around. Big blue eyes grow impossibly wider as he takes in the number of people in the large room. Then, a ridiculously loud wail of a scream is ripped from his throat before Amelia takes him from Sam.

"Prince." I clap Sam on the back. "Not exactly like the poker nights we used to have." Back in high school, Becks used to call me "Saint," and Sam "Prince," since his father was the mafia king in town. Of course, Becks dubbed himself "King," like everything the Kingstons touch. That all changed two years ago when Sam took his father's place. But we can't call them both "King," so Sammy's stuck with "Prince."

Sam throws his arm over my shoulder. "Saint, have you met Declan?"

Declan Sinclair is the quarterback for the Kings football team. He's only been in Kroydon Hills for a few years, but he's already become somewhat of a legend since he's brought the championship home twice. I offer him my hand. "We've met at Hart & Soul. My daughter takes classes with Annabelle and the girls."

His smile grows as he looks around for the girls. "She must be the third musketeer I saw running away with them a minute ago."

"Yeah, that's her. Sorry about that. I saw your wife. I should probably go make sure Brynlee's behaving herself."

I'm handed a beer. "Don't worry about it. Belle's not shy. If she needs you, she'll come get you." Declan sips his beer. "So, I hear congratulations are in order." He tips his head toward the far corner where Scarlet and Lenny are standing.

"Thanks." My eyes stay locked with hers. "Excuse me, guys."

I cross the room quickly and insert myself into the women's circle. "Ladies," I greet and place my palm on the small of Scarlet's back. Lenny welcomes me and then quickly excuses herself as if she'd planned it that way all along.

Scarlet watches her go before meeting my gaze. She doesn't move away though, so I'll count that as a small victory. "I'm surprised to see you here, Cade." Her tired eyes scan the crowded room. "Actually, let me rephrase. I'm surprised to see everyone here. I thought this was going to be a quiet girls' night. I guess my family had other plans."

I cup her elbow and am grateful when she lets me guide her over to a sofa. "You feeling okay, Scarlet?"

"Is that a nice way of telling me I look tired?" She looks up at me through inky black lashes. "Because you wouldn't be the first person to tell me that tonight." We sit down, and she leans her head back against the arm I stretch out over the top of the sofa.

It's so damn easy to fall back into old habits.

Scarlet was never one who like being touched.

She wasn't that girl who hugged everyone.

But she never pulled away from me.

I guess not everything changed.

"Are you tired? I can take you home if you don't feel like driving." I'm sure she has her own car with her, but the offer flows freely anyway.

"I'm not planning on staying long. It's just been a busy few weeks. I guess it's catching up with me. But I don't plan on leaving my apartment this weekend. I have some work I need to get done. Then I plan to relax for the rest of the weekend. Who knows? Maybe I'll even get a massage."

I'm not sure why I hate the idea of someone having their hands all over her body.

But I do.

"How about I bring you dinner?"

Scarlet's eyes open about as wide as Sam's baby's did earlier. But before she can answer, Becket joins our conversation by forcing himself down between the two of us on the couch, inserting himself like a nun telling us to make room for the Holy Spirit.

"Well, shit. Looks like we've got the baby mama and baby daddy together. You guys want in the pool?"

For an intelligent man, Becks is a fucking moron when he wants to be.

And he should be terrified, judging by the look on Scarlet's face. "What pool, Becket?" The words are spoken with icy precision through gritted teeth.

Becks swallows. "The pool we've got going on for whether the baby is a boy or girl and when Baby Kingston will make its grand entrance into the world."

I shove him away since he's practically sitting in my lap. "Get off me, fucker." I scoot over to put some space between us. "And it's Baby St. James."

Scarlet's brow shoots straight up. "Oh, is it, now?" She tilts her head to the side like one of those dinosaurs in Jurassic Park, studying its prey.

Fuck.

I'm the prey this time.

"I must have missed that conversation." She stands from the couch with a little more color in her face and smiles deviously at her brother and me. She points at Becks. "You're an ass, Becket." Then her eyes hold me hostage until she lets her smile show. "And we still have to discuss what we're going to call baby girl Kingston. But she will carry my last name."

She walks away from the two of us, smiling.

Knowing she's won.

And maybe she has.

But I don't know if I'm thinking straight since all the blood has rushed from my head to my dick as I watch her perfectly heart-shaped ass, encased in tight jeans, walking away. Fingers snap in front of my face, and if they were anyone else's, I'd probably have broken them as quickly as someone swats a fly. But they're Becks's. So I play nice.

"Listen. I know you've nailed my sister since she's carrying your spawn. But if you could possibly keep the sexcapades to the bedroom and wipe the fucking drool from your face, I'd appreciate it." He finally moves over so he's not so close I can smell the beer on his breath.

"No sexcapades, man. I told you, we aren't together." But only because this woman is not giving me a fucking inch to work with.

The thought shocks me.

Do I want more than a co-parenting relationship with Scarlet Kingston?

Hudson drops into the chair across from us, and I eye the beer in his hand skeptically.

"Come on, man. It's one beer." Hudson has a fight coming up but not close enough to be in full-blown camp yet. That doesn't mean he should be polluting his body with that shit.

Becks ignores Hudson and looks back at me. "Seriously? You and Scarlet aren't a thing?" He sounds stunned, like this isn't exactly what I told him weeks ago.

"That's the same line she fed me," Hudson adds.

"It's not a line, guys. We're not a thing. Your sister is way above my pay grade." I may be hoping to change that, but I don't need to let them know.

Not yet.

Becks puts his crystal tumbler down, and Hudson leans in as if readying to hear what wisdom his brother is about to impart. "You realize you're worthy, right, Saint? Like seriously, I was pissed at first, but if any man was ever going to be the man to challenge Scarlet Kingston and come out a winner on the other side, it would be you."

Hudson shakes his head and blinks his eyes a few times. "What Becket is trying to say but may be mixing too many movie references to be clear about, is we love our sisters. We were raised to put them on pedestals no one else could reach. But you're a good guy and a great dad, Saint. And Scarlet could use someone to get her to remember that there's more to life than work."

Pretty sure these two just gave me their blessing to date their sister, but I could be wrong.

"So, let me get this straight. You both were pissed as hell when you found out that Scarlet and I had hooked up, but now you what . . . give us your blessing?" I laugh. "Not so sure she'd appreciate that." My eyes search the room but don't find Scarlet anywhere.

Lenny, however, drops down on the other side of Becket. "Sounds like you know my sister pretty well, Cade. Better than these two, at least. And you're right. She'd hate knowing anyone had given any type of permission. But at least you know that." Len flashes a beautiful smile my way, then shoves Becks off the couch. "So . . . it's time to figure out what you need to do to get the girl."

SCARLET

Since my doctor's office is in the city, I agreed to let Cade pick me up at the Kings offices and drive us over, rather than backtracking to get him in Kroydon Hills and then needing to double back into the city. So I'm not surprised when Connor tells me Mr. St. James is here to see me.

He's early.

Seeing him Friday night was confusing. The attraction between us is visceral. It always was. So it's no wonder we got together in Vegas when finally given the opportunity. The pull to him is as powerful now as it was when we were teenagers. But I'm stronger now.

I stand from my chair and smooth my hands down my black cigar pants as Connor escorts Cade into my office. "Thanks, Connor. We'll be leaving in a few minutes. I'm not sure what time I'll be back."

"No problem, Scarlet." He looks between Cade and me and smiles. "I cleared your schedule for the afternoon."

I scrutinize his face. "I thought I had a four o'clock?"

"Nope. You're good for the rest of the day." He shuts the door behind him, and I can't help but wonder what's going on. "Well, okay then. Just give me a minute, and I'll be ready to leave." I sit back down and finish the email I was sending, albeit a little slower than I usually would because my eyes keep straying to Cade.

He's wearing gray and white workout pants that taper to

the ankle and another Crucible shirt. Today's is red. And right now, he's perusing the credenza along the wall of my office. It's filled with pictures. One of the last games we were all at together, as a family, before Lenny's mom died and she ran off to England. One of all of us as little kids in matching Kings jerseys. Dad and Grandpa together when the new stadium was built. And my most favorite recent one of Max, Becks, me, and Lenny with her fiancé, Sebastian, after he played in and won our most recent championship game.

He may not be married to Lenny yet, but he's already part of the family. There was something extraordinary about having a family member playing in that game.

"There's a whole lot of history on these shelves, Scarlet." Cade picks up a frame and turns it so I can see it. "But I think this is my favorite." It's a picture of Max, Becks, and me as teenagers in our jerseys.

There's absolutely nothing special about that one. "Really?"

"Yup. This is the *you* that was mine." And damn, if the sexy as sin smile that accompanies that statement doesn't make my panties damp.

"Okay, Romeo." I hit send on my email, close my laptop, and add it to my bag in case I don't want to come back today. Working from home is always an option.

A few minutes later, the two of us are in Cade's truck, taking the ten-minute drive to the doctor's office, the tension in the air blanketing both of us. It's not until Cade parks and we get out of the truck that one of us finally breaks the silence. "How have you been feeling, Scarlet?"

I don't get a chance to answer him before his phone rings. "You can take that. I'm going to go get signed in."

Luckily, I'm called back immediately and let the nurse know that Cade will join us in just a minute. After I've peed in a cup and been weighed like a prized pig, I'm escorted to one of the exam rooms. My blood pressure is taken, and I'm told to sit on the table. The doctor should be right in.

"Wait. Don't I have to get changed?" I mean, where's the itchy pink paper gown?

The older woman smiles warmly at me. "First baby, honey?"

I hate being called "honey." "Yes. I guess it's obvious?" Okay. That was the polite answer. It may have taken more energy than I had to give, but I was nice. What I wanted to say was, *"Could you answer my fucking question instead of asking me another one?"* But no need to piss off the people I'm going to need over the next few months.

My nerves are fried, and the exam hasn't even started.

Just as she's leaving, I hear Cade's voice before he enters the room. "Sorry about that. Imogen picked Brynlee up from school today and was just letting me know her teacher pulled her aside to talk to her." He leans against the wall and crosses his ankles and then his arms over his chest.

"Everything okay with Brynlee?"

"Well, let's see. She called a little boy a 'fucknut.'" He rolls both his lips in, keeping his laughter murmured.

I, however, laugh out loud. "Oh my God. No. Where did she hear that?"

"Let's just say I'm going to make your brother clean the bathrooms at the gym for a fucking month." He crosses the room and leans a hip next to me on the table. "It's good to see you laugh, duchess." His fingers run through my hair as the door opens, and Dr. Esher walks in.

"Hi, Scarlet." She looks over at Cade. "And Mr . . . ?"

Cade doesn't answer right away though. He looks to me for permission first, then offers her his hand. "Cade St James. I'm the baby's father."

Dr. Esher tosses her hair over her shoulder and smiles before offering him her hand. "Very nice to meet you, Mr. St.

James." If she's flirting with him, I might actually strangle her with the stethoscope around her neck. "How are you feeling, Scarlet?" I never really thought about it before, but Dr. Esher looks like she can't be any older than I am. How many babies could she have possibly delivered? Shit. Maybe I need to find a new doctor.

"I feel great." I plaster my best PR smile on my face and sit tall until Cade clears his throat. One look his way, and I know I'm about to get ratted out. Damnit. "Well, I feel pretty good, but I guess I've been tired."

She sits down on her wheelie stool and scans what's on the computer, then rolls over to me. "Okay, let's get a quick look and listen, shall we? First, I need you to lie back. Then unbutton your pants and pull them down a bit."

Cade stands next to me, watching Dr. Esher as she squeezes cold jelly on my stomach and starts pushing down with a small wand. I've been quietly dreading this appointment. What if something is wrong? What if they were wrong last time? It's only been a month. Four short weeks. But it only took the first beat of her heart on the very first day for my entire world to tilt on its axis, and I've spent those four weeks since that moment figuring out how I needed that world to look, so I could give my daughter the best life.

She's surpassed every other priority I had.

She's it now.

She's the priority.

It only takes a minute before a quick, strong heartbeat fills the room, and overwhelming relief fills my body.

Cade's fingers grasp mine, and he squeezes, then wipes away the tears I didn't realize were falling down my face.

The doctor moves the wand around and pushes a little harder. "That's a good, strong heartbeat. Everything looks good in there."

Cade bends down and kisses my forehead, then leans his head against mine.

The move surprises me.

It's intimate.

I don't hate it.

I kinda wish I did.

The doctor wipes my stomach clean, then moves back to her computer. "Well, everything looks good with the baby, but I'd like to take your blood pressure again." She sets the cuff on my arm and presses a button to start the process.

"Why do you need to do this again? Is something off with my blood pressure?"

She waits until it's done before recording the numbers and finally answering me. It seems like it takes hours but is probably less than sixty seconds.

"I wanted to make sure the reading the nurse got earlier was right. I'm a little concerned with your blood pressure, Scarlet. You've always been right around one ten over seventy. But you were just one forty-eight over eighty-six. And that's what you were earlier too."

Cade sits next to me on the table and wraps an arm protectively around my shoulder. "What does that mean, Doc?"

"It means I have some questions. Are you still exercising?"

"Yes. Four to five days a week. Cardio and some light weights with my trainer."

She nods her head. "Are you eating right? Getting enough sleep?"

"Is there ever enough time in the day to get enough sleep?" I mean, seriously. I'm thirty, not eighty.

"How's your stress level?"

"I handle crises and make multi-billion-dollar decisions for a living. In my world, that's not stress. It's just a Tuesday."

Dr. Esher looks at me with pity in her eyes, and I want to

rip her pretty, blonde hair extensions out. "I want you to try to take it a little easier, Scarlet. I need you to try to watch what you eat. You can maintain your exercise routine for now. But I want you to make sure you get more rest and lower your stress level. Hypertension, this early in the pregnancy, can lead to other complications I'd rather not see you have to deal with." She turns back to the desk, scribbles something on a pad and hands it to me.

"What's this?" I ask.

"It's a type of blood pressure cuff I want you to get. If you need a nurse to help you coordinate with your insurance, just let us know. I want you to take your blood pressure every morning and night and jot down the results for me. I want to see you back in two weeks."

Cade's arm has slipped down and is rubbing comforting circles on my back. "What should I be doing to help her, Doc?"

"She needs to rest and control her stress, Mr. St. James. I need you both to know that gestational hypertension is something to be taken very seriously, or it can lead to serious complications to both Scarlet and the baby."

"What complications?" I don't do well with maybes and what ifs. I need facts.

Dr. Esher stands from her stool. "Preeclampsia. Hospitalization. Pre-term delivery. We need to make sure we take this seriously and watch your blood pressure, Scarlet. If we aren't able to control it over these next few weeks, you're going to spend your pregnancy on bed rest. And I'm sure you'd like to avoid that."

How am I supposed to cut out stress when I'm about to take over the Revolution?

CADE

SCARLET IS QUIET AS WE DRIVE BACK TO HER OFFICE. WHEN WE left the doctor's office, I asked her if she was okay, and the look she gave me was glacial. But now, as we get closer to her office, my chances of getting her to open up about how she's feeling are dwindling. "Talk to me, Scarlet. I'm worried about you."

She doesn't turn her face toward me. Handicapping me by not giving me her eyes. "I've managed to survive thirteen years without your worry or help, Cade. I think I've got this."

Her cold words cut like ice.

She's good at that.

It would be foolish to correct her.

To remind her that the eighteen-year-old punk I used to be might not have been able to take care of her. But he's long gone. The man I am today takes care of what's his.

Is she mine? She was once. At least I thought she was.

Frustration keeps me from telling her that she needs to get over herself and let me help since she's carrying my child. I'm a lot of things, but I'm not a fool.

When we pull into the Kings parking garage, she gives me directions to her car instead of the entrance to the offices. I take that as a small win.

The passenger side door opens, and she moves to get out without saying anything, so I reach out and grab her wrist, stopping her. "Scarlet."

She finally turns her gorgeous face my way, only to break

my heart when I see tears in those midnight-blue eyes of hers. Instead of staying in the truck, I hop out and walk around the front of it until I'm face to face with this infuriating woman. When I reach out for her, she tries to push me away, but I don't give in. Instead, I wrap my arms around her and pull her into my chest.

I might as well be holding granite at first.

But after a moment's hesitation, her arms wrap around my waist, and she lays her head against my chest, finally taking the small comfort I can give.

I run my fingers over her hair and cup her face. "Let me help you, Scarlet. You don't have to do this alone."

She lifts her head. "I wish you were right. But don't worry about me. I'm good at being alone."

"Scarlet . . ."

She pushes away and adjusts the bag on her shoulder. "Thanks for coming with me today, Cade. We'll talk this weekend, okay?"

I stand there, stuck in place as she settles herself inside her sporty little car.

Not sure how much I can push her without it being too much.

Frustrated, I get back into the truck. My phone is ringing with a call from Rylie.

"Hello?" I watch Scarlet's car in the rearview mirror as I exit the parking garage, hoping she's going home.

"Umm, Cade? Any chance you can stop by?" My older sister sounds frantic.

"What's going on, Rylie?" I send the call to my Bluetooth and turn on the car.

There's a loud screech in the background and then the sound of wood scratching against wood. "OH MY GOD! There's a really big snake in my kitchen. Like really big. I can deal with mice and spiders. Hell, I can deal with bats. But I don't do snakes, Cade. And Jillian is at work. Please come get it."

"I'm on my way. I'm just leaving Kings Stadium now. Where are you?"

A semi-hysterical laugh escapes from Rylie's lips. "Well, I'm currently sitting on my kitchen table, watching the damn thing sun itself in front of the sliding glass doors. Was the doctor's appointment today or were you just meeting up with Scarlet?"

Rylie was great when I told her about Scarlet and the baby. There was no guilt trip with her like there was with Mom. "It was the appointment. Scarlet and I haven't progressed to the meeting up for lunch kind of friends yet."

"You'll get there. I never met a girl you couldn't charm. How was the appointment?"

I take the dig at my former player ways in stride. I earned them. I definitely spent my twenties playing the field once I was back home. "Not so good. Scarlet's blood pressure was up. Doc wants her to cut back on the stress in her life, watch what she eats. That kind of thing." I picture the tears gathering in her eyes and wish to God I could fix this for her.

I take a deep breath and then admit, "I don't know how to help her, Ry."

Rylie screeches again. "It moved. Fucking speed, Cade. Help me. Then I'll help you help her. I'm a registered dietician, and I'm married to a stubborn woman. I can help you figure out a few meals to bring to her, so it's one less thing for her to stress over. And I can help you figure out how to get out of the friend zone."

When I don't answer my sister, she laughs. "It's obvious you want her. Your voice changes when you talk about her. It goes kinda soft. And you are not soft. I mean, she's incredible. She's gorgeous. She's strong-willed. She's a powerful woman who won't put up with your shit. You've got that whole, alpha male fighter, protector thing going on, but Scarlet Kingston is the ultimate alpha female, and you know it. Seriously . . . all of Philadelphia knows it."

"She's pretty incredible, Ry." She always was.

"Then come get the snake. And in return, I'll help you get the girl."

The snake Rylie was screaming about was a little garter snake, perfectly harmless and happy to be rehomed into the woods behind their house. Less than five minutes later, I'm sitting at the kitchen table she'd just been sitting on while she makes a pot of soup for me to take to Scarlet. According to her, it freezes well, and is heart, and therefore, blood pressure friendly. Low salt, healthy protein, and chunks of fresh veggies.

God, I love my sister.

As the soup simmers on the stove, she offers me a glass of iced tea and sits down at the table with me. "Tell me about her, Cade. Tell me something I don't know from *Philadelphia Magazine* or from growing up here. Tell me why you're drawn to her, and why I should help you."

I study my sister. Yet another fiery red-head in my life with the passion and excitability all red-heads are known for. I decide it's time to finally tell someone the truth. "Scarlet and I were together in some way or another for almost two years in high school. She begged me to keep it from her brothers, and, at first, I was okay with it because she was a sophomore and I was a junior.

We were young.

What did hiding matter?

I think at first, sneaking around was part of the fun. But it turned into more pretty quickly."

I lean forward on the table and wipe the condensation from my glass. Talking about this isn't something I'm completely comfortable with, even with my sister. Scarlet has always been mine. I've never shared any of this before, not like this. "Even back then, she was the strongest person I'd ever met. She knew who she was and what she wanted. She wasn't afraid to go after whatever that was. And for a long time, it was me." I think of her back then. She was beautiful in such a natural way. She could have ruled the school, but she didn't. She wasn't interested. "Scarlet had this way about her. Her energy just sucked me in, and I loved it. She was fearless. Except when it came to her brothers."

"I thought Becket was one of your best friends."

"He was." I think back to those years I spent lying to him. I hated it. I didn't hate it enough to give her up though. "He still is. And he still doesn't know. I was in love with her. But I was a dumb kid. What the hell did I know?" I'm not sure if I'm trying to convince her or myself.

"We all are when we're teenagers, Cade. We haven't experienced living enough to have any real clue about life." Rylie stands back up to stir the soup, then cocks a hip and points the wooden spoon at me. "If you two were so in love, why did it end?"

"I was graduating and going into the marines. I wanted to talk to Becks about everything. I wanted to bring us out into the open. I wanted to do the long-distance thing. But she didn't want any of that. She ended it." At least, that's what I remember thinking back then. Now, I can't help but wonder what would have happened if I'd have fought for her.

Rylie turns the stove off and covers the pot, then starts doing the dishes in the sink. "So you left for the marines, and that was it? You never talked to her again?"

"I wrote her a few letters that summer but never heard back from her."

Water from the sprayer on the sink flies at me across the room when my crazy sister decided I need to be wet. "What the hell, Rylie?"

"You are such a dumb man. Seriously. You're sitting here telling me that for two years you were willing to go sneaking around your best friend's back. Which, by the way, makes you a shitty friend, and I would love to be a fly on the wall when you finally fess up to Becket Kingston. I mean seriously, if I didn't play for the other team, I'd be willing to take him for a test drive. But I digress."

I grimace and close my eyes. "Oh, God. That's a visual I never needed."

"But if you cared so much, maybe even loved her, why did you let her go so easily?"

I think back to those last few months of high school. "I think it had started to get harder. Harder to find time to be together without anyone finding out. Harder to hide it from Becks and Sam. I think I wanted her to be willing to fight for us. She knew I wanted to be a marine. That wasn't new. And yet, she was so willing to let me go. I trusted her in a way I'd never trusted anyone, and she broke that trust."

"How did she break your trust? By breaking up with you?" Rylie offers me a towel but doesn't give me a chance to answer. "Maybe it wasn't meant to be back then. She might have broken up with you, but it sounds like she was upfront about it. I think she broke your heart, not your trust, Cade." Her green eyes soften around the edges. "Maybe you both needed to grow up and live your lives alone before it was time to live it together. Maybe now, it's time to live it together."

"She's always been the one who got away."

"Build back the trust you used to have, Cade. You have so much to gain if you think this is what you want. Build that back. Be there for her. Make sure she knows that you want to be more than her friend, but don't pressure her."

I lean back in my seat. "Yeah. Because that should be easy."

"Nothing worth having is ever easy. You guys had it once before it broke. Fix it, Cade. It might just be the most important thing you ever do."

I hang my head, knowing Rylie's right. Getting Scarlet Kingston to give us a chance is sure to be the hardest fight I've ever won. But no fight has ever been more worth it.

Rylie leans against the counter, a smug smile in place. "Oh, and Cade . . ."

"Yeah?"

"You've got to come clean to Becket."

Fuck.

Once I leave Rylie's house, I check in with Imogen to make sure Brynlee's set, then text Becks.

Cade: Hey can I have Scarlet's address?
Becks: Is she going to kick me in the balls the next time I see her?
Cade: Why would she do that?
Becks: Why are you asking me for her address instead of asking her?
Becks: And if you two are so close, why don't you know it already?
Becks: Should I be worried you're a stalker?
Cade: No dumbass. Rylie made some soup for Scarlet. I want to stop by and surprise her with it.
Cade: Kinda loses the surprise if I ask her where she lives first.

Becks: Well I wouldn't stop by now.

Cade: Why?

Becks: Because she's not there. She's in her office. I saw her five minutes ago.

Becks: Us corporate dumbasses are usually in the office until five or six.

Becks: Scarlet rarely leaves before seven.

Cade: Can you send me her address anyway?

The dots start and stop a few times before Becks shoots off her address.

Cade: Thanks, man.

Becks: Don't make me regret it.

With a plan in place and my mind made up, I head back to Crucible.

If she needs space, I'll give her what she needs.

For now.

SCARLET

I HAD EVERY INTENTION OF COMING STRAIGHT HOME WHEN Cade dropped me off earlier. I even got in my damn car. But then the phone rang, and I knew I had to answer it. Connor wouldn't have called unless it was something important. So, like a moth to the flame, I answered, and now, nearly six hours later, I'm finally home.

Our star wide receiver could find trouble in a church.

And usually does.

Once that fire was contained, Max brought Becks, Len, and me into his office to discuss the details of the acquisition. Our lawyers have looked everything over and given us the go-ahead to move forward. It appears we're going to be closing this deal next month.

I should be thrilled.

This is my chance to do what I've always wanted.

I'll be running the organization.

So why, as I sit in front of my television, eating ice cream and binging *Schitt's Creek* on Netflix for the millionth time, do I just want to cry? Stupid freaking hormones. At least that's what I'm blaming it on. Because admitting it's fear would make it real. Admitting I'm scared my end goal is finally within my reach if I stretch my fingers in front of myself but it might not be what's best for me right now is too awful to consider.

It scares me. And I don't scare easily.

I'm Scarlet Kingston, and I refuse to believe there isn't a way I can have it all.

I'm stronger, smarter, and tougher than this.

I'm also a klutz who nearly drops my tablespoon full of rocky road on my cream carpet when my doorbell rings. My siblings are generally the only people who have drop-in privileges with my doormen. So unless I specifically tell Bob not to let someone up, like I did last week with Hudson—not that it worked—they can sign in and come right up without being screened first. But I wasn't expecting any of them tonight.

I plant my spoon in the carton of ice cream then pull on my white, fuzzy sweater to cover my silk nightgown. No need to give Max a show when he's probably here to hammer out more details on the Revolution acquisition. Typical Max. I'm not sure how many times, since Dad died and Max had to fill his shoes, he's shown up at my door, briefcase in hand, needing to talk something through that just couldn't wait.

He's a type A workaholic.

Not necessarily by nature but by need.

He's carrying a heavy weight on his shoulders.

But when I open the door, it's not Max.

Cade stands at the threshold. He's dressed in the same shirt from earlier, but now he has on basketball shorts instead of his athletic pants. Can calves be sexy? Because this man's calves are definitely sexy. Sculpted and defined.

"You gonna let me in, duchess?" If the nickname wasn't enough to make my insides clench, like they do every time he says it, the way he's eyeing up my body right now certainly does. I cross my arms to cover my chest and hold my sweater in place. Then stepping aside, I motion for him to come in. "How did you get up here?"

"Let's just say Bob is a fan."

I may have to have a talk with my doorman. "Well, by all means, if Bob's a fan, you should come right in, Saint."

"Where's your kitchen?" He holds up the bag he's carrying, and I lead him to the kitchen. "Rylie made you blood pressure friendly soup, some fresh bread, and she threw in a few cookies." He places the bag on my white marble counter and turns to me. "She said these are all okay for you to have." Once the cartons are out of the bag, his eyes burn their way up my body again before finally landing on my face. The same damn twinkle in his forest-green eyes that used to be my undoing years ago sparkles back at me.

I've been with my fair share of men.

Friends. Lovers.

Never relationships. Not since Cade.

And I don't know if that can technically be classified as a relationship.

I've spent my twenties in mutually beneficial agreements.

Men friends who were looking for the same thing I was.

Who had lofty aspirations.

They didn't have time for a relationship that would hold them back.

It's worked for me. It's worked for years.

But I've been busy, and that itch hasn't been scratched since my night in Vegas. At least not by something that didn't require batteries or recharging. That's always how it goes surrounding the football draft each year.

There's no time.

The team is my life.

The organization is my choice.

That must be why my brain is short-circuiting, reminding me the man standing in front of me was the best sex of my life and questioning whether it would be so bad to take a dip in that pool one more time. I mean, what's the worst thing that could happen? It's not like I can get pregnant again.

"So, I thought you were going to go home and rest after the appointment today."

Okay, well him thinking he gets a say in how I live my life is definitely one of the worst things that could happen. "There was an emergency that needed to be handled, and it's my job to handle it, thank you very much." I take a step toward him, my hands on my hips, firing myself up further. "Then a few things popped up. I do help run a multi-billion-dollar organization, you know."

He takes a step forward, ready to answer, when I cut him off. "Wait a second. How did you know I went back to work?" My blood starts pumping with the annoyance that's begun to course through my veins.

"I texted Becket for your address." Cade's voice raises to meet mine. We were always good at arguing. Two strong-willed people. Neither ever willing to give an inch. "I wanted to stop by to talk, to see how you were feeling. Today was rough, and I thought maybe you'd want to talk about it since you shut me out on the ride back."

"It's my body, Cade. You don't get a say." I take a step closer to him as his hands reach for me.

Those same hands grip my hips as mine push against his muscled chest.

Not pushing him away but not pulling him close either.

A war between what my body wants to make it feel good and what my brain knows is a stupid fucking idea.

"It's my baby in this body. I might not get much of a say, but you can't shut me out either." His hands move. Callused palms slide up my neck and under my hair. "Tell me to stop, duchess."

"Don't stop." I don't have the strength to fight it. Not now. Possibly not ever.

Strong hands lift me up, and spin me around, pinning me against the wall as his hungry lips crash down over mine. With one hand on my back, holding me to him, and the other on my face, angling me just the way he wants, I give in. I release all the fear, all the stress, all unknowns of the day and bask in this moment.

In the feel of his tongue sliding against mine.

Deepening the kiss.

I moan as my core tightens when those same lips trail along my jaw, then my throat. At the electricity pulsing between the two of us when he pushes my sweater and the strap of my nightgown off my shoulder and grinds his impressive erection against the silk covering my body.

Wanting more.

Needing this.

Until I feel a vibration against my thigh. I ignore it momentarily when those skilled lips make their way to my breast, pulling on my nipple with his teeth through the silk of my nightgown.

Pleasure and pain. God, I missed that.

Fuck. What is that vibration? I throw my head back against the wall, ignoring it. Until it dawns on me. Breathlessly, I pull Cade's head away from my breast. "Saint."

His lust-filled, green eyes meet mine.

"Your phone." I gasp as the hand that had been wrapped around my waist slips under my panties and runs along my sex.

"What?" His brain isn't catching up.

I wish I could shut mine off.

"Your phone is vibrating."

Knowing he can't ignore it, I slide my legs from his waist and watch as he pulls out his phone.

"Shit. It's your brother." He silences the phone and moves to put it back in his pocket. "He can wait."

"He's called twice. It might be important."

He answers his phone with an annoyed groan, and I take the minute to pull myself together. Watching him walk across the room gives me the distance I need to clear the fog of lust from my head.

What the hell was I thinking?

After a minute, he walks back into the kitchen, lines of frustration pulling at his face. "Duchess . . ." Those talented hands reach for me, but I step away.

Both of us try to speak at the same time.

With Cade telling me, "Becks set off the alarm at Crucible."

As I say to him, "This shouldn't have happened."

His long legs easily swallow the space between us, and one hand grips my face. "This *should* have happened, duchess. This was always going to happen. You were mine all those years ago, and I was a stupid fucking kid who didn't know what to do with you. Well, I know now. And you're still mine, Scarlet."

His thumb runs over my bottom lip. "But I'm not gonna beg." Cade kisses my forehead and drops his hand from my face. "Let me know when you've accepted it, Scarlet." He places one hand on my still flat stomach. "In the meantime, you'd better get used to seeing me. Because while you take care of everything for your players and your company, I'm going to be taking care of you and our baby."

I rest my hand over his, letting those words sink in.

"Let me know when your brain catches up to what I already know." He turns to leave, but I stop him.

"And what do you think you already know?"

He doesn't turn around as he answers, but there's no mistaking his words. "You'll know when you figure it out." Cade opens my door but stops and looks back at me. "I'm stopping by Crucible on my way home. I'm telling Becket about us tonight."

"Cade . . ."

"I'm telling him everything."

Then he walks out of my condo.
Leaving me frustrated.
Completely caught off guard.
Turned on.
And maybe . . . just maybe, a little bit hopeful.

CAD E

As I drive to Crucible with the taste of Scarlet still lingering on my lips, I know I made the right move. When Becket called, it was because he'd set off the alarm at Crucible. Imogen changed the code last week, and I guess I forgot to tell him. His timing sucked, but it was also perfect. As much as I wanted Scarlet earlier, I want her more in all the moments to come.

Had we gone further tonight, she may have regretted it tomorrow and built back the walls I'm working on lowering, fortifying them even stronger.

When I walk into Crucible, Becks is beating the shit out of a heavy bag. I'm about to make what's likely a shitty night for him shittier. Nobody beats on a bag like that without reason. "Yo," I call from the door, but he doesn't hear me over the Fort Minor song blasting from his phone.

He slows down when I move into his line of sight, then hold the bag steady for him

"Sorry, Saint. I didn't mean for you to come out here. I just didn't want you to get a call from the security company." He jabs the bag a few more times. "You ever have a woman who drives you insane?" He doesn't wait for my answer. "I swear to God, Kendall is one person when it's just us and a completely different person around everyone else." One last punch to the bag, way harder than he should be hitting it, then he backs off. "I don't know, man. She drives me crazy." He pulls his gloves off and throws them on the floor. I didn't mean to drag you out of the house. I was good once you gave me the code."

"I was with Scarlet when you called." I move around the bag and lean against the metal cage the guys practice in, watching him stretch his arms. They're gonna hurt tomorrow after that little display.

His head snaps up. "Is she okay?"

"She will be." I wait a moment before adding, "I'll make sure of it."

Becks picks his gloves up from the floor and throws them in his bag. "Yeah . . . Don't think Scarlet will be happy about that. She hates help."

"She always did."

Becks stops and stares. "Has she now? And how, exactly, would you know what Scarlet's always done, Saint?"

"Listen first, react after. Okay, King?" Becks looks at me quizzically but nods his head. "I was in love with your sister in high school. We were together for two years, and we kept it from you." I shake my head, feeling like a teenage girl for my confession. "We kept it from everyone. Your mom wouldn't let Scarlet date, and she didn't want you and Max to have to lie for her. So we kept it quiet . . . I loved her, man."

Becks's face is neutral when he asks, "When did it start?"

"Our junior year. You, me, and Sam were going to watch Max's football game, and Scarlet tagged along. I'd never met anyone like her. I knew I was a goner. The same still holds true." I remember coming out of the bathrooms by the concession stand at one point, and there she was, leaning against the massive cement wall of the bleachers. Her dark hair pulled high in a ponytail, a navy blue Kroydon Hills Prep hoodie on, and the tightest blue jeans molded to her legs with knee-high black boots. My teenage brain came up with about a hundred and twenty things I could do to her under those bleachers in three point five seconds.

When Scarlet saw me and smiled, I was sunk.

When she asked me for my phone and put her number in, the same way I did to hers a few weeks ago, I couldn't believe she was so bold. I'd never met a girl who didn't think they had to play coy at our age. But not Scarlet. She texted me that night, and we talked all week.

Just us.

She asked me not to say anything to Becket, and at first, it didn't seem like a big deal. By the time it did, it was too late. I was in love and willing to do whatever it took to keep her.

"It's about goddamn time, Saint."

I stare at Becks. "What the hell are you talking about?" He couldn't . . .

"I know you two thought Sam and I didn't know. But we did. We figured it out our senior year." His brow lifts with a devilish smile. "Come on, now. We're not idiots, and you two were not as fucking careful as you thought you were." He leans next to me against the cage. "I wondered if you were ever going to man up."

"Why didn't you say anything?" This doesn't make any sense.

Scarlet's family is the most intrusive family I've ever met.

His dopey smile grows. "It wasn't my business. It was Scarlet's and yours. She was safe with you. I knew you'd never let anything happen to her. So I just figured when you guys were ready to tell us, you would. It was easy to figure out you two ended things when you left for the marines. She moped around all fucking summer but never said a word. I figured if she wanted me to know, she'd tell me, and she didn't." He shoves my shoulder. "I never thought you'd knock her up a decade later though. I didn't see that one coming."

"Yeah. Me either. But I think us getting back together was what was always meant to happen. The baby just pushed us in that direction. Now, I just gotta get Scarlet on the same page."

Becks laughs. "Sounds like we've both got women problems, brother."

"Yeah. I guess we do."

Imogen's waiting for me when I get home after my stop at Crucible. She's sitting at the kitchen table with hot pink noise-canceling headphones covering her ears and a pencil in her hand, tapping out a beat. Her laptop is in front of her, covered in stickers with sheets of music spread out next to it and a notebook open with lyrics scribbled inside. Gen's never been overly organized when it came to her music, but it works for her.

I pull at one of the padded speakers covering her ear. "Hey."

Startled, she yanks them from her ears, tilts her head, and gives me her pissed-off eyes. "Jesus Christ, Cade. You scared the shit out of me."

"Sorry," I laugh. "I didn't realize you were so engrossed. Thanks for watching Brynlee for me. Everything go alright tonight? Did she give you a hard time?"

Imogen closes her MacBook and pushes it aside, then puts her pencil inside her notebook and lays it on top of her laptop before sitting back in her chair. "Let's see . . . that's a two-part question with a really fucking strange answer. Brynlee was fine. She wanted to stay up later and watch *Tangled* again, so she wasn't thrilled when I put her to bed. But she went."

I wait for her to elaborate on the fucked up part, but she doesn't. "Okay. Well, that's normal for Brynn. So, what went wrong?"

"Well, let's see . . . When Brynnie and I got home from the gym, there was a car parked across the street from the house. It drove away as we pulled into the driveway, but I'm pretty sure it was Daria."

Fuck. I cross the room to the security screen. "Did you check the cameras?"

Gen nods. "I did. It looks like her. You've got to deal with this, Cade. Ignoring her isn't working."

My address isn't listed.

She shouldn't know where we live.

"The only good thing she's ever done is give me Brynlee. I don't want to invite her back into our lives."

"I hate to tell you this, big brother. But she's Brynlee's mother. It's time to call the bitch back."

If I do this, will I be opening Pandora's box?

Turns out, I'm not actually opening anything.

"You still haven't heard from her?" Jax asks as we stand next to the cage, watching Hudson spar with Dave.

"Watch your leg," I holler, trying to get Hudson to concentrate. He's sloppy today. "No, man. Not a word, and it's been over a week." I left Daria a message the day after my security feed confirmed she'd sat in front of my house for over an hour, waiting for something . . . For what, we're not sure.

Jax's fingers wrap tighter around the cage. "You think maybe she just wanted to lay eyes on Brynlee?"

I shrug, not sure what the hell my ex is thinking.

"That bitch doesn't deserve to breathe the same air as your kid." Jax is family. He knows exactly what went down when Daria decided she didn't want to be a mother. He's been here for all of it. "You call your lawyers yet?"

"Yeah." I look back to the front desk where Brynlee's laughing while she helps Imogen fold the new t-shirt stock that just came in. Not so much folding as making a mess. "I called them the next day. She's not getting near my baby girl."

When Hudson finally gets Dave to submit, I tell them both to go again.

"So, how are things going with your new baby mama?" At least Jax lowers his voice this time.

I glare back at him. "I don't fucking know, man. Scarlet runs hot and cold. She's supposed to be taking it easy, but I don't think she is. We've talked a few times this week, and I know work's kicking her ass." I don't think she even realizes how stressed she's sounded when we've talked. It's just her normal frequency. "We have another checkup to go to Saturday morning. We'll see what they say then."

"What do you mean, she's supposed to be taking it easy?" Hudson leaves Dave lying on his back in the center of the mat as he looks down at me from the cage. "Is she alright?"

"Her blood pressure was up at her last appointment. They wanted her to try to eliminate stress." I give Hud a hard stare. "Do not share that with your whole family, Hud. That's up to her. Not you."

"Does Max know?" he pushes.

Max Kingston was only a year ahead of Becks, Sam, and me in school. He's been groomed his entire life to run his family and their empire. And while I know that there's more to Max than meets the eye, I also know that that empire and his family come before absolutely everything else. I wouldn't call him a friend, but he's always had my respect.

I know him enough to know that if he was aware Scarlet was supposed to be eliminating stress from her life, he'd have her locked in a gilded cage. That might not sound like such a bad thing to me at the moment, but Scarlet would hate it. Instead of voicing that, I tell Hudson, "No clue. But either way, you do not tell him. If the doc says we need to be concerned this week, I'll talk to Scarlet."

When Hudson moves to speak, I cut him off. "No, Hud. Don't do it. Your sister will destroy you before you ever get the chance to defend your title. Got it?" I wish I were kidding. Scarlet would eviscerate him.

And she might very well flay me alive for letting it slip to Hudson.

"Then man the fuck up and take care of my sister, Saint." He throws the door open on the octagon and walks down the steps. "Someone has to."

Fuck if he's not right.

I stop Jax from going after Hud. "Don't. He's not wrong. Can you hold the fort down here for a little while?"

He slaps me on the back. "Yeah, man. Do what you gotta do."

Once I'm in my truck, I call Scarlet's cell phone and get forwarded to her office.

Her assistant's voice greets me, "Good morning, Scarlet Kingston's office. This is Connor."

"Hi, Connor. I need to speak with Scarlet."

"Sorry, she's not available right now. May I take a message?"

"This is Cade St. . . ."

"Mr. St. James. Ms. Kingston should be out of her meeting in fifteen minutes and has a two-hour opening after that."

I sit there, waiting for him to continue, but he doesn't. "Do you always give out Ms. Kingston's schedule so freely, Connor?" That idea doesn't sit well with me.

"Only for people who are good for Ms. Kingston, Mr. St.

James. And between the two of us, I think you're one of those people. So don't take this the wrong way if I say she hasn't had lunch yet and loves the balsamic tomato salad from Bagliani's on Second Street."

Well, shit.

The kid's actually looking out for her. "Thanks, Connor. You like anything from there?"

"I'm good, thanks. You may also want to order an unsweetened iced tea with no lemon. Oh, and Becket and Lenny usually jump in when we order from there."

"Not today, Connor. Any chance you can help me out and block the next hour in Scarlet's calendar?" It's worth a try.

A second goes by. "Done."

"Thanks."

That's how I find myself sitting outside her office thirty minutes later, while Connor calls to let her know I'm here.

"Your next appointment isn't for an hour and a half, Scarlet." Connor glances my way with a grimace. I guess she isn't thrilled that I stopped by, judging by the side of the conversation I can actually hear. "No. That's tomorrow." He pauses a minute. "Right. Okay, great. I'll show him in."

Connor hangs up the phone, a victorious look on his face. "She's a bit grouchy today, so don't say I didn't warn you."

When I stand, I take a long look at this guy who barely looks old enough to not be considered a kid himself. "Thanks for the help."

He eyes me up. "Don't make me regret it."

One more person who's protective of Scarlet Kingston.

I can respect that, even if it would drive her crazy.

But what all these people don't realize is that she'll never need another protector again

That position's been filled.

SCARLET

No matter how vain you try not to admit you are, when a sexy man is about to walk through your door, you can't help but do a last-minute check to make sure everything's in place. At least that's what I tell myself as I tug my bra up just a little bit, then reach into the wrap dress I'm wearing and tug my boobs up too. The girls are getting bigger already, and I need to make some time to get new bras in a larger size. I just haven't had the energy to do anything after work this past week.

Once everything is sitting nice and perky where it's supposed to be, I smooth my hands over my hair just before the knock sounds at the door and Connor opens it for Cade to walk through.

Normally sweatpants do nothing for me.

They look sloppy.

Like someone threw them on with no thought about how they'd appear in public.

Adeline never allowed Max, Becket, or me to wear sweatpants.

She'd have had a fit.

Sweats on Cade St. James could never look sloppy.

No. Not when he fills them out perfectly, leaving very little to the imagination.

And I've had quite an imagination since the last time we were together.

He's wearing a short-sleeved, black Crucible t-shirt that

stretches tightly over his muscled chest and around his bulky biceps today.

It's showcasing every muscle he has and then some.

And that combination of the tight shirt and the loose sweats is potent.

I should have known if anyone would pull off this look, it'd be Cade.

Now, that's how you look put together in a pair of grey sweats.

I may have spent this last week more exhausted than I thought I could ever be, but I've also spent it wearing out my vibrator while I thought about the man who's currently standing at my door with a bag in one hand and a cup carrier from Bagliani's in the other. A mix of memories and fantasies played out in my mind all week.

Callused hands on my hot skin.

Strong lips controlling mine.

Teeth scraping against my breast.

Leaving me to wonder if the memory was doing justice to the night or if I was viewing it through rose-colored glasses every time I've tried to make myself come. "Try" being the keyword. I haven't been able to come since that night. It's as if my body rejects the idea of doing this alone when what it wants is within reach.

Stupid pregnancy hormones.

Pulling myself together, I pop up from my desk and dart around it. The scent of garlic and balsamic vinegar teases my nose, and my stomach growls in response. "Oh, my. Please tell me there's a salad from Bagliani's in there. Please, please, please. I'm starving."

Cade chuckles, a deep throaty laugh that vibrates through my entire body, and hands me the bag. "There is. There's a few garlic knots in there too." He takes the cup carrier and pulls out one of the teas. "Unsweetened iced tea. No lemon."

133

He pushes a paper straw through the lid and then hands me the cup before moving across my office and sitting down on the white leather sofa situated under the windows overlooking the stadium.

Cade stares at me, waiting. "Sit down, Scarlet. Eat while you have time."

I should be bristling at being told what to do, but for once, it's nice not to have to think.

I've done nothing but think all week.

Making decision after decision.

Putting out fire after fire.

Finalizing the acquisition.

Instead of telling him any of that, I sit next to him on the couch and place the salad on the table. "To what do I owe the pleasure of this lovely lunch, Cade?" I wrap my lips around the straw and sip my tea.

As I peek up through my lashes, I could swear he's staring.

"Thank you for lunch. This was sweet."

"I've been called a lot of things in my life, duchess. But sweet has never been one of them." He grabs a garlic knot from the bag and throws it in his mouth before removing the lid from his tea and taking a gulp.

My eyes linger on the thick column of his throat as he swallows, and I realize it's turning me on.

What the hell is wrong with me?

I take a bite of the tomato, mozzarella, and arugula and moan. "This is so good."

"When's the last time you ate, duchess?" He leans back in the chair and stretches his legs out in front of him, letting them rub up against mine.

Why is that sending every nerve I have into hyperdrive?

I try to remember his question. Breakfast, right. "I had

half a toasted English muffin with peanut butter and a decaf coffee for breakfast."

"Oh, yeah?" He pulls his phone from his pocket, glancing down at it. "And what time was that? Because it's noon now."

I swallow my mozzarella and bite back the icy retort on the tip of my tongue. Reminding myself he did something nice for me, I sit a little taller and bring the straw back up to my lips. "It was around 6:00 a.m., right after I finished the workout with my trainer."

Cade runs his fingers through his silky blonde hair that's in desperate need of a trim.

I'd know. I used to love to run my fingers through it while he was fucking me.

Goddamn, my libido today.

Seriously, is this what pregnancy hormones do? I've got to remember to ask Amelia.

"You feeling okay? Has your blood pressure changed at all since the last time we talked?"

I tilt my head to the side and take a deep breath in, then blow it out slowly through my nose. I'm only a few days shy of eighteen-weeks pregnant. That means I have twenty-two more weeks of people asking me how I'm feeling and telling me I look tired, if these last few weeks are any indicator of what's to come. I'm not thrilled with either.

"I'm okay. Still tired. My blood pressure has gone up just a tad. But we'll have to wait until Saturday to see what the doctor says. They'll have to do something. Cutting stress out isn't happening. And I'm doing everything else they've told me to do."

"Scarlet . . ." Cade's voice is calm and kind. But the look he's throwing my way is exasperated

I place my fork down on the table and push my salad away before I stand up. "Don't, Cade. I'm doing the best I can." And I'm not in the mood to be lectured by him or anyone else. I walk to the door and wrap my hand around the knob. "I think it's time you get back to the gym, don't you?"

Something about the way Cade crosses the room has goosebumps racing down my flesh.

Both his hands gently grab my face and hold me in place, his hot breath tickling my nose. "I'm not trying to pick a fight with you." His thumb runs over my cheek. "Tell me what I can do to help you, duchess."

And instead of opening the door, I lock it.

I lean my face into his palm, close my eyes, and sigh.

My body is screaming for more. More contact. More heat. More Cade.

I don't think.

I don't stress.

I just act.

All it takes is for my body to lean in the tiniest bit, and without hesitation, Cade's lips capture mine, and I melt into him.

Give over control.

His hands slide down the soft material of my dress and drag it up to my hips before they cup my ass, dragging me against him and lifting me into the air. He walks us back to the leather sofa and sits us down with me on his lap.

"Cade . . ." Desperate for more, I untie the knot at the waist of my wrap dress, then revel in the groan that leaves his lips at the sight of my bigger breasts.

Breasts that are bigger than the last time he'd seen them.

Breasts that are barely contained in a sheer black lace bra.

I finally let my fingers run through his soft hair and pull him to me. A moan of ecstasy escapes my lips when his tongue licks around my nipple through my bra, sending shivers dancing across my heated skin.

My breath gets caught in my throat when his hands glide

up my thighs. He draws his head back and pulls my face to his. "I like these, duchess." Strong fingers play with the silk band at the top of my thigh-highs, making me so grateful I opted for this dress today and that I haven't given up my addiction to beautiful lingerie just yet.

Cade licks a line up my neck, and my head spins, while his other hand slips under my panties and skims the lips of my pussy. "You want me to make you come?"

"God, yes." My stomach quivers. "I need more."

His tongue slides over my lips. Devouring. Then he pushes inside my mouth as he does the same with his finger. "Do you want to come on my cock or my hand?"

I throw my head back and close my eyes as I ride his hand.

"Eyes on me, duchess. Remember who's making you feel good."

My eyes snap open and lock on his.

Fuck. I shouldn't like that command, but I do. I really do.

"Both," I pant.

A wicked smile spreads across his lips right before he goes back to teasing my nipple. This time the cup of my lace bra is shoved roughly down. His teeth tug as his fingers rub the inner walls of my pussy and his thumb circles my clit. A fire erupts in my body, heating me from the inside as I finally find the orgasm I've been searching for since he left my house a week ago.

Cade swallows what would have been my screams with a searing kiss and continues to work me, knowing exactly what I need as I ride the wave of euphoria.

He's always known.

When I can think again, my lips trail down his neck, and my hands, that had been anchored in his hair, go to the waistband of his sweats just as the phone on my desk rings.

I freeze for a moment before realizing we're in my office

and Cade's not the only one in control. "Ignore it." I'll call whoever it is back later.

My hand continues its exploration, skimming over the velvety smooth erection straining against his boxer briefs, but I need more.

We need more.

I stand, and he reaches for me, but I back up just a step, then grip his waistband with both hands and pull at his sweats and boxers until he lifts his lap and I'm able to move them down his thighs. "I'm clean. I haven't been with anyone since our night in Vegas. And you can't get me more pregnant." I let my panties fall to the floor and kick the scrap of black lace aside.

His hands are on my hips in an instant.

Lifting me back onto his lap.

"It's only been you for me for a lot longer than that, Scarlet."

My eyes snap back to his, and the honesty there scares me a little.

His warm palms slide up my sides, leaving goosebumps in their trail and pulling me back into the moment.

My knees dig into the soft leather on either side of his hips as I line my body up, ready to take him inside. When I lower myself onto his cock, our foreheads meet as we both hiss at the contact. "Saint." God, I feel so full as my body stretches to accommodate him.

"I know, duchess." His tongue licks into my mouth. "Me too."

I slowly lift my body just enough to drop back down again without losing this contact.

My phone rings again. But neither of us acknowledge it.

Cade's palm holds me to him, resting flat against the small of my back as the other grips the back of my neck, anchored in my hair. It's possessive and protective and so utterly Cade.

We breathe into each other as I ride him into oblivion.

There's a knock at my door, but I ignore it.

It's just us.

Him. Me.

In our bubble.

Our heavy breathing.

The slide of our skin.

Complete desperation.

"Scarlet." His voice is strained as I scrape my nails against his scalp.

My grip on his hair grows tighter. "I know. I'm so close."

His head tips back.

His firm lips drink in my skin, then my lips again. The hand that had been resting on my back wraps around my waist, pulling me closer to his firm chest, holding me tighter and changing our angle. What had been just out of reach is being rubbed over and over again now. Friction and feelings. Sensation and sanity. Memories. Reality. It's all meshing together, driving me higher and higher again, until I freefall from the cliff's peak.

I come on a silent scream.

My breath caught in my throat.

My world tilting on its axis.

Every single neuron in my brain firing at once and yet, not working at all.

Cade leans his head against my chest as he thrusts up again and again, holding me to him. Whispering words I shouldn't want to hear but couldn't possibly thrill me more. Until he finally can't hold back anymore and follows me off that cliff with my name whispered like a benediction from his lips.

The power of it is overwhelming.

Oh, God. What did we just do?

My brain doesn't get a chance to ruin the euphoria coursing through my body when another knock sounds at the door. This time it's followed by Max's powerful voice. "Scarlet."

Max knocks again as Cade lifts me to my feet, and then pulls up his pants.

"Give me a second, Max." I start sliding everything into place as Cade picks up my panties and stuffs them in his pocket. I'm about to give him hell and rip the lace away from him when he places one finger over my lips, then kisses me quickly.

"Can I see you before Saturday?" There's no twinkle in his forest-green eyes. No cocky smirk on his handsome face. Just a man asking me to make time for him.

"Cade . . ."

Max knocks again as the phone on my desk rings. I heave out a deep breath, knowing what this is going to look like— exactly what it was. Damnit. Caught in the act like a teenager.

Who am I kidding?

We were never caught as teenagers.

When I unlock and swing my office door open, Max marches right through, then slams a folder down on my desk. He looks around as Cade moves across the room but doesn't even have the decency to look surprised. "St. James." Max nods, then sighs and side-eyes me. "At least you locked the door."

A nerve in my eye twitches from the strength it takes to hold back the retort that may be sitting on the tip of my tongue.

"We've got a fire to put out, Scarlet." Max opens the folder and hands me a copy of a newly leaked memo discussing every single point of the King Corp. acquisition of the Revolution.

Shit.

When my weary eyes meet Cade's, he knows exactly what I'm going to say without me needing to utter a word. He leans down and kisses my forehead. "Let me know." Seeing the confusion in my eyes, he adds, "About when I can see you." His hand quickly dances across my waist. It's just a split second in time. But there's something so powerful about that single touch.

I nod.

As Cade walks through the door, Max calls over to him. "St. James. Any chance you could wait for me in my office? I'll only be a minute. Connor can show you the way."

"Sure." Cade turns back to me. "Call me tonight, Scarlet." Then he walks through the door.

Max leans on my desk, the sleeves of his white dress shirt rolled up to his elbows, a hint of his tattoo showing. I thought Dad was going to kill him when he got it. A trace of rebellion from the perfect son. He's filled Dad's shoes better than any of us could have since Dad died, more than anyone should have had too.

So instead of giving him shit for the lecture he's probably about to lay on Cade's shoulders, I simply sit behind my desk, cross my legs, ignore the come that is most likely dripping onto my chair, and grab my pen. "Alright. What do you need me to do?"

CAD E

MAX'S OFFICE IS ON THE TOP FLOOR OF THE BUILDING. THE only offices I see up here are his and the head coach's. Jesus. These people have more elaborate offices than I've ever seen.

They exude money and power.

Don't get me wrong, I do well for myself.

I was a lucky enough bastard to be born to a well-off family. But my parents made sure we knew how important a good work ethic was in life, that we were never afraid to work hard. And that's what I've done. First as a marine, then as a fighter. Fighting made me more money than even Brynlee's kids should be able to spend in their lifetimes so long as I keep investing it well.

But the Kingstons are in a stratosphere all to themselves.

They're in the top tier of the 1 percent.

Max has a corner office overlooking the entire Kings stadium. There's a desk with two chairs opposite it, a table with four chairs surrounding it, and a couch with another two more chairs at the back of the office. My office in Crucible could fit in here at least three times with room to spare.

The credenza behind his desk looks much the same as Scarlet's but with more family photos. The Kingston kids throughout the years. In jerseys. On the field. As adults, and in the owner's box. And a single picture from Sam and Amelia's wedding last year. Sam and his bride stand in the middle of a line of happy Kingston siblings. And my friend is smiling. Never thought I'd see a picture of that.

Proof Sam Beneventi is happy.

Lucky bastard.

Taking a seat in the sleek leather chair across from Max's desk, I wait.

It doesn't take long before he walks through the door and shuts it tightly behind him. "Thanks for waiting, Cade." Max takes a seat behind his sleek desk. "Hudson mentioned that Crucible was sponsoring an exhibition to raise money for veterans."

"Yeah. We've been running it for a few years now. It's scheduled for the last Saturday in July. All of the money is split between a few different organizations that help out struggling vets in Philly." I was lucky enough to have my family here when I came home. Without them and the gym, I'm not sure how I'd have survived that first year.

"How are you doing with sponsors? Donations?"

"We're doing okay. Imogen's been taking care of most of the details." I really should give my sister a raise.

Max writes something down on a sticky note, then tears it off and hands it to me. "That's the name of the woman who runs King Corp.'s charitable division. If you need any help, give her a call. Tell her I sent you."

"Thanks, man. I appreciate it." I fold the note and place it in my wallet, then look back at Max, who's writing something on his desk. I'm surprised when he hands me a check. Not a King Corp. check but a personal check. With a whole lotta zeros. "What's this?"

Max stands. "It's my donation. I'd like it to remain anonymous, if possible. Hudson's told me about the programs you run for veterans at Crucible." He crosses his arms over his chest and takes stock. "It's impressive. And yet . . . you don't boast. You don't publicize. You don't use it to draw in more clients."

I sense there's more he wants to say but isn't sure how to say it.

"You got a question for me, Max, just ask it. It'll stay here, between us."

He moves around the desk to face me. Max Kingston's a big guy. Not as big as me but big enough. He's broad. He probably works out with a trainer a few days a week. But none of that intimidates me.

It's his presence that's impressive.

The way he wears his power.

He's the man at the top of a family empire.

And he owns it and all the power that comes with it.

"You're in love with my sister." His voice leaves no room for question.

He's not mad like Hudson.

He's not curious like Rylie.

Max isn't a man who's accustomed to asking questions unless he already knows the answers.

He controls. He commands.

I know a thing or two about that myself.

So I don't pull my punches. "I've been in love with your sister for years. The timing's never been right before."

"And now?"

I push up from my chair, standing toe to toe with him. "Now it's time to make it right. Scarlet's mine, Max. Scarlet and our baby."

"She's gonna give you hell, you know." A hint of a smile pulls at his mouth. "She's not going to make it easy on you."

She never did. "Nothing worth anything in life is ever easy. And your sister is worth everything. Not sure how long it's going to take to convince her of it. But luckily, I know a thing or two about not giving up before the bell rings."

"When do you guys go back to the doctor? I'm worried about her. She's tired. She's had two migraines in the last two weeks. Bad ones. She had to go home to sleep them off. And that's not like Scarlet."

I wonder if this woman realizes how many people love her and want to look out for her.

"I'm worried about her too. Scarlet needs to watch her stress and take better care of herself. We see the doctor Saturday. We'll see what she says."

He runs his hands over his face. "She's not watching her stress at all. I've been having her run point on the Revolution acquisition. Everything I'm setting her up for is going to be an exercise in stress management. Controlled chaos. There's not going to be a single easy day for the next two years. We won't even be officially closing the damn deal for at least another month, and it's already consumed all of us." He stops, then opens his mouth to speak but thinks better of it.

"Don't do that. Your sister will tell you what she can and can't handle. Scarlet's not shy, and she's not stupid. She's probably waiting to see what happens before she talks to you." There are very few people in this world I'd be this sure of, but I have no doubt Scarlet knows her limits. She may need a little help accepting them. A little more voicing them. But she'll have me to help with that.

"I'll give her a week, Cade. But she's got to come talk to me . . ." He leaves his words hanging. The threat of him talking to her. Of her finding out one more person just spoke about something that should have been hers to discuss is lingering.

"She'll talk to you." She has to.

After I tiptoe out of Brynlee's bedroom later that night, my cell phone ringing downstairs has me running as quickly and quietly as a man my size can. My daughter hates going to bed. Fucking hates it. She's like the princess in "The Princess and the Pea." She needs more pillows. She needs Teddy. She needs water. The house is too quiet. She'll always feel that one tiny little pea at the bottom of the mattress.

I have about two point five seconds before she wakes up, bitching that the house is too noisy.

I left my phone on the island in the kitchen, and when I come to a stop next to it, Imogen is holding it in her hand, having just silenced it. Her face is pulled tight in anger. I look down, surprised to see Daria's name flashing across the screen, and furiously swipe to answer.

"Nice of you to call me the fuck back, Daria. Want to tell me why you were sitting in front of my house a few weeks ago, then went radio silent when I called you?" Anger courses through my veins. There are few things in life I hate, but this woman is one of them. She gave her daughter away as if she were a toy she'd had enough of. For the rest of her life, Brynlee will know her mother didn't want her. I'll never be able to change that for her.

"Hello, Cade. I'm sure I don't know what you're talking about. I don't even know where you live." Her voice is sugary sweet, and I can picture, from memory, the cunning look painted on her face.

"What do you want, Daria? Why have you been calling the gym?" I don't have time for this bullshit.

She sighs, as if this were an inconvenience. "It's nice to know that club rat sister of yours has given you my messages. So, you were just ignoring them then?"

"You're not supposed to be calling at all, Daria. No contact means no contact." I'm already over this conversation.

"Cade . . ." she tries to purr. "She's my daughter too."

"No. She's *my* daughter," I answer, my blood boiling. "You signed away any right you had to her three years ago. What. Do. You. Want?" Imogen's eyes grow wide at the fire raging in my voice.

Then both of our eyes fly to the quiet knock at the front door.

We turn to the security system display sitting on the built-in desk in the kitchen.

Scarlet.

My eyes meet Gen's in silent understanding, and she moves to let Scarlet in while Daria rants on the phone. The two women couldn't be any different if they tried.

One who hid my daughter from me because I couldn't love her.

The other not ready to hear that I've never loved anyone else.

SCARLET

THE DAYS SEEM TO BE GETTING LONGER AS I GET MORE pregnant.

At least, that's what it feels like.

But tonight, as I turned the key in my car's ignition, something changed. I wasn't sure what it was at first. But then it happened again, and I knew I needed to go to Cade.

I needed to see him.

I needed him.

He said he wanted to see me.

I hope he meant it.

Especially now, because the nasty look plastered across Imogen's face as she opens the door makes it clear that she certainly doesn't want me here. I guess I need to play nice with Cade's sister if I ever expect him to deal with the full fucking coven of Kingstons. "Hey, Imogen. Any chance Cade's home?"

Without saying a word, she steps out of the way to let me walk through the door, and I decide it's time the shitty attitude she always has when she's around me comes to an end. So I stop in front of her. "What is your problem with me?" I try to ask it nicely, but I don't do *nice* very well. "Have I done something to you I'm unaware of? Because as far as I know, I've never mistreated you. But you have no problem being rude to me."

She forces the door closed behind me. "Not everything is about you, princess. Cade's on the phone, dealing with bitchy

140

baby mama number one." She spins on her heel, leaving me to follow her back to the kitchen.

Wait . . . Am I bitchy baby mama number two?

Because I do not like the sound of that.

When we enter the kitchen, Cade is arguing with someone on the phone. His back is to me, but his voice exposes the anger I can't see on his face. "You signed a fucking contract, Daria. A legally binding contract. You don't get to see her. You don't get to be in her life. And you don't get any more money." He practically yells that last part and looks ready to maim someone as he turns his head to catch Imogen motioning for him to keep his voice down.

I'm guessing *Daria* is saying something on the other end of the phone because Cade's quiet for a moment.

Then, with more restraint than I expected, he answers whatever she must have said.

His voice is eerily quiet.

Controlled.

Like the calm before the storm. "I wish you wanted to actually be in her life. But unless you're talking about consistently being in her life, day in, and day out, there's not a fucking chance in hell I'm letting you anywhere near my daughter." He pauses for a moment, listening before adding, "You'll never see another fucking dime from me. So find a new fool to fuck over."

He slams the phone down onto the counter after disconnecting the call but doesn't turn around.

He stands with his back to me, his hands hanging by his sides in fists.

Imogen hesitantly speaks up. "Cade . . ."

The silence that follows is thick enough to choke someone until Cade finally turns around. He doesn't look at me. Just Imogen. "You called it. She wanted more money. It's all she'll ever want. Brynlee deserves better."

"That fucking nasty twat waffle. She'll never realize what she's given up. It's her loss. Brynlee can't miss what she never had." I get that Imogen is trying to make Cade feel better, but she couldn't be more wrong. You absolutely can miss something you never had. Especially when that thing is a loving, caring mother. I never had what these two have. Our mother used my brothers and me as status pieces, tools to gain favor with our father. She feigned interest when it suited her and ignored us when it didn't. None of that means I didn't wish for someone different in my life, someone more like Lenny and Jace's mom.

I never had that.

But I did miss it.

Either way, I guess I'm not the only one Imogen St. James dislikes.

And . . . I could have gone forever without putting myself in the same category as Cade's ex.

I saw photos of them on social media back in the day.

She was beautiful.

She looked so much like Brynlee.

They looked happy.

But of all people, I should know that looks can be deceiving. I'm generally the one orchestrating the deception. Public relations is perception. Perception can be based on deception just as easily as truth.

Cade surprises me when he wraps his arms around me in a firm embrace.

Suspecting he needs this right now, I wrap my arms around his waist hesitantly.

His chin rests on the top of my head, and one hand moves up to the back of my neck. "I didn't expect to see you here tonight, duchess."

We're both quiet for a moment until a throat clearing breaks our bubble. "And on that note, I'm going to my room.

Goodnight." Imogen grabs a water bottle from the counter and practically runs from the room.

I tilt my head back to say something, but Cade's lips brush against mine and suspend me in the moment. "I'm sorry you had to hear that, Scarlet. But I guess I can't avoid filling you in on Daria, considering, as much as I wish it weren't true, she's the mother of my child." His eyes soften. "Well, the mother of my oldest child."

He takes a step back and tugs me with him into the connected family room and down onto his oversized, black suede couch. Cade's elbows rest on his knees for a moment before he scrubs his hands over his face and through his hair. "That woman will never stop astounding me."

I don't know what I'm supposed to say. So I just listen.

I listen to Cade tell me the story of Daria and him.

The story of a fighter enjoying his success and everything that came with it. Including Daria. Of how she wanted more, but he didn't. Not with her. Of how she eventually tried to hurt him by keeping Brynlee from him before that backfired. And how she now wants him to be her personal ATM.

Bitch.

Just as he finishes telling me his story, it happens again.

That *thing* from earlier.

"Cade . . ." I grab his hand. "I came for a reason."

"What? Shit, Scarlet, I'm sorry. Did you need something?"

I ignore his words and place his palm flat over the right side of my slightly less than flat abdomen. Then wait.

"Scarlet?"

"Just wait," I whisper.

He moves his hand slightly, so I give in and guide his palm through the opening of my wrap dress and let it rest on my skin, the heat sending frissons of awareness through my soul.

And then it happens again.

Cade scoots closer to me, eyes wide with shock and glee. "Was that . . . ?"

I nod, my throat clogging with emotions.

"I thought it was too early for this." His other hand cups my face, and the tears in his eyes, mirroring mine, let me know he feels the next flutter too. "I can feel our baby." The unmitigated awe in his voice is one of the most incredible things I've ever heard.

"She did it when I got in the car to go home. So I came here instead."

Cade pulls me to him, tucking me under one arm.

His other hand still resting on my stomach. My head resting on his chest.

We sit like that for a while.

Neither of us speaking.

Not wanting to ruin the moment with bickering or banter.

Not this moment. Not this time.

At least not until my eyes get heavy.

I think about saying something, about getting up and driving home. But instead, I decide to just close my eyes for a minute. Just a minute to rest. That's all I need.

Somewhere in the back of my consciousness, I'm aware I'm moving.

At least I think I am.

But I don't care.

I'm comfortable and warm, wrapped up in the salt-water scent of Cade.

Just a few more minutes.

Then I'll go home.

I usually don't like being warm when I sleep. But the weight and warmth of the blanket feel like heaven tonight, pulling me back under. When I slide my hand to burrow under my pillow, I realize my head isn't resting on a pillow.

No. My hand is moving against bare skin.

I slowly force one eye open but can't make out much in the dark.

It takes a moment for the fog to lift before I remember falling asleep earlier on Cade's couch.

Then a sexy, gravelly, sleepy voice whispers in the dark, "Stop thinking so hard, duchess. You were asleep. I didn't want to wake you up to drive home tired. You're in my t-shirt. And nothing happened. Any questions?"

I pull the shirt up to my nose and inhale the scent.

"Did you just sniff me?" He pulls me against him with his palm resting under the shirt I'm wearing.

I lay stiff for a moment, caught between the desire to run and the need to stay. "Why do you always smell like the ocean breeze? The beach is over an hour away."

"It's my bodywash." The arm I'm lying on circles around my waist, giving Cade the chance to lay his palm flat on my stomach. "Go back to sleep, Scarlet. The alarm's set for five. Unless you need to get up earlier, we've got two more hours."

"Five works." I hesitate. "Thanks, Cade." I try to force my body to rest.

"For what?"

Glad I can't see his eyes, I lay a truth on the line. "For taking care of me." I place a kiss on his bare chest over his heart.

"I like taking care of you, Scarlet." His lips press down against the top of my head, promising so many things without saying a word, and I relax in his arms. "Now, sleep.

You need it. Your body's working hard, keeping our baby safe. I'll wake you up in a few hours."

Keeping our baby safe . . .

One day, I'll have to tell him I haven't always done a good job of that.

SCARLET

I'M WOKEN UP THE FOLLOWING MORNING BY HOT BREATH fanning my face.

The problem with that is it's not Cade's breath.

Bright green eyes stare back at me, framed by a cherubic expression. Brynlee's strawberry-blonde hair is tangled around her face. Her pink teddy is clasped in her hands. "I had a bad dream," she whispers.

Oh, shit. I look over my shoulder, but Cade's side of the bed is empty.

What am I supposed to do now?

I don't have to worry long because she tugs on the black and grey comforter I'm currently under. "Daddy lets me sleep with him when I have a nightmare." When she starts climbing into bed, I scooch over to give her some room.

Apparently, she doesn't want it.

The tiny blonde curls herself up next to me like a cat, pulls the blanket up around us, and starts twirling my hair around her tiny fingers.

Okay, what the hell am I supposed to do?

"Why are you in Daddy's bed?"

Oh fuck.

Cade, where the hell are you?

"Umm . . ." Get it together, Scarlet, "Well, I fell asleep here last night, and your Daddy didn't want me to drive home sleepy, so he let me sleep here."

Christ. How many times can I emphasize the word sleep

to the tiny terrorist who can probably give the best interrogators the marines have a run for their money.

Does this answer satisfy the three-year-old?

No. No, it doesn't.

"When Grammy and Poppy sleep over, they sleep in the other room."

Oh. My. God. Where is Cade?

I have no idea what an acceptable answer is right now. But I don't get to worry about that for long. She yawns wide and long, then places her head in the crook of my shoulder and closes her eyes, leaving me to wonder if what I just felt was my heart cracking wide open for this kid.

Maybe she's not a terrorist.

Maybe she's astute for her age. She's obviously already mastered getting precisely what she wants. Apparently, right now, that's me. I'm kind of impressed with her skills.

Soft snores tickle my cheek, and I settle in a bit more.

My head turns slightly toward the creak of a door opening. I'm guessing it's the bathroom door as Cade steps through. Black cotton pajama bottoms hang off his lean hips, and every single ab he has is on full display.

One, two, three, four, five, six, seven, eight.

Holy shit, Lenny was right. He's got eight abs.

A cocky expression gleams across his chiseled face until he comes closer and sees who's joined me in bed. Then, the overly confident smirk slides right off his gorgeous face and is replaced by something much more tangible, an expression I'm not willing to deal with this early in the morning.

He walks over to this side of the bed and stares down at us with a longing on his face I haven't seen there before. "I can take her back to her own bed." He reaches out for her, but I stop him.

"No. Don't. She just got back to sleep." I'd hate to wake her, and I don't really want to. "What time is it?"

"It's five. I was just going to wake you up."

I can't believe I'm going to say this. "I can go in later. What time do you have to get up?"

"I'm the boss. I can go in whenever I want." He reaches down and caresses my cheek. "What'cha thinking, duchess?"

"Come back to bed. I haven't slept this well in a few weeks. I'll text Connor when we get up and let him know I'll be late." A smirk I can handle. A big goofy smile, or even the smile he flashes when something's funny . . . those aren't dangerous. But the look this giant of a man gives me is so pure. So potent. So real. I don't know what to do with the emotions tugging at my chest after seeing it.

So instead of worrying . . . instead of overanalyzing why . . . I relax against Cade when he climbs in, pressing his chest to my back. He wraps his arms around Brynlee and me. Instead of freaking out, I close my eyes and let sleep pull me back under.

Four hours, one cranky little girl that didn't want to get out of bed, one stop at my condo for a shower and a change of clothes, and a quick commute later, I'm finally walking into my office when Lenny sees me.

"Hey. You just getting in?" She glances down at her watch, then back up to me. "Did you have a doctor's appointment or something?"

I grab her wrist and look around. "Yeah. Or something. Come with me." I pull her into my office and lock the door behind us.

Of course, Lenny laughs. "The only time my door is locked is if Sebastian comes up here to see me." Her eyebrows wiggle, and my mind goes back to yesterday afternoon on my couch.

"Scarlet? You okay? You look warm."

I'm warm all right. My entire body just flushed, remembering how he made me feel. "Shut up. I need to talk to somebody about my crazy fucking morning. And you're the lucky sister who happens to be here. So, I guess you'll do."

"Gee, thanks." When she drops down onto my leather sofa and sips from the cardboard coffee cup in her hand, I cringe. "Umm . . . you might want to sit . . ." I point to one of the two chairs. "Sit over there."

Lenny manages to switch seats through fits of uncontrollable laughter. "Oh, this is priceless. I wish you could see your face right now. Swear to God, Scar." She throws her head back and practically howls.

I look her over. "Why are you dressed like that? Did someone forget to tell me we were implementing casual Fridays?" Len's in jeans and a t-shirt. Her dark hair is pulled back in a messy top-knot.

Lenny shakes her head in frustration. "Hello? Bash and I are taking the red-eye to Hawaii tonight, remember? His best friend, Murphy, is getting married, and we're both in the wedding."

"I thought that was next weekend?" I could swear she said it was next Saturday.

She finishes her coffee and starts to finger the lid. "It is. But when the bride's father is the president of the United States, you book the entire resort for privacy and give your friends a Hawaiian vacation for funsies."

"Makes sense." I sit down across from her and cross my legs. Then I proceed to tell her about last night and this morning, not leaving anything out. At the end of my verbal vomit, I finally look up at her face to gauge her reaction, but she's doing an excellent job of covering her emotions. Imogen should take a tip from Lenny.

"Okay, first things first. How was Brynlee when she woke up in bed with you? How did she react?"

How did she react? "I don't think it phased her. We were all asleep. Then I woke up to sweaty little hands on my cheeks, and I opened my eyes." I think back to that moment. I would have thought she'd have been at least a little freaked-out. But she wasn't. "She told me she wanted pancakes for breakfast and had to pee. Then she jumped off the bed and ran to the bathroom."

"Ooh. Pancakes sound good. I'm hungry."

"Focus, Eleanor. So . . . what should I do?"

"Wow. I don't think you've ever asked for my advice before." She sits back and shifts in her chair, gloating.

"That . . ." I circle my finger in the air around her face. "That look. That gloating. That doesn't look good on you, Eleanor." Although being able to talk to her like this is something I never expected when she was growing up. So if I have to deal with a little gloating, it's still worth it.

Lenny laughs. "Yeah, well, it feels good." She gets up and moves to sit next to me on the couch, eyeing it first. Until I tip my head to the other side of me, telling her that spot may be safer. "First, remind me to bring you in some disinfectant wipes. Always good to keep a container of them in your desk so your brothers don't end up sitting where your man's naked ass was a few hours before. Second, what do you want to do? I mean, obviously, there's a tremendous amount of chemistry between you and Cade. It sounds like there are real feelings there too."

"Yes to the chemistry. He and I are definitely explosive. But what if those feelings are just left over from what we felt as kids and the pregnancy magnifies them? Making them seem bigger and stronger than they are? And what if—"

Lenny cuts me off, "What if it's the most important thing you ever do? Would that be so bad?"

"Letting myself have false hope? Yeah. That sounds pretty bad, Len." For years, I've convinced myself that I didn't want this kind of relationship. That I didn't need it. Because it was easier than hoping I could have more than my parents had, more than I feel comfortable wishing for.

Lenny laces our fingers together and pulls my hand into her lap. "There's no such thing as false hope, Scarlet. Hope is always real. No matter what, there's always room for hope."

"When did you get so smart?" I spin the stunning engagement ring resting on her finger.

She squeezes my hand. "Sometime after I came home from England and started watching my badass big sister. Do you remember what you told me when I didn't know whether to keep fighting for Sebastian?" I shake my head, but she keeps pushing. "You told me we're Kingstons, and we go after what we want." She shrugs her shoulder. "It turned out pretty well for me."

"There are things he doesn't know yet."

"Then tell him. Either he'll understand, or he won't. But at least you'll have your answer."

But if he doesn't understand, will I lose him before I ever get the chance to have him?

Cade spent the drive to the doctor's office the next morning trying to make me smile. He sensed my discomfort as soon as he picked me up and incorrectly assumed it was because I was worried about the appointment. That was part of it, but my blood pressure hasn't changed in the past two weeks, so I'm fairly certain that everything is going to be okay today with baby girl Kingston. What I still haven't decided is what I'm going to do with her daddy.

As we now sit in the cold office, waiting for Dr. Esher to

do the exam, my heart speeds up at the touch of Cade's hand on the back of my neck while I lean back on the table.

"Everything is going to be alright, Scarlet." He leans in and places a chaste kiss on my lips. "I won't let anything happen to you or our girl."

I lean my head against his, whispering against his lips, "You called her a girl."

"I did. I'm pretty sure you can will anything you want into existence, duchess. God himself better move out of the way for Scarlet Kingston." He kisses my forehead as Dr. Esher walks through the door.

"How are we feeling this week, Scarlet? Any better?" She starts scrolling through her questions, as she reads through my chart. "Your blood pressure is still higher than I'd like it to be, but it's holding steady, not going up. You don't have any protein spilling into your urine. So we'll continue to monitor it. I'm not ready to put you on anything for it yet, but we may need to if anything changes."

She goes over things to look for and says I'm going to have to come back in for a blood pressure check again in two weeks but we won't need to do a full exam then. "Alright, shall we have a little look?"

I unbutton the bottom of my soft pink button-down shirt and pull down the waistband of my black leggings. I'm pregnant, but I haven't popped yet. My waist is thicker, and my breasts are bigger, but I just look like I've gained a little weight. I'm trying to find a balance between comfort and class while I try to still look cute.

I'm just not sure how much longer that will last.

The cold jelly is squeezed onto my bloated belly, and the doctor starts rolling the doppler back and forth around my abdomen. "Now we'll need you to schedule the anatomy scan for some time over the next week or so. They'll check out all the baby's organs and systems. They can usually tell you the gender too." She moves the doppler a little more, catching the speedy little thumping of our baby's heartbeat.

"Oh, wow. Well, if it's something you want to know, it looks like I can tell you the sex of the baby now. I seem to be getting flashed." She taps a few buttons on the screen, then angles it to us.

I have no idea what she was looking at.

All I see are two perfect pouty lips, that appear to be sucking on a finger.

Cade leans down and kisses the top of my head. "Your call. Do you want to know?"

I smile up at him. "I think I do." I turn back to Dr. Esher. "Can you really tell us? I mean, how accurate is it?"

"Let's just say I have no doubt, Scarlet. But it's completely up to you."

Cade squeezes the back of my neck again, and I soak in his strength.

"Okay." I reach up and grab Cade's other hand. "We want to know."

She points to a grey blob on the screen. "Your little girl isn't very shy, and she is most definitely a girl."

"Our little girl." My heart feels more full than I ever knew was possible as I stare at my little daughter on the screen and make her a million promises all at once. She will never have the life I've lived. She'll never doubt that her mother loves her. I didn't think it was possible, but my world has shifted yet again, and she's the new constant it's going to rotate around.

Suddenly, nothing else seems quite so important.

Just her.

I gasp and turn to Cade. His forest-green eyes are filled with emotion.

He wraps his arm around my shoulders, and whispers in my ear, "You were right, duchess." His voice betrays his emotions. "We're having a girl." His lips press against my temple, and I wish I could freeze this moment in time.

One perfect moment amidst the chaos yet to come.

A girl.

Our girl.

CADE

After Dr. Esher gave Scarlet instructions to continue monitoring her blood pressure daily and schedule her next appointment and the anatomy scan, I wanted nothing more than to spend the afternoon with her. But unfortunately, I've got meetings that were scheduled weeks ago with the promoter for our upcoming exhibition, so that wasn't going to happen today.

As we drive through the city, I enjoy listening to her marvel over the fact that we're really going to have a daughter.

Scarlet is even more enamored now than she was before.

She's a sight to be seen.

"You're absolutely glowing, duchess."

Her light laughter soothes my soul in a way few things ever have. "What are you doing this afternoon? Want to get some lunch?"

I settle my hand over hers. "I wish I could. Unfortunately, I've got a meeting with a fight promoter this afternoon and then have to pick up Brynlee from my older sister's house."

She pulls her hands away quickly. "Oh." Disappointment laces her tone.

"Do you have plans for tomorrow? Why don't you come over? We can have a little barbeque for Memorial Day." I reach out and grasp her hand in mine. "It would give you a chance to get to know Brynlee a little better."

Scarlet's voice betrays her hesitance. "Is Brynlee the only reason you'd like me to come over?"

"The only reason? No." I lift her hand to my lips. "But it is one of the many reasons. The loudest, silliest one. The one who asked about you a lot last night." I lower her hand and rub my thumb in circles over her soft skin. "Scarlet, I want you in my life as more than the mother of my child. And if you're going to be in my life, then Brynlee is going to be in yours."

"You want me in your life?"

I pull sharply into the garage of her building, throw the truck in park, and turn to face this frustrating woman. "Scarlet Kingston, you are the stupidest smart woman I've ever met. Yes . . . Yes, I want you there to get to know my daughter. She's a part of me." I run my hand over her hair, attempting to soothe her fear, not sure where it's coming from. "Just like our little girl is. But that doesn't mean I want you there for me . . . for us any less." My frustration grows as I try to find a way to get Scarlet to hear me.

My hands grab her face moments before my lips crash down on hers, swallowing her gasp.

Devouring.

Consuming.

Until her lips are swollen and bruised.

Until we're both gasping for breath.

"We fucked this up once, Scarlet. I'm not letting us fuck this up again. Come over tomorrow. Pack a bag. Spend the night. We can have a lazy holiday Monday doing whatever you want." My eyes dance between hers. "Stay with me."

Her hands cover mine. "Aww, Cade. You say such pretty things. *'Don't fuck this up,'* might be the sweetest thing anyone's ever said to me." She leans in and sucks my bottom lip into her mouth, scraping it with her teeth before soothing the pain with her tongue. "Pack a bag, huh? You want me to spend the night?"

She's giving me whiplash, but it's worth it.

"Yeah, duchess. Pack a bag. Come over any time tomorrow. Bring your bathing suit."

She slips the strap of her purse over her shoulder and stares at me. "It's barely eighty degrees out."

"The pool's heated, and Brynn loves to swim. She'll try to con you into it. Be ready."

Scarlet steps out of the truck before turning to face me. "Guess I'll see you tomorrow, Cade."

"Wait . . ." I call after her as she shuts the door, then jump out of my side, round the truck, and grab her, my hands on either side of her neck. I back her up against her door, a wicked smile gracing her beautiful face. "I really wish we could spend the day together."

Her arms circle my neck as her smile grows. "I swear, the only time I've ever enjoyed being manhandled is when it's been by you."

"That's because I'm the only man who's supposed to be handling you, duchess." I take her mouth in a fierce kiss. And I promise myself when I finally get this woman awake and in my bed, I'll take my time worshipping her the way she deserves, finding every sweet spot as I explore her entire body.

She whimpers when I pull back. And I want nothing more than to carry her up to her condo and sink deep into her heat. "Tomorrow."

She licks her lips and nods her head. "One day, you're going to ask me to do something, not tell me to do it. I don't know why I let you get away with that."

I step aside and open the door into her building for her, then smack her ass as she walks past. "Yeah, you do. You like when I tell you what to do." She purses her lips, and I wink. "You always have. Don't question it now."

"You're crazy." She laughs. "I'll see you tomorrow."

I watch her greet her doorman then walk to the elevator. That woman is mine.

Now I've got to get her to realize it.

Kingston Family Group Text:

Scarlet: I have some news . . .

Becks: Saint's not the father? It was an immaculate conception?

Lenny: Ummm . . . based on recent activities that may have occurred in her office, I'm pretty sure that Scarlet's no virgin.

Scarlet: You seriously just can't keep your mouth shut, can you Len?

Lenny: Mouth . . . legs . . . Us Kingstons aren't very good at keeping things shut lately.

Max: Jesus Christ. What's wrong with you people?

Hudson: I'm with Maximus. I don't want to think about my sisters having sex.

Amelia: Says the man whore. How many women have the tabloids caught you with in the last few months?

Hudson: Didn't you used to be the sweet one?

Scarlet: We've corrupted her.

Lenny: It was so much fun.

Amelia: Yeah it was.

Amelia: Wait. Are we still talking about sex or corruption? Because either way it's been so much fun.

Jace: You guys are insane. And fucking GROSS! What's your news Scar?

Sawyer: Aww. Look at little jack-off being the voice of reason.

Sawyer: Someone wanna tell him sex isn't gross, or are we teaching him abstinence?

Jace: Go fuck Huck Fin, asshole. I'm not a virgin.

Hudson: Sure you're not.

Becks: Loses some credibility when you've gotta convince people.

Scarlet: Baby Kingston is officially Baby Girl Kingston. We found out today!

Lenny: OMG! YAY!

Amelia: Love it! I can't wait to buy baby girl clothes!

Becks: That's fantastic – but don't you mean Baby Girl St. James?

Sawyer: I'm sure she's gonna be as beautiful as her momma.

Hudson: Kiss Ass! Love you Scar. Congratulations.

Max: No matter what her name is, she's a Kingston. Congratulations Scarlet.

Scarlet: Hey – any chance you can stop by this weekend?

Max: You gonna be home tonight?

Scarlet: It's Saturday night. I'm going to be out getting drunk and snorting blow with hundred-dollar bills. How about you?

Max: I can stop by before you go all Scarface.

Scarlet: Sure. But come early. I've got a hot night of binging Henry Cavil on Netflix planned out. But I'll probably pass out on the couch two episodes in.

Max: Okay. Be by after I leave work.

Scarlet: All work and no play leave Maxi pad a dull boy.

Max: See you later brat.

SCARLET

M AX IS ONE OF THOSE PEOPLE WHO HAVE WALK-UP PRIVILEGES in my building. So the only warning I get that he's here is when he texts me from my parking garage before a knock at my front door has me looking up from where I'm happily tucked under a soft blanket on my couch.

Max lets himself in like he's been doing for years. Even in jeans and a polo, he still screams work-mode. This is Max's version of dressing down. Or as close to it as he ever lets any of the employees working for King Corp. see. Colorful ink trails down his right arm, and his dirty blonde hair is messy, desperately needing a trim. "Hey." He holds a brown paper bag up in one hand and a six-pack in the other. "You hungry? I brought dinner."

As if on cue, my stomach growls, and I try to remember the last thing I ate today.

I meet him in the kitchen, loving the ginger garlic smell wafting from the bag. "I'm starving. What'cha got in there?"

Max starts taking out packages, and my mouth waters when I realize it's dim sum from Dim Sum & Noodle. "Have I told you you're my favorite brother?"

He laughs. "Seriously, like there was any competition. I mean, come on . . ."

"Don't be an ass, Maximus." I hip check him and grab a pair of chopsticks. "Want to eat on the couch?"

"Sounds good." We head back into my living room and

settle in. "So, how was the rest of your appointment this morning? How are you feeling? What's the doctor saying?"

"That's a whole lot of questions." I swallow my dumpling. "What's up with that?"

He sips his beer, not feeling at all guilty that he's the only one in the room who can enjoy alcohol at the moment. "I'm worried about you, Scarlet. I've been so tunnel-visioned with this acquisition and the parts we'd each play in it that I don't know whether I've even asked what you want."

My brother was groomed for his position within our family. Our business was always going to be his empire to run. Dad kept Max by his side for everything, and Max went along with it. Becks never showed much interest, but Dad forced him along the way. Whenever I asked if I could shadow him like they were doing, he always told me this kind of business wasn't for me.

He meant it wasn't for women.

He never thought I was as capable as my brothers.

He was wrong.

"Don't be worried. I'm taking care of myself. My blood pressure is a little higher than my doctor would like, but we're monitoring it." I pop another dumpling in my mouth and let the savory taste melt on my tongue.

Max hasn't touched his food when he places it on my coffee table. "Have you considered how much time you're going to take off after the baby comes?"

"Not yet." If someone else asked me this, I'd be ripping their heads off. But Max is asking out of concern, not lack of confidence. "But that's partly why I asked you to talk this weekend. I've been thinking . . ."

"Me too."

I point my chopsticks at him. "Let me go first. I've been doing a lot of thinking since I found out I was pregnant. About the acquisition. About my new position. About what it's going to require over the next twelve to twenty-four months."

"While I have absolutely no doubt that you'd be an incredible president for the Revolution's organization. I don't think it's the right position for you. Not right now."

I place my food on the table next to his. "What the—"

"You'd be in a new organization, trying to wrangle an old guard who's going to fight you every step of the way. You wouldn't just be putting out fires daily, Scar. You'd be attempting to contain a full-blown fucking inferno for at least the first full year. Is that really how you want to spend your first year as a mom? I don't want that for you."

It's like he's reading my mind.

Feeling my fear before I'm able to voice it.

"I don't know that I want that for me either. I mean, don't get me wrong. It's all I've ever wanted. But I don't think the timing is right." I wipe away my first errant tear. "It hurts me to say so, but I'm not the right person for president of Operations right now, Max. Maybe we could discuss appointing an interim president for the next twelve months who could report back to us until I'm ready to assume the position. I'm sure you and I could hammer out what that would look like. It's not ideal, but it could work."

"I don't think that's the answer." When I start to interrupt, he blows out a frustrated breath. "Let me finish. I don't think you should be the new president of the Revolution. I think I should take that position, and you should step into my position with the Kings."

Wait . . . what?

My brain has a hard time processing Max's words.

But he doesn't realize that and keeps speaking.

What . . . What did he just say?

"Wait . . . Can you repeat that?" I stand from the couch and look down at my brother. Waiting.

He stands and places both hands on my shoulders. Uncertainty is written all over his face. "I want you to take over as president of the Kings, and I'll move to the Revolution. You know the organization better than anyone else. You've been beside me all along. Everyone in that building is a part of the King Corp. family. It's the same job, but with less stress over the next year or two. And let's face it. Those are important years. Bring your daughter to the office. Hell, convert one of the floors to a daycare center if that's what you want. But raise her in that building the way we were."

"Max . . ." I sigh. I don't even know what to say. And I'm never speechless.

"It's the same job, Scar. But with less trouble and aggravation coming your way."

I take two steps and wrap my arms around him. "But then, you're the one taking on all the trouble and aggravation. That's not fair to you."

"Don't worry about me. I'm going to give myself a raise." He laughs a sardonic laugh and pulls us both down to the couch. "Teach my niece she can run a billion-dollar organization. Teach her she can be anything she wants. Let her see how amazing her mother is. I might be the head of the family, Scarlet. But you're the heart. You just don't want anyone to know it."

My lower lip trembles as I try to hold back the full-on sobs that threaten.

"But I know it. I see it. Take the damn job, Scar. We'll legitimately be across the street from each other. We can do this . . . If you want to."

I grab the pale blue pillow next to me and squeeze it to my chest. "Of course, I want to. It's the only job I've ever wanted. I can't believe you're just going to hand it to me."

Max picks up his beer and finishes his bottle. "The only thing we've ever been handed is our last name. Don't ever let anyone tell you differently. We've worked fucking harder than everyone else to get to where we are now. You've earned it. It's yours. But lunch is going to be on you when I need to get away from those assholes."

"They're not the enemy." At least, I hope they're not. "But if they are, just remember three-hundred-pound linemen fear me. I can make some hockey players and their management fear me just as easily."

"Yeah. I'll keep that in mind. Now on to more important matters. Who's getting custody of Becket?"

CAD E

"Daddy . . . can we go swimming yet?" Brynlee flies into the kitchen with my sister-in-law, Jillian, hot on her heels, a bottle of sunscreen in one hand and a red floppy hat, matching Brynn's red-ruffled bathing suit, in the other.

I squat down and pick up my speed demon and swing her through the air. "How about you let Aunt Jilly put some sunscreen on you first, please?" I kiss her nose when she wrinkles it in disgust.

"But that stuff is slimy, Daddy." She turns her head to my sister-in-law. "Sorry, Aunty Jilly. But it's gross."

Jillian holds her arms out for Brynlee. "Your beautiful skin will thank me for it one day, little miss." She grabs Brynn from me, then kisses Rylie on the cheek before heading into the backyard.

Rylie watches them go with a wistful expression on her face.

"You changing your mind about wanting kids, Ry?" I finish covering the chicken in barbeque sauce and set it aside to marinate. "She looks good carrying a baby." I nod toward Jillian and Brynn.

Rylie slowly shakes her head. "Nope. You can keep having all the babies until Imogen's ready to join you. I'm drooling over my wife because we had earth-shattering sex this morning. And because we don't have kids, it was loud, Cade." She smiles and goes back to stirring the pasta salad. "Really loud."

Imogen enters the kitchen with Hudson tagging along

behind her, then high-fives Rylie. "Good sex always puts me in a great mood." She turns back to Hud with a devious expression. "Wouldn't you agree, Hud?"

A groan escapes Hudson's mouth. "Listen, as long as we can keep the sex talk going about your sister and not your brother, I'm all for this conversation. I just don't want to have to think about *my* sister and *your* brother together, okay?" He grimaces and fakes a gag.

I think he fakes it.

"Dumbass," I greet my fighter, who just so happens to be one of my sister's closest friends. He's ditched his training gear for a pair of board shorts and a tank top.

"Whatever. Just wanted to get that out of the way. No sex talk about Scarlet."

I shove a bowl of chips at him, and then another. "Here. Make yourself useful and take these outside. Jax and Dave are back there already with Jillian and Brynn."

Imogen opens the door for Hud and follows him out.

"Do you think the two of them . . . ?" Rylie points her spoon to where they just exited.

I think about it for a split second and mimic Hudson's earlier gag. "I try not to think about it." They've known each other for years, and he's a man. No doubt he's thought about it. But I don't think he's ever acted on it. "He's crashed here a few times, but Imogen swears they're just friends. I don't question it."

Rylie rolls her eyes. "Of course, you believe her."

Whatever. I refuse to focus on that right now.

We manage to finish all the meal prep and throw the chicken, burgers, and hot dogs on the grill before Scarlet arrives. I texted her earlier that we were out back and to just come around the house. But when she gets here, I wish I'd met her inside, if only so I could act on my first instinct.

She's wearing one of those long flowy dresses that comes

all the way down to her heeled sandals. It's white with an orangey-pink swirling pattern that dips down between her breasts. There's no way she's wearing a bra under that thing since skinny straps sit on top of her shoulders. Laces, that same orangey-pink color, crisscross under her chest above her waist and tie in a bow, accenting the tiniest beginning of a baby bump I got to see yesterday.

My mouth waters, thinking about untying her later.

But for now, I'm a perfect gentleman.

I meet her at the edge of the patio, wrap my hand around the back of her neck and kiss her. The world stands still for a moment, and the previously noisy backyard quiets until Brynn starts giggling.

"Daddy's kissing Scarlet, like Flynn Rider kisses Rapunzel," she squeals.

"Aww. Come on," comes from a far more masculine voice, and Scarlet buries her head in my neck.

"Why is my brother here?"

I run my fingers over the curls of her soft hair cascading down her even softer skin. "Because my sister invited him. Sorry." After taking her leather overnight bag from her, I hold her hand in mine and ask Rylie to keep an eye on Brynlee while I guide Scarlet into the house.

I pull her up the stairs and into my bedroom where I drop her bag on the bed. "You look amazing, duchess." My fingers trail along the naked skin of her shoulders and down her arms, leaving goosebumps in their place. "Did you wear this dress for me?"

Her hands grip my t-shirt and pull me toward her. "Do you think I wore this dress for anyone besides myself, Saint?" She licks up my neck and trails her tongue along my earlobe. Then she whispers in my ear, "Now the panties . . . the panties I wore for you." A quick tug of her teeth on my ear and she backs away, staring at the erection rising under my army-green board shorts. "Umm." She bites down on her bottom lip. "You might want to do something about that before you go back outside, hotshot."

Scarlet darts for the door, but she forgets who she's dealing with. In two strides, I've caught up, snaked an arm around her waist, and lifted her off her feet. She starts laughing and yelling for me to put her down as we walk through the house to the backyard. "Put me down right now. I swear to God, Cade St. James, if you throw me in that pool, I will hurt you."

Her legs kick, and I have to angle us differently, so she doesn't manage to bring her heel up into my balls. I lower my voice next to her ear. "Careful, duchess. You may want to use parts of my body later that you're dangerously close to damaging now."

Scarlet relaxes once I put her down in a chair next to Rylie.

Brynlee scrambles out of the pool and comes running over.

Water drips down from her wet curls and body, but that doesn't stop my daughter from reaching her hands out for a hug. And does my duchess even hesitate about getting wet?

Nope.

She opens her arms and lets my daughter climb up onto her lap, soaking what I'm betting is a very expensive dress.

"Hi, Scarlet. I like your dress." She fingers the laces I've been fantasizing about. "Are you gonna sleep over again tonight? Daddy just bought me a new movie we could watch."

I rub the heel of my palm over my eye and groan.

My sisters' eyes whip to me.

But it's Imogen who goes for the jugular. "And where exactly did Scarlet sleep for this sleepover, Brynnie?"

Hudson clears his throat and kicks Gen's chair. "Hey, kid. What movie did your dad buy you?"

Okay, maybe I'll lay off his running a little next week.

Brynlee looks between Hudson and Scarlet for a long moment. Then she focuses her attention on me. "Ohhh, Daddy? Can we have a giant sleepover? Can everyone spend the night?" Her big green eyes shimmer with anticipation of what would, no doubt, be the most exciting night ever in my daughter's little life. She clasps her chubby hands together. Begging. "Please. Please. Please."

"Not tonight, baby." I pick her up from Scarlet's lap. "But maybe we could do that another night, okay?" I walk over to the table with the food and thank Jax and Dave for taking the chicken, burgers, and dogs off the grill, then make Brynlee's plate. "Food's ready."

The rest of the afternoon passes with a ton of laughter, accented by an uncomfortable hard-on I can't seem to get rid of for more than a few moments at a time.

Every time Scarlet Kingston laughs or rolls those gorgeous blue eyes of hers, I'm reminded of nights in the desert spent staring into the stars, searching for that exact color. Wondering what she was doing back home. If she was happy. If she was thinking about me.

Every time she moves or looks at me from across the yard, I want to find out what her panties look like. I want to lay claim to her in front of everyone in this yard. At one point, she's talking to Imogen about the upcoming exhibition, and Dave sits down and starts telling her what Crucible has meant to him since he came home from the navy.

She places her hand on his arm.

There's nothing sexual about it.

I have no doubt it's a comforting action.

And yet, I swear I've never wanted to rip another man to pieces over a woman before. But at that moment, I have the caveman-like urge to throw her over my shoulder and take her to my bedroom for the rest of the night.

I don't. Mainly because she'd kill me. But also because I know this woman, and I trust her. And I have to admit I trust him too.

These people in my yard are my family.

And they're some of the best people I've ever known.

Even Hudson.

By the time the party winds down that night, my daughter has absolutely exhausted herself. Any thoughts she may have had of watching a movie are forgotten as she rubs her eyes, tucked into Scarlet's lap as they lay on one of the lounge chairs while Scarlet talks Imogen through a few marketing ideas she hadn't thought of for the gym. Rylie, Jillian, Jaxon, and Dave are long gone. The food has been cleaned up, and Hudson and I are sitting around the fire pit, talking about strategy for his next fight while he enjoys his only beer of the day.

Everyone likes to think MMA fighters are hard-partying assholes, and we might be some of the time. But to compete at the level Hudson and I have, your body has to be your temple. And to have it running at peak efficiency, you have to watch everything you put in it. Beer included. So he's savoring the one he's allowing himself today.

"You love my sister, Saint?"

My brows shoot up. These Kingston men think the exact fucking same way. "You love mine, Hud?"

"I love yours the same way I love Scarlet, Lenny, and Amelia. I'd do anything for Imogen. She's my best friend. But that's it." He sips his beer, his lips twitching. "I bet you can't say the same thing."

"Would it be so bad if I were in love with her? Would you hate it that much?" I sit, waiting for an answer that doesn't come when Imogen interrupts our conversation.

"Time to go, Hud." She holds her hand out to pull Hudson up from the Adirondack chair. "We promised we'd hit that other party tonight, remember?" Gen leans down and kisses my cheek. "Your girls are falling asleep over there, Cade."

"Thanks." I stand, shake hands with Hudson and tell Gen to be safe.

She was right. When I get to the lounge chairs, I see Brynlee's asleep on Scarlet's lap. Her tiny fingers are wrapped around Scarlet's dark hair while Scarlet runs her fingers absentmindedly through Brynn's strawberry-blonde locks with her eyes closed, humming a familiar song.

My entire world is on that one chair.

And nothing.

Not one single thing has ever been more right.

SCARLET

I SENSE CADE'S PRESENCE WITHOUT OPENING MY EYES. I HAVE no doubt he's standing over us, watching. I can imagine Brynlee and I make quite a pretty picture. For a woman who's never cared much for children, the one currently asleep on my lap certainly figured out how to crawl into my heart and quickly make a nice little spot for herself. And I didn't even fight it. I guess I'm not quite the ice queen I once thought I was.

It feels right.

Being here.

In his home.

In his space.

With his family.

There's a weird sense of peace I enjoyed today. Contentment.

A callused finger runs over the apple of my cheek. I slowly open my eyes to see this gorgeous man, who I'm tired of trying to deny my feelings for, standing over us, just as I knew he was. "You okay, duchess?"

When he's quiet and unassuming, I almost don't know what to do with my typically loud and overly confident man. But I appreciate both sides. "I'm really good, Saint." The sun has started to set in the sky, leaving a pretty purple hue in its place. It's exquisite. Serene.

Gentle arms lift Brynlee from my lap and embrace her.

He kisses her tangled hair and quietly calms her when she starts to stir. "Time for bed, baby girl."

"I want Scarlet," she whines against her father's chest, and I feel yet another fissure in my heart form.

I stand on legs that tingle from having stayed in one position for too long and run my hand in circles over her back. "I'm right here, sweetheart. Go with your daddy, and I'll help tuck you in, okay?"

She looks at me with those big eyes framed by long pale blonde lashes and yawns, blinking her eyes closed slowly before tucking her arms under her chest and snuggling against her father.

Cade goes through her nighttime routine, then gets her changed into her Rapunzel nightgown. He tucks her into bed and lays next to her to read a quick story while I lean against the doorframe, watching.

An invited intruder.

Not her mother. But a woman who could easily fall in love with her.

With them both.

He was incredible with her today. I darted out of here pretty quickly the morning after my impromptu sleepover, needing to get my head on straight after the flurry of crazy emotions I was left to deal with. But in doing so, I missed this. I missed real life. I missed my opportunity to watch the two of them together.

And oh, what a sight to be seen it is.

I'm not sure if watching this big, strong man parent his sweet daughter should be sexy or not, but it is incredibly so. I always thought I was attracted to brains over brawn. Apparently, a good father ranks higher than a smart stockbroker.

Brynlee is so smart for such a young child. She questions everything, and the adults in her life answer her questions as thoroughly as they can for a child her age. It's obvious Cade encourages his child to question the world around her. To feel safe in her skin. To know that she's loved and wanted. That she's safe to explore.

I'm not sure every child gets to feel that kind of unconditional love, but his does.

She's a lucky little girl.

Both of the St. James girls will be lucky little girls.

When a finger lifts my chin up to meet dark green eyes, I realize what I just thought and gasp.

Cade raises that finger to my lips, silencing me until we walk into his bedroom across the hall. His brow furrows in question to my earlier reaction, and I sigh. Unable to believe what I'm about to say. "I just realized Baby Girl Kingston needs to be Baby Girl St. James."

His face transforms from confusion to elation in the span of one single beat of my heart. "And what brought on this revelation?" His hands reach under my hair and wrap around my neck. "Not that I'm complaining."

"Brynlee did. Our daughter is going to have an amazing big sister, whose last name is St. James. I want them to have the bond I have with my siblings. I want our girls to be the St. James girls and to know their name means something. That's important to me."

Cade sucks in a breath. "Our girls?"

There's no smile on his face.

No teasing in his tone.

I blow out the breath I'd been holding. "You know what I mean."

The door is kicked shut behind him, and he starts walking us backward until my knees hit the bed. Cade stares down at me. "I don't know what you mean, Scarlet. I know what I want you to mean. I know what I hope you mean. But I have no clue what you actually mean."

183

"Tell me," I whisper tentatively. "Tell me what you want me to mean."

Scared to voice what I want, only for the universe to smack me down for reaching too high. For wanting too much. For not being satisfied with the career of my dreams but also wanting to love and be loved.

Scared there's no way I'm going to get to have it all. And yet, praying to a God who hasn't heard from me since I was seventeen years old that this is my second chance at everything I've ever dreamed of having.

"I want you, Scarlet. I want you in my life. I want you in my house. I want you to give us a chance. And by us, I mean you and me. But I also mean you and Brynlee because we're a package deal." His thumb traces my bottom lip. "I want the world to know you're mine. Not because you're the mother of my child. But because you were mine a decade ago, and I was a stupid kid who listened when you didn't want anyone to know. I was a stupid kid who let you go, who didn't fight hard enough, but I never got over you. If you give me the chance, I swear to God, I'll never let go again."

"Cade . . ." I purse my lips and kiss his thumb.

"You're mine, Scarlet Kingston. You always have been. And I've been yours since the very first time you smiled at me."

I can't help but smile again as his lips gently touch mine. "I'm yours, Cade. I've never been anyone else's. There's never been another man who meant anything to me. Just you." My hands slide up his back, gripping his shirt. "Just us."

He presses his lips against mine, and my knees go weak. "Just this." His strong hands skate down my sides before he fumbles with the tie on my dress.

"It's fake, Saint. You can't untie it." A pout fit for a little boy, instead of the incredibly sexy, grown man standing in front of me, appears on his face, sulking.

I place one hand on his firm chest and force him to take a step back, then unzip the hidden zipper on the side of my dress and let it pool at my feet. I kick my shoes off and step back in nothing but tiny white lace panties that tie on either hip.

His pupils dilate as his hands begin to trace the curves of my body.

My hands shove under his shirt and rip it over his head.

Once the shirt hits the floor, he takes my face in his hands and kisses my lips, then my neck, leaving a hot trail as he works his way down my body until I'm aching with need. Rough fingers rub the delicate skin of my breasts as his tongue swirls around my peaked nipple, scraping it with his teeth and eliciting a hiss of pleasure and pain, mixing together.

Cade drops to his knees, kissing and dragging his lips down my stomach. Tickling my hypersensitive skin. Swirling his tongue around my belly button, then nipping at my hip bones before carefully untying my panties and stuffing them into his pocket.

"Hey." I hold his head in my hands and force him to look up at me. "I'm not going to have any left if you keep stealing them."

His hands grip my hips and guide me back to sit on the bed. "If you can still think, I'm doing this wrong." Then he gently places one leg over his shoulder and sucks on the soft skin of my leg as he trails his hot tongue up to my pussy. His groan of approval vibrates through me, and my pulse beats rapidly in response.

"I've been dying to taste your skin all day, duchess. So much sun-kissed skin on display. Taunting me."

I grip his hair when he leans in and slowly licks his flat-tened tongue up the length of my pussy, then circles my clit and sucks. "Jesus, Cade."

Within seconds, my body is ablaze with need.

He traces the smooth, bare lips of my sex before pushing two callused fingers inside me, fucking me with his fingers and mouth. He slowly brings me to the brink of orgasm, only to back off as my walls clench around him. Prolonging my need. Delaying my orgasm. Until finally, my entire body is strung tight on the verge of snapping at any moment.

"Cade . . ." His eyes meet mine, saying so many things.

His mouth slides up my body. Leisurely exploring.

Demanding words wrap around my skin in a caress.

Mine.

Yours.

More.

He shucks his shorts and stands before me with his cock fisted in his hand, and I lick my lips with eager anticipation. Needy . . . so needy.

I sit up and take his thick cock in my hand, then lean down to wrap my lips around him. Wanting the control. Wanting to know I can bring this man to his knees too.

"Not tonight, duchess. Tonight, is about you." The bed dips with the weight of one knee, then the other. "Tonight, I want to make you feel good. I want to worship you in my bed, where I've thought of you so many fucking times. I want to take my time and explore every inch of your body."

Both hands cup my ass and pull me toward him until he's settled between my thighs, and a breathless moan leaves my lips. He rubs his cock along my drenched sex, and I lift my hips, encouraging him to move. To take what he wants. To give us both what we need.

My body trembles with anticipation.

My pussy throbs with need in sync with the beat of my heart.

The air grows thick with want.

When he finally pushes inside me, it isn't slow or careful.

He seats himself fully in one strong thrust, and my already heightened senses explode in a kaleidoscope of color behind my eyes. Then he pulls out entirely and thrusts again. And again. Driving us higher and higher.

I know I can't hold out long.

He leans down and kisses me reverently, and I wonder how I ever lived without him.

Strong hands wrap around my back and pull me up to him. Straddling his lap, my legs wrap around his waist as we sit chest to chest. With every inch I move, his hard body rubs my soft skin, the friction driving me higher.

No space is left between us.

My nails rake over his shoulders, holding him to me.

Breathing him in as he controls our rhythm.

I can't get enough.

Sex has never been like this.

It's us.

It's only ever been us.

When my orgasm finally washes over me like a warm wave pulling me under, it's with my mouth on Cade's. Gasping for breath. Clinging to him. To us.

Refusing to let this moment end.

I lay limply in his arms, draped against his body as he pulls his cock out once more before pushing deep inside me and coming on a long, low groan.

Kissing my lips. My neck. My head.

Holding me to him.

Worshipping me.

Breaking me beyond repair, yet healing all my broken pieces.

CAD E

LATER THAT NIGHT, WHILE SCARLET LAYS NAKED AND SATED, draped over my chest after having reached for each other yet again, I internally debate whether now is a good time to bring up the elephant in the house. But really, if not now . . . when?

My fingers dance along her spine as they trail up and down the soft skin of her back. "Duchess . . ."

Her lips graze my skin. "Hmm?"

"I want to tell Brynlee about the baby."

The fingers that had been tracing circles on my chest freeze, and Scarlet sits up, not bothering to bring the sheet with her.

And God, my mouth waters at the sight before me. Her tits are fucking magnificent.

"Cade." She smacks me with one of the pillows. "Eyes up here, buddy." Unfortunately, she hugs that same pillow to her chest, wrecking my view. "Okay, so you want to tell Brynlee. I think that makes sense. It gives her time to get used to the idea of having to share you with a baby sister. She's had you to herself for years. She might resent sharing you with the baby at first."

I sit up and lean against the headboard. "I'm more concerned with the immediate questions she's going to throw our way."

"Our way? Oh, no. This is all on you, mister." She cracks a smile and starts laughing as I grab for her leg and tickle the soft spot behind her knee. "I'm kidding, I'm kidding. I guess it makes sense for me to be there with you when you tell her. But seriously, she might be smarter than us, so we need to be careful."

She bites down on her thumbnail, mulling the idea around. "I mean, she's definitely smarter than you."

I slide my hand up her leg. "Oh, you are so going to pay for that."

In hindsight, we probably should have discussed this more in-depth instead of going for round three, considering the questions my extremely excited daughter is throwing our way over breakfast the following morning. She squealed when we told her she was going to be a big sister. And while it was ear piercingly loud, it was the only easy thing that's come out of her mouth since.

"And Scarlet's the mommy?" She looks hopefully between Scarlet and me. "Is she going to move in here with us? Oh, oh, oh, can Scarlet take turns sleeping in my room too? My bed fits me and you, Daddy. And Scarlet's smaller than you. Maybe not as small as me. But way smaller than you. Where's my baby sister going to sleep? Wait . . . Wait. Wait. Wait. Do I have to share a room with her? I don't know if I want to share my room with her."

I dip my napkin in my glass of water and wipe the syrup from her sticky face. I can handle her being a messy eater, but I draw the line when her hair starts sticking to the syrup already plastered on her face. "Slow your roll, baby girl. One question at a time."

I glance Scarlet's way and realize she looks about ready to bolt.

Okay.

Time to calm my girls down.

I take Scarlet's hand in mine and squeeze, then place them on the table so Brynlee can see it. "Yes, baby. Scarlet is the mommy. Your sister is inside her belly. She has to get big and strong before she can come out and meet you. But once she does, she's going to love you so much. You know how much Aunt Rylie loves Aunt Immie and me? Well, Aunt Rylie is our big sister. It takes a really special person to be a big sister. Do you think you can handle it?"

She tilts her head, thinking about it.

And I swear to God, she looks thirteen instead of three.

Please let time slow down.

"I think I can do it, Daddy. Now on to the room situation."

Scarlet snorts out a laugh, then quickly covers her mouth.

Brynn whips her head to Scarlet and points her chubby little finger in her face. "It's not funny. I like my toys a certain way, and a baby won't know how to do that." Brynn's blonde head turns my way. "I really think she needs a name and her own room, Daddy. Scarlet can stay with me because I know she'll clean up after herself like you make me do. But baby needs her own room."

I look over at Scarlet and watch her try with all her strength not to laugh at my three-year-old, who thinks she's negotiating a UN peace treaty at our kitchen table. "I agree. Baby needs a name, and she will absolutely get her own room. But you know our rule about Daddy sleeping in your bed or you sleeping in my bed?" She nods her head. "Well, it's going to be the same thing with Scarlet, honey. When she spends the night, you still have to sleep in your own bed. By yourself."

Little hands fly to little hips. "That's not fair."

"You've got to learn to sleep alone, Brynlee. It's a rule for a reason."

"But . . ." When I give her what Imogen calls *'the look,'* Brynn closes her mouth with a huff. "Fine. But you're no fun."

"I know." I stand from the table and get a washcloth out of one of the drawers in the kitchen. "Come here, sweetheart."

She runs over, and I lift her to sit on the counter next to the sink and wash her face and hands. "What do you want to do today?"

Brynlee looks over at Scarlet then back to me. "Will Scarlet come with us?"

"She will. We've got her today." I look over Brynn's head and wink at Scarlet, who's looking a little less petrified than she was a few minutes ago.

Brynlee taps her finger to her lips like she must have seen in some cartoon somewhere, thinking. Then her eyes light up. "I know! Let's go to the zoo!"

That's how we find ourselves sitting on the cement steps outside the polar bear enclosure at the Philadelphia Zoo a few hours later. Brynlee's face is smooshed up against the glass, watching the giant white bear play with a red ball and splashing in the water. The polar bear is her favorite thing to see here.

"You handled that well this morning, Cade. She's a tough little cookie. When she started rattling off all her questions, I froze when I didn't have any answers. But not you. You knew exactly what to say."

My eyes stay locked on Brynn in front of us, but my hand clasps Scarlet's. "You'll get used to it. It comes with practice and experience. Never let them smell fear." I smile and drop a quick kiss on her head. "It feels better now that everyone knows, anyway."

"Not everyone."

"What?" I glance quickly at Scarlet before looking back over to Brynn. "Who doesn't know?"

Scarlet hesitates, pulling her hand back.

I hate that she's still pulling away from me.

"I haven't told my mom yet. I don't exactly have the best relationship with Adeline."

From what I remember, none of them had a great relationship with their mom. But still. "You've got to tell her. You can't just throw a grandchild on her out of the blue."

"You don't get it, Cade. Your mom was like June fucking Cleaver. And mine was like . . . I don't even know what fucked up TV family to compare her to. She ruins everything."

I take back the hand she yanked away and hold it tighter. "She's still your mom, Scarlet."

"I promise I'll tell her before the baby comes. I just want to avoid any extra stress if I can. And Adaline is the queen of stress and unwanted drama."

"Scarlet—"

She's saved by the bell when Brynlee runs over and takes Scarlet's hand. "Can you get us pretzels now, Daddy? Don't you want a pretzel, Scarlet?"

Scarlet stands up and swings their clasped hands between the two of them. "A pretzel sounds perfect."

And just like that, our conversation is forgotten, and we're on the hunt for the perfect pretzel.

SCARLET

THOUGHTS OF MY MOM RATTLE AROUND IN MY BRAIN FOR THE next two weeks. It doesn't matter if I'm alone at home, surrounded by people at work, or even with Cade and Brynlee at his house. I replayed my conversation about her over so many times in my head, I think I might be losing my mind. I know I need to call her. But I have no desire to listen to the disappointment that'll be evident in her voice.

I have very little relationship with Adaline. I can count on one hand how many times I've seen her these last few years.

Max has zero tolerance for her.

Becket is the only one of the three of us who keeps in touch. And that's because *he* keeps in touch, not the other way around. I might have a bit of a daddy complex, but Becks rocks a definite mommy complex.

But if I'm willing to work for what I want in my career and my relationship, I need to be woman enough to call my mother and see if she'd be willing to meet me halfway in order for us to have a relationship. I'd like my daughter to know the only parent I have left.

But on my terms.

That's how I find myself FaceTiming her nearly two weeks after my zoo date.

I wait until the office has cleared out for the day and know it's time.

There's no hiding that my baby bump has popped in person, but we're not in person. I'm sitting behind my

193

monitor at work, so she won't be getting that view. This is on my terms, even if she doesn't realize it.

Once I find her contact on my FaceTime app, I sit back and wait for her to answer.

Hoping for a moment she won't answer but knowing it'll be better to get this over with like the strong confident woman I am. My therapist would be so proud.

Until she answers and I regress back to that young woman who let Adaline manipulate me at will. "Scarlet, darling. It's so good to see you. You look tired, dear. Are you getting enough sleep?"

I haven't spoken to my mother since Christmas. And in the first five seconds of speaking to me, that's what she says.

"I'm fine, Mother. How are you?"

I study her while she spends the next few minutes regaling me of the week she and her latest boyfriend just spent on a yacht in Lake Cuomo. Her blonde hair is cut in a short bob, just skimming her chin. Her makeup is perfectly applied to an incredibly botoxed face. She's had so much work done, she looks more like my older sister than my mother. It's a shame. She'd be a beautiful sixty-year-old woman if she let herself age gracefully. But that was never an option for her.

I wait until she finally takes a breath before I interrupt her, having already had enough of this conversation. "I'm pregnant."

I throw it out there without any fanfare. I just need her to know so I can get off this call before I crawl out of my skin.

There's a knock on my door, followed by Lenny's head popping in just as Adaline starts to go off like a rocket. "What? You can't be pregnant. You're not married. Scarlet Kingston, what will the papers say? What do you know about being a mother?"

I wave my hand at Lenny out of the view of the camera,

knowing this call isn't going to last much longer, and she closes the door quietly behind her, tiptoeing over to one of the seats across from me without Adaline seeing.

"The papers aren't going to say anything, Mother. They have more important things to write about than me being pregnant. The Kings have won the Championship two years in a row. We're going for a third this year, and we're going to be doing it with me as president of Operations and my daughter in my arms while I do it." There. I said it, and my voice didn't even shake like the child she makes me feel like I still am.

Her throat clears dramatically, and Lenny makes a silly face, causing me to hold back a laugh. "This is not funny, Scarlet. How in the world do you think you're going to have a baby and that kind of career? Take it from me, you can't have it all. It's impossible. And who, exactly, is the father? Is he going to make this right and marry you?"

"It's not 1955, Mother. I don't have to marry the father if I don't want to. I'm a grown woman with the means to take care of my own child if I want to do it alone. But that won't be the case. The father is Cade St. James, and he is very much in my life."

If Adaline could move her forehead at all, I'm fairly sure her eyebrows would be touching her hairline right now.

Ahh. The beauty of botox.

"The same boy—"

I spare a glance at my sister and cut my mother off, not wanting her to finish that sentence in front of Lenny. "Yes, Mother. The same boy. Only he's a man now. An incredible man. And the father of your granddaughter."

"Scarlet, you can't be serious."

"I'm very serious. I didn't call to get your opinion or advice. I just wanted to tell you that you're going to be a grandmother in a few more months." Before she gets the chance to say anything, I take the high road and lie. "Mother, I just realized I have a meeting to get to. I've got to go. We'll talk soon. Bye."

"Scarlet—" I close FaceTime before she gets the chance to finish her sentence and lean back against my chair, looking at Lenny. "I'm so sorry you had to hear that."

"I barged into your office. You've got nothing to be sorry for. That was painful. God. I haven't seen your mom since Dad's funeral." Lenny was lucky. Her mother was nothing like mine. We lost her right before Len graduated from high school. She tried to mother all of us, and we let her. It was the first time anyone ever had. "She's wrong, you know."

I close my computer and tap the lid. "She's wrong about a lot of things."

"Oh, I have no doubt about that. But you're going to be an amazing mother, Scarlet. And you're going to have it all. You'll just have to learn how to balance it all. Then, maybe you can teach me."

"Thanks, Len. I appreciate it. Thank God, I've got time to figure it all out before I need to teach you anything. Because I have absolutely no idea what I'm doing." But that idea isn't as scary as it used to be, thanks to Cade.

Lenny purses her lips before she smiles. "Well, that's what I came to talk to you about. I wanted you to be the first one to know."

I remove my glasses and study my sister. "Know what, Eleanor?"

Her entire face lights up. "I'm pregnant."

I jump up from my chair and pull Lenny into a tight hug. "Oh, Len. I'm so happy for you. When are you due?"

"February third. Can you even believe it, Scarlet? The Kingston girls are having babies together. First Amelia, then you, and now me."

I squeeze her again, then laugh. "You always did want to do everything I did."

"I did. But Bash and I had a little too much to drink after our friends' bachelorette and bachelor parties, and as they say, the rest is history. We're trying to keep it quiet for now. You know, our friends Nattie and Brady are getting married next month, and we don't want to announce it before then. I don't want to steal her thunder."

"Nice *Friends* reference there, Len."

"Yeah, well it's Nat's favorite show. But that's not everything. I need your help. Sebastian and I want to get married at Dad's house next month. We want something really small. Intimate. Can you help me pull it together?"

"Oh, Lenny Lou. I would love to." I pull back and frame her face with my hands. "Sebastian is a lucky man, Len"

She hugs me again. "Love you, Scar."

"Love you too, little sister."

As I lie in bed, wrapped up in Cade's arms, I fill him in on my conversation with Adaline. I know I need to tell him what happened after we broke up. Adaline nearly said it earlier while Lenny was in the room. I guess it's just a matter of time before the truth comes out.

But I'm not ready to pop our perfect little bubble.

I never imagined we'd find our way back to each other.

I never thought I'd find this.

The tips of Cade's fingers trace circles on my bare back. "You seem lost in thought, duchess. What are you thinkin' so hard about?"

I rest my palm over his heart and close my eyes. "Lenny's pregnant. Sebastian and she are finally getting married."

"It's about time. They've been engaged for what . . . two years?"

I lean up, my chin resting on his chest. "A year and a half. He asked right after he got drafted." With one bulky arm resting behind his head and the other on me, Cade's eyes are sleepy but locked on mine. "Do you think that would have been us if I didn't break us?"

"I don't know . . . maybe. Or maybe we needed that time apart. Tell me . . . Did you do what you thought you had to or were you just over us?"

I suck in a breath, his words bringing me back to such a painful time in my life. "I thought I was saving us both from what I thought would be a worse breakup eventually. But now, I don't know if it could have been worse than it was. I wonder if I stole all those years from us."

Cade rolls us over so he's bracing himself above me. "You're here now, and I'm not letting you go this time. Go ahead and try." His lips brush over mine gently, reverently, before he places his lips against my stomach.

"I told Adaline today."

I'm tucked back into his arms, and his palm rests gently on my bump. "How'd that go?"

"About as good as you'd expect. But it's done." I let out the breath I think I've been holding since I ended the call. "Thank you for pushing me to call her. She needed to know, and now it's done."

"I'm glad you did it. It's always better to just get it out there."

I wonder if he'll think that once he knows my secret.

SCARLET

"So, you're both coming to the exhibition, right? I promised Imogen I would firm up how many tickets I need by the end of this week. They're going quickly, and we only have two weeks left." Lenny, Amelia, and I are sitting outside a local bistro, enjoying the last rays of warmth from the setting July sun. We just left the bridal salon where Lenny was fitted for her gown. We're supposed to be planning her wedding.

She and Sebastian finally set a date and are getting married at Dad's house in a few weeks.

Amelia sips her iced tea with a knowing smile on her face. "So, things between you and Cade are good?" Her lips quirk up in a sarcastic smile.

She already knows the answer.

My cheeks grow hot at the thought of us having been caught making out like teenagers last week, when the family got together at Kingdom to celebrate the acquisition of the Revolution being finalized. The deal is done, and Max and I both moved into our new positions a few days ago.

It's weird not having him in the building.

Definitely going to take some getting used to.

One more thing that seems to have fallen into place like it was always meant to be.

"Things are good between us. Too good, if I'm honest. Life almost doesn't seem real lately. Like it can't actually be this good, can it? I feel like a commercial for having it all,

199

only I find myself constantly waiting for the other shoe to drop." Frustrated, I stuff a French fry in my mouth and sigh at the exquisite taste of grease and salt.

Both foods I've been trying to avoid while I watch my blood pressure.

But this place has the best fries in the city.

I swear I've never wanted greasy, salty foods as much as I do now that I'm pregnant and can't have them.

Lenny reaches across the round cast iron table and steals a fry. "You know how I feel about this, Scarlet. You control when that other shoe drops. Or if it drops. I know there are things Amelia and I don't know. I know you're not ready to talk about them. But I think you need to talk to Cade about whatever they are. It's going to continue to eat at you until you do."

"Scarlet," Amelia sits back in her chair, pinning me with her eyes. "Whatever it is, he's going to understand. You'll make him understand. But it's going to become harder the longer you wait to do it."

I wish I could believe that. "How can you be so sure?"

"That's easy." Lenny swipes another fry. "It's the way he looks at you. Like you're the only person in the room."

"Like you're the only person in the world," Amelia corrects.

The waiter comes by and places a chocolate lava cake with a side of vanilla ice cream and three spoons in the center of the table, then disappears. I take a bite of the cake and debate my next move. "Cade's been so busy making sure everything is ready for next weekend, he and I have barely seen each other this week. But I think I need to talk to him soon. This can't wait forever. It's not fair to him." None of this is fair. But life rarely is.

"You'll know when it's the right time, Scarlet. But like I said, it's going to become harder the longer you put it off."

Amelia never picks up her spoon, staring at the dessert as if it personally offended her because it didn't come from her bakery.

More for me.

I scoop up another spoonful of chocolate and ice cream and savor every last decadent drop. "Okay. Enough about Cade and me. Now that we've got your dress decided, Len, what do you want us to wear for the wedding?" I glance over at Amelia, then back to Lenny. "And keep in mind, if you put us in pink, we might boycott."

When I get in bed later that night, the urge to call Cade and come clean is strong.

So strong.

But not strong enough to follow through.

He deserves to know the truth. But I don't know if I can bear to look into his eyes and see the disappointment I know will be staring back at me. I don't know if we can get past that. I don't know if he'll even want to try or if he's going to think I lied to him like Daria did.

I should have known this is where we'd end up.

Falling in love with him as a teenager was the easiest thing I'd ever done. And the consequences of it shattered me. They shaped me into who I am today. The stakes weren't nearly as high then as they are now. And that scares me.

Almost as much as the realization that I never stopped loving him.

My stomach churns when my phone rings, but after a quick glance at the screen, it calms down. I settle back against my pillows. "Maximus."

"You owe me one. You know that, right? I took one for the team with these goddamn assholes. Remind me why we thought buying a hockey team was a good idea? These people are so fucking frustrating." He starts grumbling, so I can't make out exactly what he's saying. At least, not until I hear, "Swear to God, Scarlet. I've never met anyone more infuriating."

"Take a breath, Max, and tell me who we're talking about exactly." I'm fairly certain I've been described this way a time or two. Not that I want to mention that to my brother when he sounds like he's about to burst a blood vessel.

Max groans, and a door slams on his end of the call. "Daphne Brenner."

"Will's daughter?"

He grunts in response, and I almost laugh out loud. This entire call is so unlike Max that I feel the need to make sure it's not really Becket I'm talking to, even though I know it's not.

"If I said the sky was blue, she'd say it's green. If I say we need to increase revenue, she throws a piece of paper across my desk showing me we don't. She's the most infuriating person I've ever met." The thud of something hitting the wall, or possibly the floor, echoes across the line. "I need an ally."

"Well, when you paint such a pretty picture, I'll just jump right in." I know that's not what he means, but I'm at a loss for words. "Who are you thinking?"

"Don't worry. I'm not taking any of your team. I've got my eyes on a different King." His voice trails off as a doorbell sounds in the background.

"Max?"

"Sorry, Scarlet. Thanks for letting me vent. We'll catch up next week." He disconnects the call, leaving me to wonder what the hell that was.

CAD E

"DADDY, I DON'T FEEL SO GOOD." BRYNLEE'S BRIGHT GREEN eyes are covered in a sheen of unshed tears as she grips her pink teddy to her chest while she drags her feet into the kitchen.

Scarlet is sipping a cup of coffee while I make a protein shake before the crazy starts today. We have interviews scheduled all afternoon and a photoshoot at the end of the day, all to keep up the hype for next weekend's exhibition. There are four fights planned in total, with mine being the last one of the event.

They're supposed to be friendly fights.

But no one wants to lose.

Even if it's for charity.

"Come here, sweetheart." I lift her in my arms and sit her on the granite counter while I take the thermometer out of the kitchen drawer filled to the brim with supplies. Band-Aids, alcohol wipes, hair ties, and nail clippers all live in this drawer. Of course, I have the same things in a drawer in Brynlee's bathroom too. But having them on each floor of the house has made my life easier more than once.

She opens her mouth for the thermometer, and I lean my cheek against her forehead.

Yup. She feels warm.

Scarlet stands and crosses the kitchen to run a hand over Brynn's strawberry-blonde curls while we both wait for the thermometer to beep, alerting us that it's done. And yes, she does have a temperature.

Shit.

"Okay, sweetie. You're running a little fever. Nothing too bad. Let's get some Tylenol in you, and Daddy will come up with a plan." Once Brynn's comfortable on the couch with her favorite Disney movie playing on the television, I try to come up with a way to handle this today.

Imogen is already at Crucible, ensuring everything is set up for the press. This event is her baby. She and Scarlet have actually seemed to get along a bit better lately as they've discussed different aspects of the exhibition.

Rylie and Jillian are in the Keys, visiting my parents.

When I walk back into the kitchen, I rest my hands against the counter on either side of Scarlet, caging her in and leaning my head against her chest. "Some days, being a single parent fucking sucks."

She runs her fingers soothingly through my hair. "What time do you have to be at Crucible?"

I look at the clock on the oven. "In an hour."

"Okay. So go get ready, and I'll stay here with Brynlee. She doesn't need to go to Crucible today, but you do." Her hands lift my face, then her lips brush gently over mine. "Go. Get dressed, get to the gym, and do your thing." She laughs lightly, then places my palm against her growing bump and pushes down.

When our daughter pushes back against my hand, I drop to my knees and kiss where my hand just was.

"Go, Cade. I've got our girls covered. Do your thing."

When I stand back up, I wrap a hand around the back of her neck and kiss her with a promise for later.

A hunger. A thank you. A lifeline.

Is this what it's like to have a partner?

Someone to pick up the slack when you can t?

Someone to share your life with?

With one hand still resting against our daughter and the other gripping her neck, I get lost in the ocean-like depths of her blue eyes. "Scarlet . . ."

"Go."

The words are there. Sitting on my lips. Waiting to be said. Needing to be heard. But not now. Not yet. "Thank you." I kiss her one more time before pulling away. Her responding smile is small. Hesitant. Beautiful.

"Go. This is your event. We'll be right here when you get back."

This might be my event, but everything that matters will be waiting for me in this house.

Hudson Kingston isn't fighting in the exhibition. He has a title to defend, and his fight is just a few short months away. You don't risk getting hurt in a charity event before a fight like that. Instead, he's agreed to be our MC for the night and is thoroughly enjoying that he doesn't have to answer questions or have his picture taken. Instead, Hud's reveling in watching us all perform.

Most of us don't mind this part, charity or not.

When you fight for a living, you tend to be an extrovert. I loved the spotlight back then. I loved the attention. The glory. And all the things that came with it. But not now. Now, I'd rather be home with my girls instead of watching the clock, waiting for this to be over.

The event is a week away, and we've already raised more money for my veteran's charity this year than in the last few years combined. Thanks, in part, to Max Kingston's check.

I pull my phone from my pocket, making sure I haven't missed any calls from Scarlet. "Why do you keep checking your phone?" Hudson and I are standing back from the crowd surrounding Jax and his opponent as they go through their interviews and pictures.

"Brynlee's home sick. Scarlet's staying with her. I guess I keep waiting for the text telling me I need to come home." I shove my phone back into my pocket and shrug.

"If there's one thing I know about my sister, it's when she says she has something under control, she has it under control. So, you've got nothing to worry about. Brynlee seems to really like her too. How's that going?"

A reporter walks by, trying to get Hudson's attention, but he just nods and waits expectantly for my answer.

"How's what going? Brynlee's relationship with Scarlet?"

Hud nods.

"It's good, man. Brynlee loves Scarlet. I thought she was getting the motherly attention she needed from Imogen, Rylie, and Jillian. But I don't think it's the same when it comes to your sister. She gets something different from her. I'm not sure I can put it into words. But it's pretty amazing to watch." I thought Brynn would give me a hard time when I told her I was leaving this morning. But she didn't. She was snuggled up under a blanket with her head resting on Scarlet's lap, watching the last of her movie. She let me kiss her goodbye but didn't seem to care that I was leaving. "Her little world used to revolve around me, but she had no problem making room for Scarlet."

"You ready to have another kid?" He looks at me, then shakes his head. "I still can't believe you and my sister." I try to interrupt him, but he puts his hand out, stopping me. "I'm not saying it's a bad thing. I just never figured the guy who would finally tame Scarlet would be you. Or a guy like you, for that matter."

"What's that supposed to mean, asshole?"

"Calm down. I just meant you're rough, Saint. You're a

former MMA World Champion. I've watched you with her. You don't let her steamroll you the way she does most people. It's a good thing. I think Scarlet needed someone who was as strong as her. I guess she found it."

I guess she did.

"Don't fuck it up, Saint," Hudson smirks as Imogen taps me on the shoulder, letting me know it's my turn to be interviewed. "You'll never find someone better than my sister."

Like he needs to tell me that.

Scarlet Kingston has always been too good for me.

She's also always been mine.

SCARLET

There have been so many princess movies added to Disney's vault since Lenny was a little girl, and my younger sister, Madeline, has never really been into princess movies. So I never really noticed the new ones. Actually Ashlyn, my third and final stepmother, was never fond of Madeline watching much television at all, let alone princess movies, which is surprising, considering Ashlyn resembles the embodiment of a cartoon princess. But Brynlee and I have camped out on the couch most of the day, binging all the princess goodness Disney Plus has to offer.

The poor kid feels awful, but luckily for both of us, she was able to keep down the chicken noodle soup I made earlier for lunch. I'm not sure what it says about me that I fed Cade's daughter soup that came out of a box, but that's what was in the pantry, and that's what she wanted. It was actually pretty good.

Brynlee fell asleep about halfway through the last movie. Now this one I could get behind. A badass little red-headed princess wanted to be able to control her own life. Finally, a little girl power instead of a princess needing to be saved.

Once I make sure Brynlee is asleep, I gently slide a pillow under her head and get up to clean the mess I managed to make in the kitchen.

I've never been much of a cook. I grew up with someone else always taking care of it. And once I was old enough to have to deal with it myself, I was also old enough to have a meal service deliver fresh meals directly to my refrigerator. How was I supposed to know the soup would bubble up and over the top of the pot? It didn't say anything about that on the instructions on the back of the box.

Once that's handled, I grab my laptop out of Cade's room and set myself up at the kitchen table, ready to jump into the report Lenny sent me about the first week of training camp last week, when a knock at the front door catches my attention. A quick glance at the security feed, sitting in the corner of the desk in the kitchen, shows a petite brunette. She looks familiar, but I can't place her.

Not wanting Brynlee to wake up, I hurry to the door before she can knock again. Once the rounded oak door opens, the smile falls from the pretty woman's face, replaced by a sneer. "So, you *are* living here. I thought he was wrong."

"Excuse me?" I don't like the entitled tone to this woman's voice. "And who, exactly, are you?"

"I'm here to see my daughter." She glances down at my pregnant belly, and an even uglier look passes over her face.

Shit. This is Cade's ex, Daria. She's dyed her blonde hair to a stark brown. That's why I didn't recognize her. "If you want to see Brynlee, you'll have to talk to Cade." I step through the door and close it behind me, putting more distance between Daria and Brynlee. "Now, please leave."

"You think you're so fucking special because you're a Kingston. Well, guess what, honey. You spread your legs the same damn way I did, so when he's done using you and then tosses you away like he did me, maybe you won't feel so superior."

I look Daria over from top to toe. Her clothes are ill-fitting. Too big. They hang off her frail frame and are in desperate need of a wash. Her eyes are sunken and wild, and her skin is sallow.

What's wrong with her?

Is she sick?

Is that why she wants to see Brynlee so badly?

She's out of her mind if she thinks she can get past me. I take a step closer. I'm Scarlet fucking Kingston, and it will take a hell of a lot more than this little bitch to intimidate me. "You need to leave. Now." I take another step forward, backing her down the stairs. "I'll let Cade know you stopped by." I wave my fingers in the air. "I'm sure he'll be in touch. Bye-bye."

I'm sure he'll be calling his lawyers first.

If not, I might just call mine for him.

There's something about this woman that isn't sitting right with me.

For someone who supposedly came to see Brynlee, she only mentioned her once.

"Oh, I look forward to it." She turns to leave, then looks back over her shoulder. "I'll see you real soon, princess."

"It's King, not princess."

A princess needs to be saved.

I can save my own damn self.

When I go back inside, I breathe a sigh of relief to see Brynlee still sound asleep on the couch. I'm not sure how that woman could hold this beautiful little girl in her arms and then decide to just give her away to her father. Sign away all her parental rights. Take what I'm sure was a hefty payment, and then think she has the right to come back in and disrupt her life.

Brynn rolls over, and her little eyes flutter open when her hand meets the cool couch instead of me. "Scarlet . . ." She turns and looks around until her eyes land on me. "I feel yucky." Her arms go out in front of her, reaching for me, so I sit down and pull her onto my lap. Resting my cheek against her face, I feel her warm skin.

"Come on, baby. Let's get you some more medicine." I run

my fingers along her temple. "Do you want to take a bath? It might make you feel better."

She shakes her head from side to side. "No. Can we lay in Daddy's bed?"

"We can do anything you want, sweets." I stand up and reach out my hand for hers. "Don't forget Teddy."

She holds him tightly against her chest. "Can we bring up juice too?"

"Okay." We make a pit stop in the kitchen for an apple juice box, and I have an inkling that I'm getting played. But when she looks up at me with pitiful green eyes, I don't really care. Let her play me if it means she'll feel better.

I stop by the security feed in the kitchen, make sure it's armed, and then grab the apple juice and Tylenol before following Brynlee upstairs. It doesn't take long for us to find a new movie to turn on. We've moved on from animation to live action. Only now she's picked one of my favorites —*Beauty and the Beast.*

The two of us lie snuggled up in the center of Cade's king-sized bed, the soft gray blanket that typically lies draped across the foot wrapped around us. Brynlee is playing with my hair while her head lays against my shoulder. "Scarlet . . . When my baby sister comes, are you going to live with Daddy and me?"

My brain is screaming, *"It's a trap."*

There's no easy way to answer this question.

And it's not something Cade and I have discussed yet. He's brought it up, but I backpedaled a bit and changed the subject. He needs to know the truth about the past before we plan for the future.

"I'm not sure what we're going to do yet. Your daddy and I are still figuring that out." Okay. Good. That was good. Noncommittal. But still good.

"Oh." Disappointment laces her tone. "I like when you're here. I never had a mommy before."

Oh, my . . . That's not playing fair. "Oh, honey." I wrap my arm around her tightly, not sure what to say. "I love you, Brynlee." I press my lips against her head.

"I love you too, Scarlet."

I would have never thought the first time I said those words to someone outside of my family, it would be to this little girl who stole my heart.

I never stood a chance.

CAD E

I COULDN'T WAIT TO GET HOME TO MY GIRLS ONCE THE PARADE of press was finally over this afternoon. They're a necessary evil if we want this event to be a success and to raise as much as we can for vets trying to return to civilian life. Not everyone has the support system I came home to or even the one we try to provide with the program at Crucible. And some kind of a support system can make all the difference for these men and women.

As of right now, we're already on track for our biggest year yet.

Imogen's done a great job getting everything set up. Now we just have to show up and put on a great show. I'm excited to share this with Scarlet. She's never seen me fight. Never seen what my gym is capable of, not from this perspective.

Scarlet is used to being at the top of the food chain in her world.

But this isn't her world. It's mine.

Being with a Kingston could be intimidating for a lesser man.

But I'm no lesser man.

And I've got plenty to be proud of in my business and my life.

When I walk into the house, the only noise is the dull hum of the air conditioner. The family room and kitchen are both empty. Brynlee's blanket from this morning sits in a ball on the couch.

Where are they?

I take the stairs two at a time, following the light flickering through my open bedroom door. And there they are. My whole heart tangled together in the center of my bed.

As I push the door open further, Scarlet's head shoots up. She places a finger to her lips, letting me know to be quiet, then looks down at a sleeping Brynlee before carefully attempting to extricate herself without waking my daughter. She's in the same soft gray, cotton shorts from this morning, showing off her long, lean legs, and one of my ribbed, white Crucible tanks that would normally be too big for her, but instead snugly hugs her growing belly. Her wild, dark hair is down around her shoulders, and her skin glows with a pretty pink flush.

She's stunning.

And she's mine.

She tiptoes over to me and pushes me through the door before closing it behind us.

My hands grip her face as my lips devour hers. "You are so beautiful." I back her against the wall, my hands trailing down her sides.

"Cade," she mewls against my lips as her fingers grip the front of my shirt, then push back. "Wait . . ." she pants, as a concerned look ghosts across her face.

"What's wrong?" I rest a hand against her stomach. "Is it the baby? Brynlee?"

Scarlet takes my hand and leads me away from the bedroom door. "It's Daria. She was here earlier. She knocked on the door and demanded to see Brynlee. But there was no way that was happening. I meant to call you but got distracted."

"What the fuck?" Adrenaline courses through my body. Daria's gone too far this time. "When?"

"A few hours ago. She knocked on the door while Brynlee

was napping on the couch. I went outside so Brynn had no idea anyone was here, let alone who it was. Daria insisted she needed to see her, and when I told her no, she seemed more angry that I was here and with you than she was that she couldn't see Brynlee. The whole thing was bizarre. It felt off. Forced. I think she may have been on something. I knew you'd be home soon, so I just locked us inside the house and armed the alarm. It wasn't anything I couldn't handle, so I didn't see a need for you to stop what you were doing and run home."

"Scarlet . . ." I reach up and tuck a lock of her hair behind her ear. "You shouldn't have to handle her."

Soft fingers skim along my shoulders. "I've dealt with much worse than your ex, Cade. Handling people is my job."

"Not anymore, it's not. Not when it's her. Not when it's my daughter. Let me deal with it." I pull her into my arms, tucking her against my chest. My protective instincts want to put her and the girls in nice little bubbles forever. But Scarlet would hate that.

"I'm fine, Cade." She kisses the underside of my jaw, soothing me. "Brynlee and the baby are fine. When I came back inside, Brynn asked to watch television in your room, and I couldn't tell her no. Then we had our own version of an intense conversation, and we've been lost in *Beauty and the Beast* since." She lifts my hand to her lips and presses them against me. "Well, I've been watching. She's been snoring. But I think her fever broke. She's a sweaty little mess in there."

I tug her behind me down the stairs and sit her on the couch so she can tell me exactly what Daria said before I leave a message with my attorney. "I want a restraining order. She signed away her rights. If she wants them back, she can take me to court and fight me for them. I will not let her come in and out of Brynlee's life on a whim, confusing her. That woman may have given birth to her, but she is not her mother."

Scarlet grabs my hand and places it against her stomach, just as our daughter rolls.

Not a kick, but what feels like a full-body Imanari roll. A classic MMA move I've used to take down more than one opponent. And she's using it on her mother. I shove her tank up and kiss her belly.

Her nails scratch gently along my scalp. "Tonight, Brynlee asked me where her sister and I were going to live."

"Did she?" It's not really surprising. Brynlee is firmly planted in the team Scarlet column. She put herself there after the very first time she fell asleep in Scarlet's arms and has dug her feet in deep ever since.

Can't say that I blame her. If you're lucky enough to be allowed to see past her icy exterior, the woman she hides from the world is pretty fucking amazing.

Scarlet leans back against the pillow and absently rubs her hand against our very active little girl. "She did. Right before she told me she never had a mommy before." Scarlet's big, blue eyes glisten, and her lower lip trembles.

"Duchess . . . what's wrong?" She went from smiling to tears faster than I knew was possible. This seems to be happening more often lately. According to Sam, it's the pregnancy hormones hard at work. He made it a point to remind me not to tell her that though. Something about Amelia smashing a cupcake in his face when he made the mistake of mentioning that to her.

"What happens if we don't work out? What happens to Brynlee?" She looks down at her stomach. "What happens to this little girl? Are we being stupid? Selfish? If this ends, will our daughter have two parents who hate each other like mine did? Because that was a horrible way to grow up. It was painful, and I want so much more for them than that."

I take her hands in mine, wanting her to feel my strength.

Needing to ground her before she spins out. "Do you love me, Scarlet?"

She nods her head as the first tear falls.

"Because I love you, duchess. I loved the teenager you were, but that was young love. First love. I'd have done anything you asked back then and did. I hid what we had from your brothers because that's what you needed, and I was a kid who figured having a piece of you was better than having nothing." I pull her onto my lap and brush my lips over hers. "But loving the woman you've become is so much more than what we had back then. There's nothing on earth that could make me hide how I feel about you now, Scarlet. I don't want to be your friend. I want to be your everything. I want to be your lover, your protector, your partner. I want it all."

With our foreheads touching, she kisses me, then whispers against my lips, "I think you're the only person I've ever loved, Cade."

"I know your parents fucked up your views on marriage and love. But we're not your parents." Scarlet wraps her arms around my neck, and I'm enveloped in the spicy vanilla scent that's only ever been hers. "We're not going to agree on everything. We're going to fight. We're going to get frustrated and mad. But the key is going to be never giving up. We can't ever stop fighting for us. Because we're worth fighting for. I know you've got to feel it too."

"I do feel it, Cade. But I'm broken."

My girl looks terrified. "Scarlet . . ."

"What if I can't do it? I've spent my life letting everyone think I'm invincible. That I've got all the answers. That nothing they say or do can affect me. What if it's all a lie? A façade? What if I'm not strong enough to give you want you want? What you need and our girls deserve?"

My rough palms rub her bare arms, leaving goosebumps in their wake. "Then you let me be strong enough for the two of us. Outside these walls, you can be whoever you need to be. The King in charge of her kingdom. Be strong. Be fierce. Be whatever you need to be. But inside these walls, just be yourself. And if that means you need to lean on me for strength, then let me give you mine."

With tears streaming down her face, Scarlet moves one leg to the other side of my lap, straddling me. Her hands skim up under my shirt as her lips slide over mine. "I need you, Cade. I need to feel you. To feel us."

My thumbs swipe the tears away from her eyes. "Duchess . . ." My face gives away my hesitance.

"Ignore the tears. It's the hormones. They're happy tears." She tugs my shirt over my head and drops it to the floor before adding her own to the growing pile. Her fingers trace the muscles of my chest, followed by her tongue. "Have I told you how much I love your body?" Teeth scrape along my nipple, sending a shiver down my spine, before she stands up and slides my shorts down, followed by hers.

From behind, you can't even tell Scarlet's pregnant. But from the front . . . there's no denying this incredible woman is carrying my baby. And it is so fucking sexy. My hands reach for her.

Needing to feel her skin.

To worship her swollen breasts.

To love her.

But Scarlet has other ideas. She drops to her knees, her breasts bouncing at the abrupt movement, and my cock jumps at the sight. Her small hands wrap around my cock and pump me once . . . twice.

"Duchess—"

Her pink tongue darts out and swirls around the tip of my dick as she licks a pearl of precum and smiles. And holy hell, my entire body comes to life. She lifts her midnight-blue eyes and looks up at me through long dark lashes as her soft hands cup my balls. "Jesus . . ." I groan and anchor my fingers in her hair as Scarlet swallows me down her throat, tugging at what little restraint I have. Her soft, warm, wet mouth gliding up and down my cock in a torturously slow pace, combined with the friction of her tongue and the sound of her moan, give me sensory overload.

My spine tightens, and my hips jerk up at the exquisite sensation, and Scarlet speeds up in response.

But this isn't how I'm gonna come.

Not tonight.

I move my hands to her shoulders and tug. "Come here, duchess. Let me love you."

She takes me deep once more, hollowing her cheeks and sucking with a pop as she pulls away and pouts. "Fine." Her palms press against my chest until I lay down on the couch, and I let her think she's in control. "But I want to ride you tonight."

Like I'm gonna tell her no. I move a pillow behind my head so I can watch her with ease and dig my fingers into her hips as she lowers herself slowly down onto my dick.

"Mmm. You feel so good, Saint." Her body shimmies, and her breasts sway as she takes me inside her.

Stretching her.

Filling her.

She rests her delicate palms against my pecs once she's fully seated and starts to slowly rock her hips, her wet pussy grinding against me.

My hands cup her perfect ass. Fingers sliding forward to dip in her drenched sex before they slide back up to her perfect puckered hole, pressing just enough.

Scarlet throws her head back and moans.

"That's it, duchess. Take it all."

One of her hands slides up her beautiful body and cups a breast, then tweaks her nipple, eliciting another moan, so I sit up and band one arm around her waist, then take that breast in my mouth, tugging on her perfect pink nipple with my teeth while her walls tighten around me. "God, I love fucking you. You were made for me, Scarlet."

Her fingers lace through my hair and pull. "Make me come, Cade. I need to come."

I lift my hips, thrusting up with each grind of her hips. "Mine. Only ever mine."

Our mouths crash together in a tangle of tongues and teeth.

We swallow the moans and the screams as we push our bodies higher until we can't take any more. Can't hold out any longer. Her tight heat swallows me whole, clamping down on my cock, milking it as my stomach tightens when I finally let go of the orgasm that's been building.

"I love you, Scarlet Kingston." I push the curtain of her hair away from her face and hold her to me.

She grazes a spot at the hollow of my throat with her teeth before resting her lips there and licking it with her tongue. "Don't ever let go, Cade."

"Never."

CADE

THE FIRST TIME CRUCIBLE SPONSORED THIS EXHIBITION, MY dad had no idea what he was doing. We figured it out as we chugged along. That first year, we were able to host it at the gym because it was a new and relatively small event, but we still managed to raise a few thousand dollars for charity and were happy with the result.

By the time we started planning it the following year, I had begun making a name for myself in professional fighting, and we were able to leverage that to draw in a bigger crowd with deeper pockets. That meant we needed a larger space to accommodate everyone. That was the first year we moved the exhibition to the 2300 Arena in South Philly, just a few minutes away from the legendary Blue Horizon boxing gym. That place may have closed when I was a kid, but its legacy is a Philadelphia legend.

The 2300 Arena seats two thousand, and this year, we sold the place out.

I'd hoped my parents would fly up for the event. I'd like them to meet Scarlet. But they had other plans. Mom said they'd be up for a few weeks once Scarlet had the baby. She said they'd be more helpful then. Not that I can imagine Scarlet accepting help, especially from a virtual stranger.

Imogen and I watch as they finish setting up the cage in the center of the arena. The event doesn't start until seven tonight, but we all have to be back to mingle before the doors open at six. Each fight consists of three, five-minute rounds between two professional fighters. One retired, and one up-and-comer. It's all for charity, but one of the up-and-comers will likely attempt to take the opportunity to make a name for himself.

I'm not worried.

But I hope my opponent isn't that guy this year.

I don't feel like embarrassing him in front of two thousand people.

"You about ready to leave?" Imogen bumps me with her shoulder, clearly already over the amount of work that's gone into today.

"I appreciate everything you've done to pull this together, Gen. You really did a great job."

She stuffs her hands in the pockets of her shorts and doesn't look up. "Yeah well, having Scarlet to bounce some things off this year really helped. I hate to admit it, but she's good."

"You ever gonna tell me what you've got against Scarlet?"

Imogen mumbles something, but I can't understand her.

"What are you, five? Just say it."

"Fine. Whatever. I was always a little jealous of Hudson's sisters. They make it look so easy." Imogen's pale skin turns a flaming red to match her fiery red hair.

I tug her back around, forcing her to look at me. "Make what look easy?" Sometimes I fucking hate being a man because if growing up with two sisters has taught me anything, it's that they speak an entirely different language than me.

And I learned early on to tread lightly when trying to translate it.

"The whole fancy girl thing. They know how to dress. They know how to speak. They know how to attract every man in the room. It's annoying and frustrating and so fucking intimidating. And Hudson and Sawyer both hold them up on pedestals, like they're the most precious things in the world." She looks up at me like I'm stupid. "It's really annoying."

I wrap an arm around my sister that she promptly shakes off. "I hold you up on a pedestal."

"No, you don't. You treat me like one of the guys. Just like Dad did. Just like everyone in the gym does. And everyone in the band and bar do."

Oh, shit. This may be a bigger issue than I thought.

"Whatever, Cade. It's fine. I guess I just really didn't want to like her in the beginning. I convinced myself she was a stuck-up bitch and you were too good for her." I try to interrupt her, but she doesn't give me a chance. "But I was wrong. She's not so bad. She's actually pretty cool once you get to know her. And she loves Brynlee."

Gen hip-checks me, then wraps her arm around mine. "I think she even loves you too. So I'll admit I was wrong. But if you tell her I said that, I swear to God, I'll cut your balls off with dull kitchen shears, then make you watch while I pop them like tiny little balloons."

The pain I feel in my abdomen from that horrifically detailed visual has me covering my balls and turning away from her. "What is wrong with you?"

Her brows lift as she smiles. "I was raised in the gym. Did you expect anything less?"

"Are you telling me this is going to be Brynlee in twenty years?" Jesus. I think I need to lock my little girl in a tower.

"Maybe." But as Hudson approaches us from the other side of the cage, her smile fades. "I'm outta here. I'll be waiting in the car."

Gen walks away without looking back as Hudson joins me.

"What's up with her? You two have a fight or something?" The words leave my mouth before I think better of it.

"Yeah. Or something." He stands next to me as we watch the final pieces of the octagon being put together.

I'm not sure why I'm asking. I don't think I actually want to hear the answer. But I must be a glutton for punishment because I ask anyway, "Do I want to know?"

"Nope." Hudson pops the "p" at the end of the word and shoves his hands in the pockets of his cargo shorts, the same damn way my sister just did.

I drag my hand down my face. I can't fucking believe I'm about to wade into these waters. "What happened?"

"Not happening, Saint. Remember what you told me a few months ago?" When I look blankly at him, he continues, "If you've got questions, ask your sister. But know that absolutely nothing happened between the two of us." He turns to leave. "I'm outta here. I'll see you tonight."

The women in my life are driving me crazy. And the guys aren't any better.

SCARLET

"CADE LEFT FOR THE ARENA AN HOUR AGO, AND I'M STILL trying to decide what to wear." I hold my black empire-waist dress up in front of the mirror again. "Seriously, Amelia. How did you always look so cute when you were pregnant with Maddox? I feel like a beached whale."

My sister stares back at me through FaceTime. "You don't look like a beached whale yet, Scarlet. That'll come in a few more months. Now, which one is more comfortable? The black or the green?"

"The green. But it isn't as dressy." I pick the green maxi dress up from the bed and hold it in front of the mirror. It crisscrosses over my chest with contrasting piping, cap sleeves, and a ruffle at the bottom. It's also the color of Cade's eyes.

"That one, Scar. Definitely the green. Put it on, and let me see." She waits patiently while I slip it on and fluff my hair. "Yup. That one. It's perfect."

I slide my slightly swollen feet into my favorite pair of heeled espadrilles and grab my purse. "Thanks, Amelia. I owe you one."

Laughter flutters through the iPad. "Oh, yeah. It was really rough helping you pick something to wear out of your dream closet. Be careful in those heels, Scarlet. You're seven months pregnant. Your balance isn't what it used to be."

"Blasphemy. I'll have you know I plan on walking into the delivery room in heels." A quick look at the time, and I realize I'm already running behind. "Damn. I've got to go, Amelia."

"Have fun. I can't wait to hear all about it." The iPad moves, and I'm able to see my sister sitting on the floor of her living room, surrounded by squishy blocks.

"Are you sure you don't want to come? I'm sure I could find you a ticket."

My nephew army crawls toward her on chubby little arms and legs. "Nope. I'm good here with the little man. But say hi to my husband for me."

A pudgy hand moves toward the camera before the call cuts off.

I guess it's time to go.

It's not a long drive from my condo to the arena in South Philly, and traffic is light for a Saturday night in the city, so I somehow manage to make it to the event on time. Once I get to the door, security whisks me to what they're using as the backstage area tonight. A handful of fighters and their teams are scattered throughout the large room. Everyone is in their own camp. This may be an exhibition, but judging by the unsmiling faces back here, they're still taking this seriously.

You can taste the testosterone in the air.

After a moment, I spot Cade and the guys from Crucible in the far back corner. And oh, my . . . my man is breathtaking. His black grappling shorts stretch across his muscular thighs. His chest is bronzed from the summer sun. Every sinewy indent and hard-earned muscle is on full display, and I have to fight the urge to run my hands over his chest. I've seen Cade fight on television, but never in person. If I had, I might have kickstarted our new relationship years ago. How anyone could possibly resist all that is beyond me.

When he runs his black-gloved hand through his dirty blonde hair and smiles at me, my body goes up in flames.

Desire courses through my veins.

Pregnancy hormones are no joke.

I swear I used to be someone who would never have even considered PDA. Now I have to take a moment to compose myself, so everyone doesn't know I'm remembering the way Cade made me come on his face last night.

When did I turn into this person?

Instead of dwelling, I navigate the crowded room and join the Crucible corner.

Cade's hands immediately lift to my face and my baby bump, cradling both as his lips brush gently over mine. "Hi, duchess."

I glance around at the guys surrounding us, who are now whistling as if they've never seen a chaste kiss before. Pulling back slightly, I greet them all with my middle finger raised, then turn my attention back to Cade. "It looks like you've got a great turnout. The arena is packed. You ready for your big fight?"

"You worried about me, Scarlet?" Cocky green eyes sparkle back at me.

I lean in and brush my lips over his ear. "Of course not. I just want to know how long it's going to take you to finish this so you can take me home. Your sister is keeping Brynlee tonight. We have the house to ourselves."

Imogen clears her throat. "Um, you know I'll still be there, right?"

I guess I wasn't as quiet as I thought. "You might want to sleep with headphones on then."

"Oh, come on. Just go to your place instead of his. Ewww." Imogen sticks her tongue out and fakes a gag.

I wrap my arms around Cade's shoulders and squeeze him as I kiss his cheek. "Kick some ass tonight, Saint." I don't wait for the heckles I know are coming from the peanut gallery and quickly walk away without looking back.

As I walk down the aisle, looking for my family occupying the row closest to the cage, Hudson stands in the middle of the octagon with a mic in his hand, going over tonight's rules with the audience and letting them know all the ways they can help make a difference. One hundred percent of the proceeds from the merchandise, silent auction, and donations are being distributed between a few different local veteran's charities.

I take the open seat between Lenny and Max and wait anxiously for Cade's fight.

I know it's the final one of the night, but I had no idea it was going to take close to two hours before he'd come down the makeshift tunnel. All the fighters have put on a good show. And Hudson has hammed it up in between rounds and matches like the hot dog he is.

The air in the arena is thick with excitement as a heavy beat begins blasting over the speakers to a song I don't know while Hudson stands in the center of the ring. "And now, for the final fight of the night, we've got a local up-and-coming heavyweight fighter with four wins to his name this past year. Standing at six-foot-five and weighing in at two hundred and sixty-one point five pounds, put your hands together for Jake 'The Snake' Jones."

The lights lower, and the crowd cheers as what seems like every person in the arena starts clapping their hands or stomping their feet while they nod in time with Johnny Cash's "God's Gonna Cut You Down." This tells me Cade is heading slowly toward the cage.

"And now, the brains behind this event. Philly's own former MMA champion and my favorite trainer." Hudson winks at Cade. "Standing at six-foot-five and weighing in at two hundred and fifty-one pounds neat, Cade 'The Saint' St. James!"

The crowd roars with excitement.

He looks like a god in his black shorts and black robe. As he walks by me, the Crucible logo stitched in a dark green across his back shines. The hood's up over his head, so I don't see his eyes until he removes the hood at the foot of the stairs.

I watched all his fights on television back in the day, but nothing compares to the chills overcoming my entire body when I see the fierce look in his eyes as he gets patted down by the ref before he climbs the steps of the cage and goes through the gate.

I turn to Max. "This is for charity. He looks like he's gonna kill somebody."

"He's a professional, Scarlet. I don't think you've got to worry about that." Max laughs, and I look back at the cage where the ref goes over the last-minute instructions. "But I wouldn't want to be his opponent."

Yeah. Me either.

Then suddenly, seeing The Snake stretching his arms out as he swings them by his side and bounces on his toes, my heart decides to take up residence in my throat. It was easier to watch this from the privacy of my own home when I was in denial about being in love with The Saint.

The bell rings, and the two fighters tap gloves.

Cade turns his head and smiles at me, showing me his dark-green mouthguard.

He takes a step back, giving his younger opponent a chance to get his footing in the ring.

They trade a few jabs, trying to give the people a show

Then The Snake throws some kind of high kick that looks like it's going to connect with Cade's jaw but doesn't.

It barely misses when Cade steps out.

I grab Max's hand. "Did this guy not get the charity memo? This is for fun. What the hell?"

Cade bounces on his toes, ready for this guy's next move. Throwing blocks with his arms. Making it look easy. Like he's not breaking a sweat. I guess it is for him. But I feel like I'm going to puke every time a hand or foot comes near his face.

They each go to their corners after the first five-minute round ends. It's easy to hear Jax, who's changed out of his fighting gear after winning his earlier match and is cornering Cade. He's bitching about how close a few of those moves came to connecting. But I can also see the smile on Cade's face clear as day. He loves this. He nods his head toward me as the bell rings again, and his mouthguard goes back in.

It's not long into the second round when my man's had enough.

I see the look in his eyes change. He was enjoying this. Now, he looks feral.

And the next time his opponent misses his mark with his leg, Cade connects his foot with the guy's jaw.

That's it.

Everyone in the arena watches as The Snake falls to the mat and bounces from the momentum.

He's out cold.

The Saint wins again.

CADE

"I HAD TO TAKE MY SHOT, MAN." JAKE OFFERS ME HIS HAND IN the dressing room after the fight's over.

"I know you did. But your cockiness cost you. You've got a lot going for you, kid. But you've fought cake fights till now. Your manager isn't doing you any favors. If you ever want to train at Crucible, give me a call." This kid has a lot going for him. But his trainer is also his manager. And he's an asshole in both positions. I pound him on the back just as Hudson escorts Scarlet into the dressing room.

The smile on her face drops when she sees who I'm talking to and marches across the room. She hooks her arm through mine and stares at Jake. "Didn't anyone tell you this was an exhibition?" My ice queen looks him over from head to toe and practically snarls at him.

"Hey, now. I'm the one who got knocked out, ma'am." When he smiles, twin dimples pop in his cheeks, making him appear even younger than he already is.

Jesus. I was fighting a baby.

"Serves you right. Are you even out of high school? What are you? Fifteen?" She turns her back on Jake and throws her arms around my neck. "I did not like watching that at all."

I run a hand down her back. "I'm fine, duchess. I won."

"You let him hit you." Oh, this woman. She owns me entirely.

I take a step back and grasp her face in my hands. "I hit him harder, duchess."

Scarlet lifts up on her toes and kisses me in front of everyone. It's a claim, and it's fucking perfect. "I love you. Now take me home."

Scarlet pulls out of the parking lot and laces her fingers through mine. "Are we going to my place or yours?"

"You know, duchess, if you'd just move in with me, there wouldn't be any question about whose place we're going to."

She ignores my question and turns toward the city. "My place it is, then."

"You didn't answer my question." I bring her hand up to my lips and kiss her knuckles, but she just smiles and pulls her hand away.

"That's because you didn't ask one."

"Move in with me, Scarlet." We've talked about it a few times over the last month but have always been interrupted. "You, me, Brynlee, and Baby St. James. You know we need to come up with a name still."

She laughs and turns toward her condo. "You're right. We haven't come up with a name yet. What do you think of Olivia?"

"Olivia St. James . . . I like it. Think of how much easier it'll be after she's here if we're living in the same home."

Once we're at a red light, she turns her head toward mine. "You want me to move in for the baby?"

"I want you to move in because I love you, Scarlet. And I don't want to waste any more time. We've wasted enough." She stares at me. No snarky retort at the ready until the light turns green and the car behind us beeps.

"Fine. I'll move in with you." Scarlet sounds like a petulant child, and it takes more strength than I needed for my earlier fight not to laugh at her.

"I love you, Scarlet."
"Yeah. Yeah. Yeah. I love you too."

SCARLET

"I SWEAR IT'S A GOOD THING I LOVE YOU BECAUSE YOU SMELL worse than the Kings locker room." I try to back away from Cade as he wraps his stinky arm around me in retaliation, but the elevator wall blocks my escape.

"How about you help me get clean before I get you dirty, duchess?"

I love this.

I love playful Cade.

When the doors of the elevator slide open, I scoot under his arm and dart to my condo with Cade hot on my heels. His mouth lowers to my shoulder as I unlock the door. "I can't wait to get inside you. Seeing you there, watching me fight . . ." he growls.

"Oh, yeah? Did you like that?" The teasing tone of my words promising him all sorts of other things he likes tonight.

One hand smooths down my side as his teeth lightly scrape against my skin. He pulls me back into the impressive erection straining against my ass, and need pools in my belly. "The question is . . . did *you* like it?"

I push the door open and spin to face him, throwing my arms around his shoulders as he lifts me from the ground. "I fucking loved it." My lips crash down on his as I push my tongue into his mouth.

Cade shoves the door closed and carries me into my condo.

In my lust-filled haze, I think I hear a throat clearing behind us.

It takes a moment to register.

Oh dear God. I know that awful sound.

"Oh, no." I tear my lips from Cade's as he places me back on my feet, and I lean my head against his chest for a split second to gain my composure before turning to face Adaline. "Mother. What are you doing in Philadelphia? And in my condo, no less?"

She's sitting at my dining room table in a pink Chanel sheath dress and gorgeous matching shoes. Not a single, perfectly dyed hair is out of place as she flips through this month's *Vogue* with a glass of wine in her hand and a half-empty bottle resting next to her.

How the hell did she get in here?

A pit begins to form in my stomach.

This can't be good.

"Darling." She stands and extends her arms toward me. "It's good to see you." She takes a few steps in my direction, then glances over my shoulder at Cade and scrunches up her nose, then lowers her voice. "Does he usually smell like this, dear?"

I grab Cade's hand and pull him next to me. "Cade just won a fight, Mother. It was an exhibition his gym hosted that raised hundreds of thousands of dollars for local veterans." Why, why, why do I revert back to a child trying to gain my mother's approval whenever I'm in her presence?

Cade offers Adaline his hand. "Nice to see you again, Mrs. Kingston."

Adaline refused to change her last name when she divorced my father. She always said it was because it was Max, Becket's, and my name, but we all agree she likes the notoriety that comes with it more than she cares about any connection to us.

She eyes Cade's hand like it's a fly she'd like to swat before bringing her eyes back to mine. "Darling, perhaps you can ask your friend to leave so you and I can talk."

Cade loosens the hold he has on my hand. I refuse to let him pull away but don't take my eyes off her. "I had no idea you were coming to town, Mother. I'm sorry, but I have plans tonight. Why don't we meet tomorrow for brunch?"

The forced smile falls from Adaline's face.

She never liked it when I pushed back.

"Really, dear. I've flown across the world to see you, and you're asking me to leave?" When I don't answer but instead continue looking at her, praying she'll just leave, she purses her lips like she just sucked a lemon, and the pit that's currently residing in my stomach begins churning like an angry storm. "Fine. We'll do this now in front of the barbarian, who I'm well aware had a fight tonight. Scarlet, how can you seriously consider having this man's child? I thought you learned your lessen after the first time he did this to you."

And there's the whole reason she came.

To ruin my life because it's not the life she thinks I should have.

Cade's hand drops mine.

I don't even know if he realizes he did it.

He sways back on his feet slightly, like he just took another hit tonight.

Except Jake The Snake and all his training did less damage than that perfectly aimed uppercut.

I knew he'd find out eventually.

I knew I needed to tell him, and I still didn't.

This is my fault.

"Get out." My words are barely audible over the ringing in my ears, so I raise my voice. "I said get out."

"You can't be serious." Shock is apparent in every word

she utters, but I'm not sure she's genuinely surprised by my reaction.

"I'm deadly serious, Mother. I want you to leave. You're not welcome here. You never were."

She reaches for me, but I step back. "Scarlet, you're not thinking straight. He has you all mixed up again. He—"

I march to the table and pick up Adaline's purse, then grab her hand and pull her to my door. "I should have done this years ago." I shove her through the door and slap her purse against her chest. "Don't come back, Adaline. You're not welcome in my life."

Adaline sputters in shock that she's being disrespected. "But I'm your mother."

"The only thing I've ever learned from you is the type of mother I do not want to be. Goodbye, Adaline." I shut the door and bolt it, then walk into the kitchen, pick up my phone, and dial the front desk of my building. "Yes, this is Scarlet Kingston. My mother has just been asked to leave my home, and she's not welcome back. Please do not let her in." I hang up the phone and finally look over at Cade, who hasn't moved a muscle since my mother dropped her bomb.

"Cade . . ."

He drops the gym bag that had been resting on his shoulder this whole time. The muscles in his face are clenched tight, and I can't read his eyes. "Is it true?"

"Cade, I—"

"Were you pregnant before? Is that why you broke up with me?" His voice is laced with hurt. With pain. But the anger I was expecting isn't there . . . yet. I take another step toward him, but he backs away. "Scarlet . . . tell me. Were you pregnant?"

I guess the other shoe is finally dropping.

Not dropping so much as catching fire. And now, I have to watch it burn.

I've avoided telling him this truth for months, not wanting to relive a single moment of finding out I was seventeen and pregnant. Just remembering the hell I went through is enough to make me taste the bile rising up my throat.

Looking back on my relationship with Cade this time, I'd like to think I'd do things differently. Tell him early on what I went through after he left for the marines. But I don't know that I would. At least for a few months, I got to know what it felt like to be loved by this man.

I wonder what Tennyson went through when he asked if it was better to have loved and lost than to never have loved at all.

Only one way to find out.

"Just stay there for a minute." He starts to speak, but I cut him off. "Please. Just give me one minute. I'll be right back." I walk down the hall to my bedroom and step into my closet, looking for a specific shoebox. One I haven't opened in ages but still know exactly where it sits on the top shelf in the far back corner. Once I have it in my hands, I bring it back out to where Cade's standing.

Exactly where I left him.

I take his hand and pull him to sit down on the couch with me.

All joking from before is gone. The happy man who wanted to do all sorts of naughty things to me has been replaced with a hard piece of granite.

"Please bear with me. I've only ever talked about this with one other person. And they were paid to listen."

He nods his agreement, and I lift the lid from the box and trace the tip of my finger over the small black-and-white ultrasound image sitting on top of the old cards and letters, ticket stubs, and dried flowers. A box full of memories of the girl I was before I became the woman I am.

Cade does as I ask and stays quiet when I hold up the old ultrasound. "Two weeks after you left for the marines, I found out I was pregnant."

CADE

"What?" I couldn't possibly have heard her right. No way Scarlet was pregnant when I left Kroydon Hills. "Scarlet . . ." She tilts her head, her soft auburn hair a stark contrast to her pale skin.

"You promised." Her blue eyes beg me to stay quiet, and even though it goes against every fiber of my being, I nod again.

"Sorry. Keep going."

She holds up an ultrasound with a date stamped on it from thirteen years ago, and my heart drops to the floor.

There's no way.

How could this be possible?

We were so careful.

How did I never know?

She holds the image reverently. "I tried so hard to act like it didn't bother me when you left. I know I told you I wanted you to go, and that the long-distance thing was never going to work out. I ended it. Ended us. But that was just a lot of big talk from a scared seventeen-year-old. I loved you in such a huge way, it was all-encompassing. You were the only person I could ever be myself with, and that was so special. I didn't want you to go. But I knew you needed to. So, I broke us."

My hand reaches for her.

Desperate to comfort her.

Not fully comprehending what she s saying.

Scarlet places the ultrasound image back in the box, then hands it to me.

As my fingers brush over it, I notice for the first time what the box is full of. I flip through old cards I'd given her. The stupid little origami birds I used to make out of my gum wrappers. The notes I'd shove in her locker when Becket wasn't with me. She has them all saved in this box.

"I broke us because I thought that's what I had to do. Then you left, and I couldn't get out of bed. I was so sad, but I was alone at my mom's penthouse, so it wasn't a big deal. She'd pop in and out like she always did, but I honestly saw her housekeeper, Sonja, more than I saw her or anyone else for that matter. Becks was staying at Dad's beach house that summer, and Max was away at college, so it was just me. And I wallowed in self-pity like only a teenage girl can. But after a few days, my sadness and wallowing turned into vomiting. And it wasn't just a queasy stomach. It was full-on can't-keep-anything-down vomiting. After two weeks, Sonja said something to my mother, who promptly informed me there were better ways to keep my weight down than bulimia."

She stands from the couch and wraps her arms around herself, covering her green dress. She's right there in front of me, but I don't think she's seeing me. Her eyes are haunted. Lost. Alone. Like I'm not there at all.

"When I finally convinced her I wasn't vomiting on purpose, she must have realized because I had an appointment after-hours that night with her gynecologist." She breathes through a dry laugh. "Because you know, no one could ever find out her picture-perfect daughter wasn't perfect. I swore there was no way I could possibly be pregnant, but she wouldn't hear me. It was the only time I ever remember my mother ignoring what I said turning out to be a good thing."

I hold up one of the old, pressed flowers from the box,

and she smiles at me. "You pulled that from your bouton-niere the night of your senior prom." She takes it from my fingers and spins it in hers. "You put it in my hair, remember? You'd just fucked me in the closet while our dates wondered where the hell we were."

"Scarlet . . ." I stand and wrap my fingers around her arms, remembering how hot it seemed at the time. She refused to let me take her to prom, so we both went with other dates when we really wanted to be with each other. Looking back now, it was cruel. She deserved so much more than that. "I can't just—"

The tears she's been holding back finally breakthrough. "You promised." She wipes her eyes. "Just let me get through this, and then I'll answer any questions you have."

"I love you."

"We'll see if you still do. So, my mom took me to the doctor's office where they confirmed I was pregnant and scheduled an abortion for me one week later."

My hands drop from her shoulders, and I take a step back.

Not sure what I was expecting her to say, but knowing it wasn't that.

"I cried the entire way home from the doctors. I didn't know what I needed to do, but I knew that wasn't it. That wasn't my answer. Don't get me wrong, I'm all for a woman's right to choose. But I wasn't given a choice. One was being forced on me." She swallows and wipes the tears from her face. "I mean, I was only seventeen, so it wasn't like I really had options. Maybe I'd have come to realize it was the right thing. Maybe not. But I never got that chance. Four days later, I woke up in the middle of the night with horrible cramps, covered in blood."

A sob rips from her throat. "I never got the chance to make the choice. It was made for me." She rubs her belly. I don't even think she realizes she's doing it. But then, she finally looks at me, and all the pain she's feeling is right there, reflected in her eyes.

"I screamed. Not from the pain. Losing our baby didn't hurt any more than awful cramps. No. I screamed because I was furious. And scared. I didn't want it to happen, but I think a tiny part of me knew this would never end any other way. Of course, my mother was actually home that night. She ran in to find out why I was screaming. And I think that was the worst part. She pulled the blankets back and looked at me sitting there in bloody sheets, and then she smiled." She puts the dried rose back down in the shoebox and picks the ultrasound image back up.

"She looked at me with that smug smile and said, *'Perfect. This way is much better. Less chance of anyone finding out.'* Any love I felt for my mother died that day, along with a piece of my soul."

SCARLET

"NOTHING IN MY LIFE HAS EVER HURT AS MUCH AS THAT NIGHT. I still remember the confusion over knowing I wasn't ready to be a mom but being devastated over what happened. I spent the next two months refusing to talk to anyone. Mom forbid me to tell anyone what had happened. Apparently, that would have been a blight on our family name. Looking back on it from an adult's perspective, I can understand why she'd think that way. But she chose not to see how acting like nothing had ever happened would fuck me up. And it really did."

It's so hard to remember the shell of myself I turned into that following year.

Cade drops back down onto my couch and stares at the floor.

He holds his shoulders tight as he tries to process everything I just laid at his feet.

So I push on while I still have the strength. "I spent the next year withdrawn. Max and Becks were away at college. You were gone. You know I've never really had a big circle of friends to start with. So I existed. I went through the motions until I graduated and left for college. My trust kicked in when I turned eighteen, so I was truly on my own for the first time. I found myself a good therapist and worked through my issues. But it took a long time to stop feeling like it was my fault. My brain knows it sometimes happens in pregnancies, and there isn't anything I could have done about it. But my heart will always hurt and wonder if what happened was my fault. Logic doesn't factor into it." My lips tremble as I tear open all these old wounds that healed so many years ago but now feel as fresh as they once were.

Cade slides my hair away from my shoulders and cups my face. Agony coursing through his veins, visible in his every movement. "There are no words that can tell you how sorry I am you had to go through that alone, Scarlet. I'm so sorry I hurt you so badly."

I step out of his hold, desperate for the distance as much as I crave his comfort. "You didn't hurt me, Cade. I had a lot of growing up to do. I was a young girl who thought she knew it all. I had no idea what a healthy relationship looked like. I'd never seen one in person. Not between my parents. Not between my mother and me. Even my relationship with my father was strained. He knew how to parent the boys. He just tucked Lenny and me into our Fabergé boxes and placed us on our pedestals. We were pretty to look at and good for decoration but not much else in his eyes. I had to learn who I was and that I was worthy. Then I needed to make my own healthy decisions as I figured out how I wanted to live my life on my own terms."

"Why not tell me years ago when it happened? My cell phone number has been the same since I was fifteen. If not then, what about months ago when we first reconnected? Why keep this from me when I should have been there to help you?"

I dig through the shoebox filled with the story of Cade and me until I pull out a bundle of envelopes tied together by a red string. They're all sealed and addressed to Cade. "I did tell you. I told you so many times. I told you twice that summer after it happened. Then I told you once I started therapy. They're all there."

I hand him the envelopes, then cross the room to stare

out my window at the city beneath us. "I'm sorry I wasn't stronger, Cade."

Cade looks at the envelopes for a long moment, then moves next to me.

His hand grabs my shoulder and turns me to face him.

What I worried I'd see in his eyes is nothing compared to the mix of hurt and anger pouring off him in waves. "Were you ever going to tell me? What the fuck, Scarlet? I didn't know my own daughter existed until she was practically dumped on my doorstep after she'd been born. Did you think I wouldn't want to know this? That I wouldn't care? Don't you trust me?"

"Cade. I . . ." I don't know how to answer him.

He drops his hand from my shoulder. "I trusted you completely. With my heart. With my daughter." He shakes his head. "Do you have any idea how hard that was? You broke my heart in high school. Then you came back into my life, and it was like things just clicked into place. They fit. We fit. It was hard to trust you, but I got over it before we became an us. It's been months. You could have told me at any point, and you chose not to. You chose to lie to my face."

"No." I shake my head. "No. I never lied."

"A lie by omission is still a lie, Scarlet." He swallows and clenches his jaw. "It's been months. Months. You could have told me at any point. But you didn't. You told me you loved me but not that we lost a baby. A baby I never knew existed."

Cade backs away from me and throws the letters I handed him moments ago at my feet. "I need some space."

"You're leaving? I thought you said you wouldn't leave, that you'd always fight for us." I may have thought I was prepared for what this would feel like, but I was wrong. Nothing could have prepared me for this—having my heart ripped out of my chest. "That's it? You're giving up?"

He shakes his head and pulls his keys from his pocket. "I need some space."

Cade walks out without so much as a backward glance.

Slamming the door behind him.

I knew this was how it would end.

But it still didn't prepare me for this misery.

CAD E

WHEN I GET HOME THAT NIGHT, IMOGEN AND HUDSON ARE ON the couch, watching the original *Harry Potter* movie like two kids. And the damn questions start before I made it to the stairs.

"Where's Scarlet?" Hudson looks around me, confused.

Gen moves a little slower. I may have woken her up. "Are Scarlet and the baby okay? Do you need something?"

"Scarlet's sleeping at her condo tonight. She's fine. Her mom stopped by, and we both just need a little space." I turn away from them. "I'm going to bed." I don't make it two steps before Hudson is next to me. Pissed.

"That must have gone well. Scarlet hates her mom. Why are you here and not there with her?" Yeah. I'd feel the same way if she were my sister. But she's not, and this doesn't concern him. Not now. Not ever.

"I'm going to bed." I get one foot on the bottom step before he opens his big mouth.

"You're supposed to be taking care of my sister, Cade. Go do your fucking job."

I don't think I've ever wanted to hit someone so badly.

But I look at Hud and see Scarlet.

He's got no idea what happened tonight.

He doesn't get to know that.

Fuck him.

But he's coming at it from a place of love and concern for his sister.

I get that. Begrudgingly. "Fuck off, Hud."

And somebody does need to check on Scarlet.

I pull my phone out and make sure she's taken care of.

Cade: Hey, man. Can you ask Amelia to check on Scarlet?
Sam: Why aren't you checking on Scarlet yourself?
Cade: We had a fight and both needed some space. She's at her place.
Sam: You left her alone?
Cade: Just ask her to call.
Sam: You're about to make enemies out of both Amelia and Lenny. You know that, right?
Sam: Bad move getting a sister involved.
Cade: Just ask.
Sam: You need me to wipe your ass for you too, Saint?
Sam: No matter what it is, you're fucking this up.

My phone rings, and I groan at Sam's name flashing across the screen. "Okay, I may grow a vagina with this conversation, but as your friend, and a man who's married to a woman who deserves so much more than me, I have to tell you, you're fucking up."

"Fuck off, Prince. We had a fight. A big one. I just need to know she's okay." I drop down on the edge of my bed and lie back. How the hell did we get here?

"You're off your fucking rocker if you think my wife is going to call her sister and then let me report back to you. That's not how this shit works. She's going to call her sister, then she and Lenny are going to come hunt you down for whatever you did to fuck shit up. Because it's always our fault. The fuck's wrong with you, brother?"

I close my eyes and picture Scarlet, her lips trembling, her fingers caressing the ultrasound as she told me her truth. A truth she'd kept from me. A fact she should have shared months ago. A reality she shared now only because she was forced to by her mother, otherwise I might never have known. A heartbreaking loss she dealt with alone.

"Fuck . . ." I drag the word out.

"Figured that all out on your own, did ya?" Sam chuffs on the other end of the phone. "Go sleep on the couch if you have to. But go back to her."

"Yeah. I hear you."

"And . . . ?" The asshole's smile might as well be glowing through the phone.

"And fuck you very much. You outkicked your coverage with your wife. You know that, right?" She's way too good for him.

"That makes two of us. But when you've got that girl, who gives a shit what everyone else thinks? Just make sure you're worthy." Sam ends the call, and I walk right back down my stairs.

Hudson glares from his spot on the couch as Imogen pops up from the other end.

"I'm going out. I won't be back tonight. Lock up behind me." I don't give either of them a chance to say anything before I'm back out the door and sliding behind the wheel of my truck.

Lucky for me, when I get back to Scarlet's, Bob is the doorman on duty, and he likes me. I also have a key to her place, so I don't have to warn her I'm coming and give her a chance to keep me out. However, as I stand outside her door, I can't decide what to do.

I'm pissed she kept this from me.

Pissed she told me she loved me but still kept it from me.

But I love her. This doesn't change that.

We don't leave. Those were my words.

I guess it's time to put my money where my mouth is.

SCARLET

I HAVEN'T MISSED ALCOHOL MUCH DURING MY PREGNANCY.

Don't get me wrong. I enjoy a glass of wine or a good dirty martini with a blue cheese olive as much as the next girl. But going without has been far from the worst thing in the world. However, replacing the glass of wine, or better yet, the shot of vodka I could really go for right now, with a cup of decaf hot tea is not really cutting it. Amelia got me one of those tea boxes, filled to the brim with different flavored tea bags.

Most of them taste like lemon furniture polish.

So I grab the vanilla and hope for the best.

It's not bad.

But it's not vodka.

It's not going to help me sleep tonight.

But hey, at least it's decaf, and I did pick the one that's supposed to have a calming effect.

So there's that.

I've just taken my first sip when the handle of my front door jiggles. And I swear to God, if one of my siblings is here, I might be the Kingston most likely to spend the night in prison tonight because there's no way I can deal with one of them right now.

The door creeps open, and I yell at them, "Go away, I'm fine." But by the time I make it to the hall, expecting to see anyone other than the man who's there, Cade is closing the door and locking it behind him.

"I thought you left." The words are out of my mouth before I have time to think better of them, but my give-a-shit-meter has been depleted tonight. "You forget something?" I hold my ground in the hall. "You know what? Don't answer that. I'm not sure why you're here, but I don't have the energy left for round two. So how about you go home, and we pick this up tomorrow?"

"That's not how this is gonna work." Cade takes my hand in his and pulls me after him. "Come with me."

Once we're in my living room, he sits me gently down on the couch and stands in front of me in the same clothes he was wearing an hour ago. Of course, I changed as soon as he left. Something I'm regretting now as I sit in front of him in one of his Crucible tanks and a pair of boy-cut, cheeky panties with my white sweater wrapped around me. Not a fashion statement. But no one was supposed to be seeing me tonight. And I'm seven months pregnant. I may still be in high heels when I walk through that door, but once I'm inside, it's comfort over fashion.

"I'm sitting. So how about you tell me how exactly this is going to work? I'm all ears." I raise my tea to my lips and blow on the hot liquid.

Cade lifts his head to the ceiling and blows out a long breath before looking at me. "Feeling feisty, are we, Scarlet?"

"I'm feeling annoyed. I'm feeling tired. I'm feeling like someone played wall-ball with my head, it's going in so many directions between you and my mother. I'm also feeling like you left and gave me just enough time to channel all my guilt and hurt into a whole lot of anger. So did you come back to talk about my feelings? Because we could be here for a long time if you did." Crossing my legs right now to add a nice little emphasis at the end of my tirade would be perfect. But since my growing belly makes that uncomfortable, I kick my legs up on my coffee table instead.

"I came here to say I shouldn't have left. I'm still mad you didn't trust me enough to talk to me sooner—"

"It's not about trust, Cade. It never was. It was about me. About my fear of ruining the only relationship I ever wanted. Why can't you see that this was the most traumatizing event of my life? My father's death and my parents' divorce aren't even in the same ballpark as this. I have so many emotions tied up in losing our baby that just the thought of it makes me want to schedule an appointment with my therapist. So, yes. Maybe I didn't make the best decision. Maybe I let my fear and pain override my common sense." I jump to my feet and immediately regret the quick movement when I wobble.

Cade's strong arms reach for my waist and steady me, but I smack them away. "You know what? Maybe I do feel feisty. You told me we'd fight and we'd disagree, but we owed it to ourselves to work through it. You told me you'd never leave."

"And you still didn't confide in me until your mother outed you to hurt me." Cade's voice rises until he's practically yelling at me. "You are the most infuriating woman."

His hand rubs my belly, and our daughter starts dancing on my damn bladder. "I'm mad as hell you kept that secret from me. It's going to take me a while to get over it."

I automatically move his hand over just a touch so he can feel our girl kicking me and leave my hand resting over his. "Then why are you here? Why did you come back?"

His other hand moves to my lower back and rests under my tank against my skin. "Because I love you, Scarlet Kingston. Nothing you can do is going to change that. I was mad earlier and needed a little space, but I shouldn't have left. I chose you. I will always choose you. But it's not easy for me to know I failed you."

"You didn't fail me, Cade. But you proved my greatest fear was right when you left. Every time I wanted to tell you about that first pregnancy . . . every single time I considered it, I backed out because I was scared it would push you away. I knew I needed to tell you, but I wasn't willing to give you up, and my biggest fear was that I'd lose you if I did. Can't you see it's not that I don't trust you? I trust you with my life. It's that I'm worried I broke us once, and that this would break us again."

Cade wraps his arms around me and pulls me to him until his chin rests on my head. "And then I went and proved you right when I left."

"I'm usually right, St. James."

He kisses the top of my head. "I'm sorry I hurt you."

"I'm sorry too."

I yelp when he lifts me, cradling me in his arms. "Let's go to bed, duchess."

Cade gently lays me down on my bed before kicking his sneakers off and turning off the lights. "I still need to get a shower. Do you mind?"

"Go." I tuck my feet under the blanket and watch him strip out of his shirt.

He drops his shirt on the chair in the corner of my room. Then he leans over the bed and kisses me sweetly. "Are you okay with me sleeping in here, or would you rather I take the couch?"

My hands tug at his face, deepening our kiss. "Shower. Then come to bed."

He doesn't shut the bathroom door when he turns the shower on.

Steam billows out into the darkness of my bedroom, and the calming sound of the shower lulls me to sleep.

Later, when the bed dips down under Cade's weight, strong arms pull me toward him, and wrap around my body. He spoons me from behind, one hand wrapped around my belly and the other positioned under my head. Heat radiates from his skin, and I'm suddenly awake and very aware of the fact he did not bring clean clothes to change into.

His lips brush the shell of my ear as he whispers, "Sleep, duchess."

"You're not making that easy when you come to bed naked, Saint." I wiggle my ass back into his hips.

"I'm sorry I made you doubt me. I don't know if I deserve your love, but I swear to God, I'll love you more than any man ever could." His lips skim over my shoulder, and goosebumps erupt over my skin.

I slip my arms out of my tank and drop it on the floor. Then, with the grace of a beached whale, I shimmy out of my cotton panties and kick them off the bed. "I love you, Cade. I think we've earned our happily ever after."

He lifts my leg up and rests it on top of his thigh, opening me up to him from behind. The cool air of the room feels so good against my hot pussy as his fingers work me into a slow frenzy.

"I didn't know you believed in fairytales, duchess." One hand gently wraps around my neck and holds my face.

I lick one of his fingers and suck it into my mouth, eliciting a delicious groan.

"I don't believe in fairytales. No one is going to come in and save us. But we've put in a lot of years working for our happiness. We've earned it. And I love you. Now make me come."

"As you wish."

He takes my lips in a punishing kiss.

Pushing his tongue into my mouth.

Owning me as he surges up with his cock. Making me his.

"Jesus. Your pussy is so fucking hot. So tight." He reaches around and fingers my clit while he fucks me from behind, and my entire soul catches fire. "I will love you until the day I die, Scarlet. Always you."

I turn my head and wrap my hand around his neck. "Always us."

"Always us, duchess."

SCARLET

I WAS MORE SHOCKED WHEN LENNY TOLD ME SHE WANTED TO get married in August than I was when she told me she was pregnant. Not because I didn't expect her to get married. She and Sebastian have been engaged for over a year. And truth be told, we all knew it was going to happen before he made it official. Lenny had no desire for a big, over-the-top Kingston wedding. The only person pushing for that was Max. I think the weight of being head of the family weighs on him more than we realize.

But even knowing she wanted something small and informal, I was still shocked when she announced she was getting married in August. While our lives may be our own, for most of us, they still revolve around football. And her husband is one of our best defensive ends.

With a bit of scheduling luck, though, she managed to pick that sweet spot in August. Our final pre-season game was last week, and our first home game of the regular season is next week. Apparently, this was the only Saturday that worked for Sebastian and Lenny as well as his two best friends, who both play for the Baltimore Sentinels.

And what does all this mean? It means I am eight and a half months pregnant, and even though the sun is setting, it's still ninety degrees outside, and I'm melting. For now, Lenny, her best friend, Juliette, Amelia, and I are in Lenny's old room, where it's at least air-conditioned, while we wait for Max to tell us it's time.

"You've still got time to run, Lenny Lou. I might not be able to move quickly, but I'm sure I could rustle up keys to a getaway car." I *seriously* don't move quickly anymore. I waddle. But I waddle in style, damnit. Even if the style is a little larger than it used to be.

Lenny gives me the finger, eliciting a laugh.

"Always keeping it classy, Len."

A light knock sounds against the door before a little strawberry-blonde head pops in. "Scarlet . . . ?"

"Yeah, baby. Come here." I hold my arms out for my girl.

"Daddy said to ask you if you had a rubber band for my hair. It's really hot outside." She wipes her little brow dramatically, then looks over at Lenny. "Wow . . . You look like a princess."

She's right. Lenny looks just like a princess. Her dark-brown hair is piled in curls on top of her head, and diamond stud earrings sparkle in her ears. A stunning, satin, strapless empire-waist gown that nips in under her chest with a light lavender ribbon accentuates her athletic frame.

No baby bump in sight for her yet.

It's understated and elegant and perfectly suits my sister.

"Well, so do you, little miss." Lenny bends over to give Brynlee a kiss, and my heart smiles.

"Wanna see the best part?" The excitement of the day is reverberating through Brynlee's little body. "Look what happens when I twirl." She spins in a small circle, and her pretty little white lace dress with a pale purple ribbon matching my sister's spins out around her legs.

Lenny and Bash asked Brynlee, Madeline, and Declan and Annabelle Sinclair's two daughters to be their flower girls. They didn't want a big wedding party. Juliette is Lenny's maid of honor, and Sam is Sebastian's best man.

When Max knocks on the door and tells us it's time, all thoughts of fixing hair are entirely forgotten. Instead, I pull

BROKEN KING

my sister into my arms. "I love you, Lenny Lou. I'm in awe of the woman you've become. Your mother would be so proud."

She wipes her eye. "Don't make me cry now. I'll ruin my makeup."

I squeeze her hand, throw a smile Amelia's way, and kiss Max on the cheek. Then I take Brynlee's hand in mine and get her where she needs to be with the other girls and the wedding coordinator. "I'm going to go sit with Daddy. You be a good girl and listen to the coordinator, okay?"

Her curls bounce against her shoulders as she nods.

"Love you, baby."

"Love you, Scarlet."

When I sit down between Cade and Becket under the stunning white wedding tent adorned with twinkling lights, fresh flowers, and greenery, I can't help but tear up even more than I already have.

It's perfect.

I slip my hand in Cade's and rest my head on his shoulder. "I love you, Saint."

"Love you too, duchess." His lips press against my head, and Becks gags.

After the ceremony ends and dinner and dancing begin, very few people actually sit back down. There are less than fifty of us here, and everyone is having a wonderful time. There's been quite a baby boom happening in our world lately. Nearly all of Lenny's friends are pregnant, but most of them aren't showing yet. I wouldn't have guessed this had Len not told me. But when my starting quarterback's wife, Annabelle Sinclair, sits next to me, not as pregnant as me but still clearly pregnant, I start to wonder what exactly is in the water around here.

259

She mimics me and kicks her feet up onto a chair next to her, her long pale blue dress covering her legs, and a chubby little one-year-old boy asleep in her arms. Nixon no longer looks like the little baby he was at last year's games. No. Now he looks like the son of our franchise quarterback. Big. Bulky. And like he's going to tower over his father one day.

Annabelle turns to me once she's settled, and a slow smile spreads over her face. "You know, I hated you when we first met."

"Yeah." I rub my stomach where I was just elbowed from the inside and think back to nearly four years ago. "At that political fundraiser. I remember."

"You were such a bitch." The words are whispered but still sting.

She isn't wrong. "In my defense, I was only doing my job. But I'm sorry for the way I treated you."

"Here's what I know now that I didn't know then." She shifts Nixon in her arms and glances lovingly at the dance floor where Declan and Cade are dancing with the girls. "You were doing what you do best. You were protecting your player, not that he needed to be protected from me or by you. But I've watched you for years, Scarlet. Before and after I knew you were my best friend's sister."

"Oh yeah, ballerina?" I smile at the nickname Amelia's husband still uses for Annabelle. He doesn't know I called her that first. "Why were you watching me so closely?"

"Because you were everything I wanted to be. You were confident and powerful. You didn't need anyone's help. When you spoke, people listened and did as you said. And after I gave you a chance, I realized you aren't mean. You aren't the ice queen you let everyone portray you as. You're just very protective about who you show the real you to. I learned that from you."

I glance back to the dance floor to see Cade spinning

Brynlee so her dress can twirl out around her, the two of them laughing. Then I turn my eyes back to Annabelle. "What did you learn from me?" For the life of me, I have no idea what she's going to say.

"To not care what the world thinks so long as Declan and my family know the real me and love me. I learned to not worry so much about the noise around me." She lifts her crystal goblet filled with fruit-infused water to her lips. "Thanks for not being the bitch I thought you were."

I lift my glass to tap hers. "I'm not sure anyone has ever said anything quite so sweet to me before." We laugh at our strange interaction, and yet I feel we may have just erased a line. No longer Amelia's sister and Amelia's friend. Or Declan's boss and Declan's wife. I think this woman just became my friend.

Possibly my first female friend who wasn't part of my family.

Maybe you *can* teach an old dog new tricks.

CAD E

"HOW'RE YOU FEELING?" SCARLET IS GLOWING UNDER THE candlelight at the table she's been watching me from all night. Her ankles are swollen, and I know she's uncomfortable. Still, I also know she'll never leave her sister's wedding a single second early. It's late. We've been here for hours, but as the band switches to a slow song, I hold out my hand anyway. "Dance with me, duchess."

A stunning smile spreads across her face, and when those midnight-blue eyes meet mine, I know I've won. Her soft hand slips into my rough one, and I pull her up from the seat and escort her to the dance floor. "Okay. But just one dance."

Scarlet leans her head against my chest, and I inhale her spicy vanilla scent. "You having fun?"

She hums her agreement. "I am. You sure do have a way with the tiny toddler crowd."

"Are they the only ones I have a way with?" I run one hand up her neck and cradle her head, forcing her to look up at me. "I love you, Scarlet."

"I love you too, Cade. I always have."

"Is this what you want? A small wedding with just family? Or do you want a big society event?" We haven't talked about getting married yet, but she's been slowly moving more things to my house lately.

None of it matters to me as long as I get to sleep with her in my arms every night.

One of her arms circles my head while the other rests

over my heart. "You're putting the cart before the horse, aren't you, Mr. St. James? You haven't asked me to marry you yet." She tugs at my tie, then straightens it out. "But if we're speaking in hypotheticals, I don't think I'd want either."

"What do you want?"

Her smile is thoughtful and serene. "I'd want you, me, Brynlee, and Baby St. James. We don't need anyone else there. We never have."

"That sounds pretty perfect."

She wraps both arms around my shoulders and lays her head back down against my chest. "Just us."

I rest my head against hers and whisper, "Marry me, duchess."

"Okay," she agrees softly.

There's no fanfare. It's quiet and subdued. And completely us.

As the song comes to an end, she pulls her head back with a bit of mischief in her blue eyes. "Can you go grab Brynlee, then meet me on the side of the house by the old tree with the wood swing? I have an idea."

"What are you up to?" Not that it matters. I'd follow her anywhere.

She runs her teeth over her bottom lip and shakes her head the tiniest bit. "Just trust me and get Brynlee. I'll be there in a minute."

When I tap on Brynlee's shoulder and ask if I can cut in on her dance with Hudson, she giggles and throws herself at me. It's late, and it's been a long day, but this is the first wedding Brynn's ever been to, and I think she's going to be flying high from the excitement of being a flower girl for days to come. "Did you have fun, baby?"

Her mouth opens wide as she yawns. "I had so, so much fun, Daddy."

We find the old tree with the wooden swing hanging by

two thick ropes, just where Scarlet said it would be, far away from the party that's still going strong. But there's no one here. Nothing special. We're so far from the massive tent tucked toward the back of the property, I can barely hear the band.

But after a moment, I hear Scarlet.

More accurately, I hear someone telling her she shouldn't be walking through the grass in her shoes because she'll get hurt. When I see who the stupid man trying to get Scarlet to give up her heels is, I'm surprised to see Declan Sinclair steadying her as her shoes sink into the soft ground.

What is she up to?

Once she's standing under the tree with me, she takes my hand in both of hers and presses it to her lips. "Want to get married tonight, Saint? Just you, me, and Brynlee? Declan agreed to officiate."

When Brynn's head pops up, much more interested than she was a minute ago, Scarlet presses her finger against her lips. "We've got to keep it a secret for tonight, okay? We don't want to take anything away from Lenny and Bash. Can you do that, Brynlee? Do you think you can keep it quiet for a few days?"

"I promise," Brynn tries to whisper, but I'm surprised everyone within five square miles didn't hear the excitement in her voice.

I place Brynlee on her feet between us and search Scarlet's face. "You sure this is what you want?"

"It's all I've ever wanted and everything I thought I'd never have."

I cup her cheek. "Then let's get married."

And that's what we do.

With Brynlee standing between us, we each hold one of her hands, and then Scarlet and I link our other hands together.

And there, in Scarlet's childhood yard, I finally get to call her my wife.

We say our goodbyes quickly, not wanting to take anything away from Lenny and Sebastian, and head back home with a sleepy Brynlee.

When it's her bedtime, she asks Scarlet to read her story to her instead of me.

Is part of me a little jealous that she wants someone other than me to read to her?

I'm man enough to admit I am. But I'm also in awe of the woman sitting on Brynn's bed with a copy of *Goodnight Moon* in her hands.

When she closes the book and brushes Brynlee's strawberry-blonde curls away from her face, she leans down and kisses my daughter, then tucks her in. "Good night, sweetheart."

Brynlee sits up as soon as Scarlet does. "Scarlet, is Madeline's mommy your mommy?"

"No, honey. Madeline and I have the same daddy. But we have different mommies."

Brynn has a bit of an unsure look on her face. Her pretty green eyes are nervous. "Like me and my sister?"

"Yes. Just like you and your sister."

"What if I don't want to have different mommies?" My daughter clutches Teddy close to her chest, toying with the white bow tied around his pink neck. "What if I want you to be my mommy too? Now that you and Daddy are married, are you my mommy? I mean, there's a boy in my class with two mommies. And my friend Heather has two mommies and two daddies." She thinks about it for a hot second, and then her eyes light up with excitement. "Oh. Oh. Oh. And

Jason has two daddies and no mommies. So if everybody gets to have what they want, can't I have the same mommy my sister does? Can't you be my mommy too?"

Oh, my little girl.

She is such an old soul.

I debate for a moment whether to join in on the conversation, not wanting to interrupt. But also pretty damn sure Scarlet won't want to say anything without talking to me first. So I walk into the room and sit at the foot of the bed. Scarlet has big pools of tears threatening to fall from her beautiful blue eyes. And I want to scoop both my girls up and hold them forever.

Instead, I wrap an arm around Scarlet, then pull Brynlee onto my lap. "Everybody's family is a little different, baby. Family means a lot of things. It comes in all shapes and sizes. But do you know the most important thing all families have in common?"

Brynn's little eyes peer into mine as if I'm about to give her the answer to all the wonders of the world. "What, Daddy?" she asks breathlessly.

I kiss the crown of her head. "Love, baby. Families are made from love. And Scarlet and I both love you very much."

"Yay! It's settled." Brynlee smiles a triumphant little smile. "I love Scarlet too. So she can be my mommy."

Scarlet traces the apple of Brynn's cheek with her fingertip and looks at me, gauging my reaction.

Like there was ever any other option.

Like this woman in my arms wasn't always destined to be the mother of my children.

I nod and pull her in tighter.

"Oh, sweet girl. I'd be the luckiest mommy in the world if I could be yours."

Brynn wraps her arms around Scarlet's neck and kisses

her cheek, then does the same to me. "I think this calls for a sleepover in my room."

"Nice try, kiddo. Nice try."

SCARLET

FIVE DAYS AFTER LENNY AND BASH'S WEDDING IS MY FAVORITE night of the entire year. It's the Kings season opener. And we have one hell of a team this year. All the commentators are already calling us the frontrunners for the championship game in January. Which means we have to work twice as hard as everyone else because the stakes are already so damn high.

When you're sitting on top, people love to watch you fall.

Tonight is my first time experiencing this game as the president of Operations of the Philadelphia Kings. And while it's a little surreal and a little sad, because the position still feels like it should belong to my father, it's also exciting.

I've decided to do things a little differently than my father did.

We only had two preseason games this year, and only one of those was a home game, so I waited to switch things up until tonight.

I wanted everyone here for this.

Dad had an owner's box he filled with high-profile guests for years.

In the years since his death, we continued that tradition. Max, Becks, Lenny, and I have had to be at each game. But the rest of my siblings come when they can, and they've all come tonight because I asked them to be here. I wanted tonight to be special.

I'm almost giddy as I push open the door of a new suite and smile as I face everyone.

"You're all welcome to watch tonight's game in the traditional owner's suite if you want. But I wanted to do something new this year. I wanted a space where we could be ourselves and bring our families without putting them on display." I run my hand over Brynlee's hair and know this is the right thing to do for my family.

Lenny bounces on her toes and claps her hands like a lunatic. "This is perfect, Scarlet. What a great surprise. Why didn't we think of this before?"

We all step into the new space that's already been equipped with an Exersaucer and playpen for Maddox, as well as a toy box filled to the brim that Brynlee spots immediately.

What's the point of being in charge if I can't make it work to suit our needs?

"I've got one more announcement to make." All my siblings stop talking amongst themselves and look to where Cade and I are standing, holding hands.

My ring finger is still bare. Cade wanted to get me a ring the day after Lenny's wedding, but I wouldn't let him. The ring doesn't matter to me at all, only this man and our daughters.

"Cade and I got married last week."

A cacophony of voices all rise at once, asking questions.

Demanding explanations.

It's chaos, but everyone is smiling.

It's drastically different from when I told them I was pregnant a few months ago.

"Calm down. I know you're probably all mad that you didn't get to be there, but in a way, you were." I hope Lenny can forgive me.

"When did this happen?" Jace looks like he doesn't believe me.

Hudson appears hurt. "Why did you wait to tell us?"

I share a quick glance with Cade before my eyes lock on my sister. "I didn't want Lenny to be mad at me for stealing a piece of her night." I wince when I hear how that sounds. "And for borrowing her officiant too. We kind of stole Declan Sinclair at your wedding and asked him to marry us under the old tree."

Cade pulls me against him. "It felt like the right moment, and we wanted it to be just the four of us."

"Aww . . . That's the sweetest thing I've ever heard." Lenny comes over and squeezes me tightly. "I'm not mad. I just wish I'd been there."

"At least you didn't wait ten years to tell us about it." Fucking Becks.

"Don't be a dick, Becket." Lenny kicks his foot, then looks over to see if Brynn was paying attention to her language. "Oops." "*Sorry*," she mouths.

Cade shakes his head and runs his palm over my belly. "I guess we deserved that." He kisses my lips, and I swear I don't remember ever being happier. "Love you, duchess."

"So . . ." Becket stands next to us, with a devilish look on his face and a beer in his hand. "Welcome to the family, Saint." He claps Cade on the back. "Does this mean I get a discounted membership to the gym?"

Cade shoves him off with a laugh. "You don't pay now, asshole."

The baby kicks, and I wince and reach out for the table in front of me.

"What's wrong? Is she kicking?" Becks reaches out to rub my belly with his hand, but I smack it away. "Hey. What was that for?"

"Never touch a woman without permission, Becket."

He looks back at me with wide, offended eyes. "You're not a woman. You're my sister."

"Oh, I assure you. She's *all* woman." Cade smirks, and Becks gags.

Then, our little girl settles down, and her momma goes to work.

The first half of the game goes well. It's not hard to spend time in the owner's box and then walk down the hall to the one for the family. This level of the stadium is all boxes. There are forty total, with a Kings Club bar set in the middle. Ten boxes and the bar separate our new box from the owner's. It's a bit of a walk, but I don't mind. If splitting my worlds means I get to keep Brynlee and her baby sister out of the public eye a little while longer, I'll do anything.

I hope they both learn to love the game and this team the way I do, but for now, I just want Brynlee to have fun. And I want to be able to bring Baby St. James with me here so I don't miss any time with her.

Lord knows this team takes up a ton of my time.

I don't know if I'll ever be able to have it all at the same time.

But I'm damn sure going to try my best to find a happy balance.

And I think this is step one in that process.

As I cross in front of the VIP Club, my arm is tugged hard, and I spin around. Daria is there with her hand clenched tightly around my arm. We're lost in a crowd of people cheering as they announce Declan Sinclair just ran the final seven yards for a touchdown.

I rip my arm away from her and wobble on my black heels. "What the hell are you doing here?"

Daria has lost even more weight since she was at the house. Her hair is greasy and stringy, and her eyes are wild and unfocused. I have no doubt she's high. And for some reason, I'm her target.

"You need to get him to give me what I want." She grabs for me again, so I step back out of reach. "I just need a little more money, then I'll leave you alone. Keep the brat. Do whatever you want. But he owes me this. I could have given her away, but I didn't. He'd have never even known she existed."

I look around for one of the security detail assigned to the owner's suite but don't see any. Max has been bugging me to get a personal bodyguard, now that I'm the face of the team, but I've ignored his nagging. Damnit. I have them set up at both boxes but hadn't thought about having them escort us between the two. "Listen, Daria. You're not getting anything from us. So stop trying. Stay away from my husband. Stay away from my daughter."

"Your daughter?" She laughs hysterically. "I gave birth to that brat, and I swear to God, I'll take her back. She's mine, and if you don't give me the money I want, I'll take her as soon as you're not looking."

The fuck she will.

I plant my foot and let her grab my arm, then scream for security.

My detail might not be here, but I know there are plain-clothes officers who patrol this area.

In less than a minute, an officer removes the chain his badge hangs on out from under his shirt, then pulls Daria off me. "Are you okay, Ms. Kingston? Was this woman assaulting you?"

When I nod, Daria screams and tries to break free from his hold, elbowing the officer in the nose in the process.

"She's lying. I didn't lay a hand on her. She's keeping my daughter from me."

"She threatened to kidnap my daughter," I tell him as a crowd begins to form.

Daria kicks her legs. "She's a lying bitch."

"You're under arrest for assault of a police officer." He slaps his cuffs on her wrists, then turns to me. "I'm going to need a statement from you, Ms. Kingston."

I nod. "Thank you. Let me go let my family know, and I'll meet you after the game."

Hopefully, this is the last time we'll have to deal with this bitch.

CADE

I look up from my seat at the table when Scarlet walks back into the suite. She stands by the door in a black pants suit with a soft gold shirt hugging her bump. Her auburn locks are down around her shoulders, and those damn heels she refuses to stop wearing make her legs look a mile long. She's more beautiful today than she was the first time I saw her smile. And I'm the luckiest son of a bitch who ever walked this earth because she's mine.

I'm so damn proud of her.

She's worked her whole life for this, and she's doing it on her own terms.

I couldn't ask for a better example for our daughters.

She motions me over with a tilt of her head, and I realize her face is flushed red.

I quickly close the distance between us. "Is everything okay, duchess?"

"No." The word comes out shaky, and she grasps my hands. "Daria just tried to get me to pay her off, and when I told her no, she threatened to kidnap Brynlee right out from under us."

I raise my hands to her face. "Are you hurt?" I'll fucking kill her.

Scarlet shakes her head. "I called for security, and they arrested her." She motions her brother over, "Becket . . ."

He joins the two of us by the door of the suite. "What's up? Is it my turn to swap boxes?"

"No." Scarlet fills him in on everything she just told me, and my anger grows with each of her words. "So what do we do?"

"We go down to the station and fill out a report." He looks at me. "Did you get the restraining order after the last time?"

"Yes. I was granted temporary restraining orders for Brynlee and me. We couldn't get one for Scarlet. She has to stay at least five hundred feet from us at all times. We go to court next month for the permanent order."

"Tell me there's something we can do, Becks." Scarlet is all but begging. "She said she'd take Brynlee."

A look of determination crosses Becket's face, and I'm reminded why I'm glad he's on our side. Becks plays the part of the joker, but he'll do anything to protect his family. Within or outside of the law. "Oh, don't worry, little sister. We've got her."

Scarlet and I leave the game early to drop Brynlee off with Rylie and Jillian before Becks meets us at the police station.

We spend the next hour with Scarlet and me giving our statements as they walk us through what needs to happen.

When we finally get back outside, Scarlet leans against the truck and rubs her belly. "So, what are we looking at, Becks?"

"Well, it's two counts of violating a temporary restraining order because Cade and Brynlee were within five hundred feet of her. It's one count of assaulting an officer, another count of criminal threats. She could be looking at five to ten years in prison. But it will probably be less with good behavior." Becket hugs his sister. "She won't be bothering you again for a long time."

Scarlet kisses his cheek. "Thanks for your help, Becks. Love you."

"Love you too. Now go home and celebrate. We won." He throws us his patented, cocky grin.

I open the truck door for her, and Scarlet closes her eyes. "Winning a football game doesn't seem so important right now."

Becks covers his heart with his hands. "I never thought the day would come where I'd hear you say those words."

"Whatever. Just don't tell the others." We watch him walk away, and she leans against my chest. "Well, today was more eventful than I planned."

I help her into the truck and shut the door, rounding the front and climbing behind the wheel. "I texted Rylie. She and Jillian are keeping Brynn for the night. She's already asleep."

Scarlet closes her eyes. "I'm sorry, Cade. I didn't know what else to do."

I reach across the truck and pull her into my arms, needing to feel her. "You're safe. Brynlee's safe. That's all that matters. I wish you hadn't been put in that position in the first place. Maybe your family was right. Maybe a gilded cage is the way to go." I kiss the top of her hair and inhale her vanilla-bourbon scent.

"Hey, we've been married for less than a week. I'm pretty sure I could still get an annulment." She laughs against my chest, and I take my first deep breath since she walked into the suite and told me what happened.

"I'm sorry this happened at your first game." I wish I could rip my ex apart with my bare hands.

"Hey." She tilts her head up and kisses my jaw. "I'm okay with how today went because now it's over. We told my family about us. My daughter saw her very first Kings game." She kisses the other side. "The first of many. Hopefully, Daria is going to jail for years. And the Kings won. Do you know what would make this day perfect?"

I run my fingers through her hair. "No, but I like where you're going with this, duchess."

"A foot rub. I've been in three-inch heels for hours, and my swollen ankles are yelling at me." She laughs and pulls away. "Let's go home, Saint."

"As you wish, duchess. As you wish."

SCARLET

THE FOLLOWING MONDAY, WHEN LENNY POPS HER HEAD INTO my office, I look up from my laptop and brace myself for the fit I'm sure she's going to throw, now that it's just the two of us. I did kind of hijack her wedding, so I wouldn't exactly say it's uncalled for. "Hey, Scarlet. Got a minute?"

"Sure. What's up?" I close the article I'm reading about the team we're playing next week and take my glasses off.

Lenny takes a seat across from me with a pensive look on her face. "So, listen . . ."

"I'm sorry, Len. You have every right to be pissed—"

Lenny interrupts me with a smile, "Stop, Scar. I'm not mad. Not at all. I get it, and I kinda like that you did it then. I wish you'd have grabbed me to be there with you though."

"Oh." Well, that's not what I was expecting. "Then what's with that look?" I point my finger in a circle toward her face. "You don't look happy."

Lenny bites down on her lower lip and scrunches up her face. "Well . . ."

"Spill it, Len."

"Amelia wants to throw you a baby shower," she says quickly, like she's ripping off a Band-Aid, and I cringe, wishing she'd left it on.

"A baby shower? As in let's get a bunch of women together and play silly games while everyone guesses how much ribbon it'll take to wrap around my stomach?" Oh, no. You've got to be kidding me. Yes, we did do this for Amelia.

But it wasn't us throwing the shower. It was Annabelle. Lenny and I are not throw-a-party-for-us kind of people. Luckily, Len planned her wedding so quickly, we didn't even have time to discuss a bridal shower. I knew she wouldn't want one.

Lenny leans back in her chair and lifts her eyes to the ceiling. "I tried to tell her it was a bad idea. I knew you wouldn't be happy, but she's insistent and determined. She's already called Cade's sisters, and his parents are flying in for it. I figured the least I could do is give you a heads-up so you can be prepared."

"Oh my God. His mother? I've never met his parents. Does Cade know about this?" I'm going to kill him.

"Oh, yeah. He knows. Amelia promised to keep it small, just family. But Becks threw a fit when we mentioned it was just the girls, so the guys will be there too." Len perks up, like that should make me feel better. "It's next Saturday night."

"Thanks, Len."

She stands, and winks. "I got your back."

Thank God one of them does.

My new favorite time of the week is Saturday mornings.

It's turned into girls' morning.

I take Brynlee to Annabelle Sinclair's dance studio, Hart & Soul, for her ballet class. Then we stop in Amelia's bakery, two doors down, for a cupcake and decaf coffee for me, hot chocolate for her. Listening to her tell me all about her class with an utterly contagious smile on her face has me praying each week that she always feels like she can talk to me about anything. And swearing on all that's holy I'll do everything in my power to make sure our relationship is everything mine never was.

When we get to dance today, Belle is behind the front desk, and her twins, Evie and Gracie, are standing next to her, waiting for Brynlee. The three of them squeal when they see each other like they hadn't just seen each other yesterday at preschool. When Miss Maddie, one of the teachers at the studio, who happens to be the sister of my Kings Center, comes out to gather the girls, the three of them grasp hands and dance their little feet across the floor, giggling.

As the door to the practice studio closes, Belle eyes me up and smiles. "Come on back to my office, Scarlet. Put your feet up."

"Thanks." I follow her down the hall, past two other studios, then awkwardly sit down on a pretty dove-gray couch.

"Here." She pushes the old coffee table in front of the couch closer to me, and I slip my shoes off and put my feet up. "Want some water?"

"Sure. How are you feeling?" Belle is around five months pregnant, if I remember correctly. She's beautiful in her pink leotard and leggings with a wispy black skirt tied under her baby bump. Meanwhile, I sit here like a beached whale who was yelled at by my doctor that I had to give up my high heels this week.

One more month.

She hands me a bottle of water and joins me on the couch. "Well, I feel like I've been run over by a Mac truck. Between the twins and Nixon, I'm constantly exhausted. My brother, Tommy, is begging to be allowed to take driver's ed, and my morning sickness never got the memo that it was supposed to end after twelve weeks. I swear this is the last baby. I can't do this again. Declan may want a whole football team, but he doesn't have to spend nine months vomiting." She props her feet up next to mine and leans her head back against the couch.

"I don't know how you do it."

She taps her water bottle to mine. "We're moms. It's what we do."

The tears come fast and hard, and I have no idea what the hell's wrong with me.

I start to laugh, and they fall harder.

"Oh my God. I'm sorry. I don't even know why I'm crying. What's wrong with me?" I stand and grab a tissue from Belle's desk, then turn back to her. "I'm a mom."

She stands and wraps her arms around my shoulders. "Oh, Scarlet. You are definitely a mom. The girls came home from preschool a few weeks ago and reported to me that Brynlee told everyone in class she has a new mommy who's the best mommy ever."

I try to dry my eyes and sniff back my tears, but it's not working.

I laugh through my tears. "I can't stop crying."

"It's the hormones. This next month, they'll be awful." She hands me the entire box of tissues, and we both burst into uncontrollable laughter.

And to my absolute horror, I think I just peed.

"Oh my God, Annabelle. I'm so sorry." I look down at the damp spot on my pants and want to die of embarrassment. "I think I just peed." I look back down, and it's not stopping.

"Uh, Scarlet . . . That's not pee. Your water just broke." She reaches over to the bag sitting on the floor and fishes out her keys. "You're having the baby. We've got to go to the hospital."

"What? No. I've still got another month. I can't have the baby. Her crib hasn't even come in yet." Annabelle grabs my bag and hands me my phone.

"Call Cade."

I do as she says and hang up when he doesn't answer. Then I call Imogen, praying she's at Crucible.

She answers after two rings. "Hey, Scarlet. What's up?"

"My water just broke, and your brother's not answering his phone." I plant both feet and double over in pain. "Shit. That's a contraction."

"Oh my God. The baby's coming!" Jesus. Imogen squeals so loud, I think she may have popped my eardrum.

I breathed through what I was sure were Braxton-Hicks contractions earlier today. "Imogen. Tell Cade to meet us at the hospital. I need you to come to the dance studio and pick up Brynlee. Annabelle's taking me to the hospital." The contraction lessens, and I can finally breathe again. "Hurry." I drop the phone back in my bag and grab onto Belle's arm as she helps me walk through the hall.

Belle stops in front of the girls' dance class, then asks Maddie to come out. "Scarlet's in labor. One of Brynlee's aunts is coming to get her at the end of class. I'm going with her, and I'll call Lexi and ask her to come get Evie and Gracie."

"Whose Lexi?" I'm not sure why I ask. It's probably because I'm in denial this is actually happening today. I'm not ready. I slide into Belle's SUV and cringe as my now-wet pants stick to my legs and her leather seats.

Belle starts the car. "Lexi's my nanny. She's amazing."

"You have a nanny?" I'm not sure why that's so shocking.

The car takes a sharp right, and I don't think we even stopped at the red light we just flew by. "Hell yes, I have a nanny. I have three babies and a teenager. Declan and I both work. I couldn't imagine my life without her."

"Don't you worry about missing everything?"

The car behind us beeps as we zoom through a yellow light, and Belle gives someone the finger. "Lexi is a huge help. But she's not me. I make sure I don't miss more than I have to. You can't be everything to everyone without help. You'll burn out, and then you won't be any good to anyone. You've got to be able to take care of yourself too. You can't drink from an empty cup."

Shit. I gasp and clutch my stomach. "Oh, God. This hurts." I breathe through the contraction and check the time.

The next one comes only five minutes later.

And luckily, we're pulling up to the hospital.

Cade is standing outside the emergency entrance, waiting for me. And I desperately wish we could just go home. That this was merely Braxton-Hicks contractions. I'm not ready.

He opens my door and helps me into a waiting wheel-chair. "You ready for this, duchess?"

"Not even a little bit."

CAE

Four hours of pushing later, and I am so fucking grateful I was born a man.

Scarlet's guttural cry bounces off the walls of the hospital room as her tight grip on my hand threatens to break every one of its bones, her white knuckles a stark contrast to my red fingers. Tears pour down her cheeks as she groans and leans back against the pillow.

By the time we got into the room and first a nurse, then her doctor came in to examine her, we'd missed the window for her to get her epidural, so my warrior is doing this naturally.

Again. So fucking glad I'm not a woman.

She didn't want anyone else in here with us, so I'm helping her hold one leg up while a nurse holds the other.

I push her hair away from her face and kiss her damp forehead. "You're doing a great job, duchess."

"Scarlet," Dr. Esher looks up from her spot between Scarlet's legs. "The baby's heart rate is dropping, and you're not progressing. We need to do a c-section."

"No," she cries. "I can do this." Her grip on my hand tightens as her lower lip trembles.

The machine to her left starts beeping, and Dr. Esher stands. "It's no longer an option. We've got to go now." Things move at lightning speed as Dr. Esher starts yelling instructions at the nurse before the door opens and my wife is wheeled out.

I try following, not letting go of Scarlet's hand, but the nurse stops me.

"Cade . . ." Scarlet calls out.

"I'm right behind you, duchess." But I'm not.

"I'm sorry, Mr. St. James, but you can't go into an emergency surgery. It won't be long before you get to meet your baby. But you've got to go to the waiting room. We'll be out to get you as soon as we can." She turns and follows the gurney, leaving me alone in the vacated hospital room.

I pull my blue scrub cap off my head and throw it across the room.

When I push through the double doors to the waiting room a minute later, a horde of Kingstons descend on me, but they let Imogen through with Brynlee in her arms. "Where's Mommy and my baby sister, Daddy?"

I kiss her head, holding back tears of frustration.

As men, they teach us to be strong.

We can do anything.

Protect anyone.

I've never felt so helpless in my life.

"Mommy had to go to a room I'm not allowed in, sweetheart. Why don't you go draw her a picture, okay?" I nod at my sister, who takes Brynlee back over to the chairs as all the Kingstons begin to talk at once.

My sister, Rylie, silences them all with a look, then takes my hand in hers.

"The baby's heart rate started dropping, and Scarlet wasn't progressing, so they had to take her back for an emergency c-section. They'll come and get me once it's over." Everyone's quiet as we sit down in the hard plastic chairs to wait.

The next fifteen minutes are the longest of my life.

I watch every one of them tick by on the clock mounted on the wall, praying my family will be alright. That we didn't come all this way after all these years for something to happen now.

Scarlet would yell at me for even thinking that.

I can hear her now.

"I'm Scarlet fucking Kingston. I've got this."

I sit with my heart in my throat, feeling smaller and more insignificant than ever before. Wanting to be in that room with Scarlet. Wishing I could be the one doing this for my wife. Thinking of all the things that could go wrong while I pray for everything to go right.

When the nurse from earlier walks through the swinging doors, I jump to my feet.

She smiles, and I nearly drop to my knees in relief.

"Mother and baby are doing just fine, Dad. Scarlet is still out, but the anesthesia should be wearing off soon. Would you like to come back and meet your son?" She holds her arm out for me to follow, but I stand there in shock.

Did I hear her wrong? "My what?"

"You have a beautiful five-pound, nine-ounce baby boy. And he has an amazing set of lungs on him. His APGARs are good, and they're cleaning him up now." She guides me back to the NICU where they're assessing my son.

Holy shit.

We have a son.

And he's perfect.

SCARLET

My eyes feel like they're covered in sandpaper as I slowly try to pry them open.

The last thing I remember was being wheeled out of the delivery room and into an operating room. But I don't think that's where I am now. As my eyes adjust to the room, Cade's soft voice catches my attention.

"I think your momma is awake." He's sitting next to me in a vinyl lounge chair, and our baby girl is wrapped up in his arms. "You are my warrior queen, Scarlet." He stands, then leans down and kisses me.

"Is she okay? It's so early. She wasn't due for weeks." My hands reach up automatically, needing to hold our baby, and Cade places her in my arms.

"He's perfect," he tells me as I move our beautiful baby girl to my chest.

I pull the soft blue hat gently from her head and run my fingers over a perfect little tuft of beautiful dark brown hair to match her long dark eyelashes, then run my finger down her nose, hoping she'll open her sleepy eyes. "Why did they put her in blue?"

She immediately begins rooting around on my chest, and I open my gown to see how this nursing thing is going to go. Thankfully, she latches on right away, and it's the strangest feeling. Tightness, but not pain, and a pulling sensation deep in my body.

"Duchess . . ." Cade whispers. "Dr. Esher was wrong. *She's a he*. We have a son."

A tiny little hand pops up, and I run the tips of my finger over his knuckles until he wraps his little fist around that finger. "A son?" I whisper, knowing I heard him right but still feeling a little fuzzy.

I have a son.

Cade sits next to me on the bed and lays his palm flat against our son's back, startling him. "A beautiful son, Scarlet. His lungs are strong. He's a little small. But they said he's perfectly healthy." He brushes his lips over mine. "We should even be able to take him home in a few days."

A son.

"So, I guess Olivia is off the table now. We need to come up with a boy name." I adjust myself to get more comfortable and lay my head against Cade's strong arm as my eyes begin to close again. "What do you think of Killian?"

"Killian St. James," he tries out the sound of the name. "It's perfect."

Welcome to the world, Killian St. James.

"Do you think you're up for seeing Brynlee yet?"

I run my hand over Killian's tiny pink cheek in absolute awe. "Yes. How about you go get our daughter so we can introduce her to her brother?"

Killian's sucking slows down as his breathing evens out until I unwrap the blanket he's bundled up in so I can see all of him. Big blue eyes look up at me slowly, and I wonder what he sees.

"Hey, baby. I'm your momma."

He's so tiny.

So perfect.

With ten little fingers and ten toes.

And the most heavenly new baby scent.

And... yup, there's a penis. She's really a *he* after all.

Minutes later, Cade pushes through the door with Brynlee on his hip. She's still wearing her pink leotard and tights, but a shirt I'm guessing someone got her from the gift shop is layered over the top of it, declaring her the "Big Sister." She looks at Killian and me with wide green eyes, so much like her father's, then whispers, "She's so little."

Cade sits back down in the chair he was in a few moments ago and pulls Brynn onto his lap. Brynlee stares at Killian and me in silence.

"Guess what, sweetheart?" Her eyes snap up to mine, and unbridled excitement shines back at me.

"What?"

"The doctor was wrong. You don't have a baby sister. You have a baby brother." And I can't remember why I was so hell-bent on having a girl all along.

Brynn's head tilts to the side, and she thinks about that for a long minute. "Are we sure it's the right baby?"

Cade and I both laugh, startling Killian again.

And oh boy, laughing does not feel good now that the meds are beginning to wear off.

I have no idea what time it is when the last of our siblings filter out.

I've slept on and off throughout the day, and I'm pretty sure I saw everyone until Lenny pops into the room with Sebastian in tow. Oops. I guess I didn't see Lenny.

Sebastian averts his eyes as Killian nurses again.

No one warned me how often babies needed to nurse or that nursing exhausts you. Amelia filled me in today when I asked, but someone should seriously warn a girl about these things. I think I'm going to write my own book, *All The Things To Expect The Day You Deliver.* Because none of this was in any of those damn books.

Lenny quietly stands next to me with tears in her eyes. "You know, there were other ways to get out of your baby shower, Scarlet."

I gently shake my head. "Yes, but I figured this would be the best excuse." I pull Killian off my chest and sit him up to burp him the way the lactation specialist showed me earlier. Then, I offer my son to Lenny. "Want to hold your nephew?"

She takes him from me, and Sebastian and Cade join us as Lenny sways with Killian in her arms. "I'm in love, Scarlet. I can't believe he's a boy. I bought so many baby girl outfits."

I laugh. "Yeah. Me too. Maybe you guys will have a girl."

Sebastian pulls my sister to his side and stares down at Killian. "So long as everybody's healthy, I don't care what we have. But it would be fun to watch Maddox and Killian make sure our daughter never dates."

"Sebastian," Lenny gasps.

He shrugs. "Come on. It's funny."

"No, it's not." Lenny looks up at me. "You gonna try for a girl?"

"Spoken like a woman who did not just have her body torn apart. I'm going to try to walk tonight, then I'm going to try to sleep. I make no promises after that, Len."

She places Killian gently into Cade's arms and kisses my cheek. "Love you, big sister."

"Love you too, Len."

A week later, I carefully roll to my side in our bed and reach over to snuggle into Cade.

The bed is cold, so I sit up to look over at the bassinet that sits within arm's reach. It's empty, and the clock reads 2:30 a.m. I've been asleep since around eleven o'clock, and the sting of my heavy breasts is definitely letting me know it's time for Killian to eat.

I grab my robe from the chair it's thrown over and pull it on before I pad across the hall and peek in on Brynlee to make sure she's okay. She's sleeping soundly in her princess bed with Teddy tucked safely under her arm. Cade and I discussed it, and Becket has already started the paperwork for me to adopt her. Legally being her mother won't change the love I have for her at all, but we agreed that it's important to both of us. I pull her blanket up and tuck her in. "Sweet dreams, baby girl."

Killian's room is the next one down, and when I push open the door, I'm not surprised to find my husband sitting in the soft white glider rocker with his feet up on the ottoman. We had a crew come in and repaint the formerly pink and gray room . . . What can I say? I let Brynlee help me pick it out. It's now a beautiful pale blue with light green accents and blue and green elephants adorning the walls. His cherrywood crib stands across from the changing table and shelving unit. He won't be sleeping in here for a few months, but the chair Cade's sitting in is pretty damn comfortable.

He's in nothing but his black boxer briefs. Golden muscles are on full display as our little man lies against his chest in a diaper. He loves the skin-on-skin time with his daddy.

It's the most beautiful thing I've ever seen.

"You gonna just stand there and stare?" Cade whispers in a raspy, sleep-deprived voice as he cracks open his eyes and kisses Killian's head.

I shrug and cross my arms over my robe. "I was thinking about it. Why didn't you wake me?"

"I wanted you to get some sleep."

I reach down and take Killian from Cade's arms, then kiss my husband. "I love you."

"It's always been you, duchess."

"It's always been us, Saint."

EPILOGUE

SCARLET

"Don't cry, Mom. It'll ruin your makeup."

I suck in a quick breath and try to get my emotions in check as I pin Brynlee's veil in place. "I'm not crying. I've just got something in my eye."

Brynn looks at me through the reflection of the antique mirror attached to the dresser, and my breath catches in my throat.

"Look out. She's gonna cry now." I spin around and nail our youngest, Olivia, with a glare.

"Zip it, you." She smiles, and the twins laugh. Everly and Gracie Sinclair have been thick as thieves with Brynlee for as long as I can remember. With Olivia following them around, doing whatever she was told just to be allowed into their group. My youngest has done everything she could to keep up with her sister who's five years older than her.

But not today.

Today is Brynlee's day to marry the man of her dreams, and I've been on the verge of tears since my husband gave his speech at the rehearsal dinner last night.

I turn to face the peanut gallery. "Can you three give us a minute?"

As the door closes behind them, Brynlee faces me, and I fluff out her dress. "You're the most beautiful thing I've ever seen in my life. I'm so incredibly proud of the woman you've become." I hold back my sob threatening to break free. "Thank you for letting me be your mother." I move her beautiful strawberry-blonde hair behind her shoulders and stare at her perfection. "I love you."

"Now, you're going to make me cry. Stop." She reaches forward and hugs me tightly, the way she used to when she was little. "There was never a better mother than you."

A knock on the door is followed by Cade's voice. "It's time, Brynn. Can I come in?"

Her eyes bore into mine. "Do I look okay?"

I nod and force the words out. "You look beautiful, baby."

I turn, open the door, and step into the hall, then I cup my husband's face. He's still the most handsome man I've ever laid eyes on. "Take a breath, Saint. Try not to cry when you see her. I'll be waiting for you at the end of the aisle."

His arm wraps around my waist, and those strong lips I love so much brush over mine before he pushes through the door.

I make my way through the beautiful inn on our favorite secluded island off the coast of New England and come to a stop on the back porch. Killian is waiting there to escort me down the aisle. He looks so handsome in his tux. His dark hair is a little too long, like his father's has always been, and a mischievous look is on his face. "Ready, Momma?"

"Ready, baby." I link my arm through his and smile at my family as he walks me down the aisle. Then, I take my seat in the front row and wait for the music to start.

The twins walk down the aisle first, one after the other.

Each one gorgeous in their mint-green gowns.

Their blonde locks shining in the sunlight.

Olivia follows them.

A stark contrast to the twins with her deep red hair.

She reaches her hand out to squeeze mine as she passes by me and takes her place at the front.

And then it's time.

The music changes to an instrumental version of "Here Comes the Sun" by the Beatles, and my heart skips a beat. Cade's green eyes are watery as he walks our oldest daughter down the aisle to the man we're entrusting to love her like we do. Once they get to the front, he lifts her veil and places a kiss on her cheek before giving her hand to her fiancé and coming to sit next to me.

Our hands reach for each other automatically, like they've done so many times before, and we watch Brynlee marry the love of her life.

Later, as they're dancing their first dance, Cade wraps his arm around me and whispers, "They're so young."

I shrug. "I don't know. I think if we'd have stayed together, we'd have gotten married young. If I hadn't wasted all those years . . ." I lean my head against his shoulder and watch our daughter.

"But then, we wouldn't have had Brynlee. Everything happens for a reason." He drops a kiss on my head. "It was always going to be us, duchess."

"And it always will be, Saint."

The End

WHAT COMES NEXT?

Not ready to say goodbye to the Scarlet & Cade just yet? Don't fret. Follow the Kingston family as they each figure out what comes next while falling in love in the new series, Restless Kings.

Max Kingston's book, Fallen King, will release May 18th. Pre-order it HERE.

Want a glimpse into Max and Daphne?

CHAPTER 1 — DAPHNE

"Have you told your mom you're not going back to California yet?" The new heels I found in a local vintage shop yesterday teeter when I step in a crack in the parking lot while getting out of my car. Okay. So maybe purple satin 1950s peep toes aren't the most practical for work. In my defense, however, they look perfect with my black lace sundress, especially once I cinched my waist in with a cute belt. Once my footing is stable again, I push my earbud back in before it falls out and continue to listen as my best friend, Carys, tells me all about her crazy weekend at her stepsister's wedding.

I take two steps toward the home offices of the Philadelphia Revolution before turning back around.

Shit.

Almost left the coffees in the car.

With my laptop bag in one hand and my purse dangerously close to slipping from my shoulder, I reach back into the car to grab both coffees, then hip-check the door shut, barely managing to avoid getting any lace caught in the door in the process.

Okay. Deep breath. I think that's everything.

My first few weeks spent as my dad's executive assistant have been intense and not at all what I thought I'd be doing a month out of college. But I figured out Monday mornings are better for both of us when I make a quick stop for coffee. So that's become part of my regular routine.

"D . . . Are you even listening to me?"

Oops. "Sorry. I'm scrambling this morning." Carys and I have been best friends since we first met in our local summer theatre program. She was eight, and I was ten, and we both wanted to be Dorothy. Instead, we ended up being the Scarecrow and Tin Man, and we've never looked back.

She knows me better than anyone.

It's not like she's surprised I'm not paying attention.

"Whatever. It's fine. When am I going to see you?" Carys flew home a week ago for the wedding, and as far as her family knows, she's only spending the summer in Kroydon Hills. I'm fairly certain only her business partner, Chloe, and I know the truth.

I push through the front doors of the offices and training facilities for the Philadelphia Revolution, and the cool air chills the bare skin of my arms as I hurry along. "I thought you were coming to the house tonight for Margarita Monday."

"Sounds good. I'll drag Chloe with me. Does seven work?" The skinny bitch is finally starting to sound winded as she jogs around Boathouse Row.

"Yup. That's perfect. See you then," I huff as I make my way to the elevator, carrying all my crap. Maybe if I ran like my bestie or danced like my roommate, Maddie, I'd be in better shape, but I've never been a fan of breaking a sweat and have no desire to start now. I mean, my ass could be a little smaller or my stomach a little more toned, but if I have to wake up early and go to the gym to do it, it's not happening.

I'd rather be curvy anyway.

When I finally make it to my desk outside of Dad's office, the area is eerily quiet, which is kind of strange for a Monday morning. Once my computer is booted up, and I've checked his schedule for the day, I grab his coffee, knock on his closed door, and then wait. The shades of his office are drawn, and I'm not even sure he's in there.

"Come in," is bellowed loudly, so I guess he must be here.

I push through the door and plaster a smile on my face.

It's a fake smile because it's a Monday morning, and nobody, not even me, is happy to be at work on a Monday morning. But it's a smile, nonetheless.

My father is dressed to the nines in a three-piece suit instead of the polo and khakis he's been rocking lately. Well . . . *trying to rock*. It hasn't been a great look for him. His hair is styled, and his face is freshly shaven. Something else he hasn't been doing lately. I'm hoping it's a good sign. Maybe he's finally getting himself out of the funk he's been in. "Good morning, Dad. Here's your coffee. I checked your schedule, and it looks like the only meeting you have today is at nine. You've got about thirty minutes before it starts. The event was locked on your calendar, so I couldn't actually see what it was. Do you need me to get you anything for it?"

Dad raises his bloodshot brown eyes to meet mine. "Sit down, Daph. We need to talk."

Oh, this can't be good.

I gingerly sit down across from my father, unsure what to expect. I've been working for him for a month. We made a deal. If I worked for him as his executive administrator/office manager for one year, he'd let me create and run the Revolution's charitable foundation. Something the organization is sorely lacking.

We're only a few weeks into our deal. I haven't even had to make travel arrangements for the team yet, so I can't imagine what I could possibly have done for him to look so disappointed in me. But apparently, I'm about to find out.

I stare at my father, who's lowered his eyes to the whiskey in his heavy crystal glass. I didn't notice that when I walked in, but now that I've seen it at eight-thirty in the morning, it's hard not to stare. "Dad . . ."

His broad shoulders rise and fall with his deep inhale and exhale before he closes his eyes and raises his face to the ceiling. "There's no easy way to say this, Daphne. So I'm just going to say it. I'm selling the Revolution." He looks down at his wrist, but his Rolex isn't there. "In about thirty minutes. That's my nine o'clock. I didn't want you to know until I was sure the deal was going through."

"You can't do that." This team was my Grandpa's pride and joy. My mom was supposed to run the organization after he died, but I guess you never plan for what happens if you outlive your child. My mom died when I was five. I barely remember her. But when this office was my Grandpa's, the shelves were covered in pictures of her growing up here.

Now that I look around the room, I see nothing but boxes.

Holy shit. He's really doing this. The office is empty, ready for its next occupant.

Dad started working with Grandpa years ago, so I wasn't surprised when he took over after we also lost Grandpa a few years ago. But this . . . This surprises me.

No.

This shocks the shit out of me.

"Why? Why do this? Is it because I don't want to run the Revolution?"

"No, Daph. I got myself into some trouble, and selling the Revolution was the only answer." He runs his shaky hand through his salt-and-pepper hair, and my eyes burn as I hold back my tears. He's selling off a piece of my family's history, and he didn't even talk to me about it first.

I play his words over in my head and get stuck on one word. "What kind of trouble, Dad?"

He raises his glass to his lips and finishes the contents with a large swallow. "The kind where this was the only answer. Now listen to me. I've negotiated for you to keep your job for a while. You and most of the management are guaranteed your positions for the next twelve months. Use that time to get the experience you need so you can get whatever job you want when you're done here." When I sit there, staring out the window instead of at my father, he slams his open palm against the desk. "Do you understand what I'm saying?"

My head snaps back to him. "I don't understand any of this."

"You don't need to understand. You just need to do as you're told. Now, go set up the conference room. The Kingstons will be here soon."

ACKNOWLEDGMENTS

M ~ I am forever grateful for you.

K. ~ No bigger cheerleader ever existed. You are the Nattie to my Belles.

Savy ~ So grateful I met you when I did, Yoda. You keep everything running smoothly no matter how crazy life really is, and you do it with a smile in your voice at all times. Thank you for all you do.

To my very own Coop ~ Another one down, and now it's almost time to work on your namesake's book. This calls for a planning session. XO

Tammy ~ How have we still not celebrated with cocktails yet!?!

Vicki ~ I cannot thank you enough for loving these characters the way you do... especially Scarlet! Your notes are EVERYTHING.

My Street Team, Kelly, Shawna, Vicki, Ashley, Heather, Oriana, Shannon, Nichole, Tash, Nicole, Hannah, Meghan, Amy, Christy, Emma, Brianna, Adanna, Jennifer, Lissete, Poppy, Jacqueline, Kathleen, Diane, Jenna, Keeza, Carissa, Kira, Kristina, Terri, Javelyn & Morgan ~ Thank you, ladies, for loving these characters and this world. Our group is my safe place, and I'm so thankful for every one of you in it. Family Meetings Rock!

Sarah ~ I'm so grateful to have you in my corner. Thank you so much for putting up with me.

My editors, Jess & Dena. You both take such good care of my words. Thank you for pushing me harder, and making me better.

Gemma – Thanks for giving it that finishing touch.

Jena ~ you are so talented! Thank you for bringing these covers to life.

To all of the Indie authors out there who have helped me along the way – you are amazing! This community is so incredibly supportive, and I am so lucky to be a part of it!

Thank you to all of the bloggers who took the time to read, review, and promote Broken King.

And finally, the biggest thank you to you, the reader. I hope you enjoyed reading Scarlet and Cade's love story as much as I enjoyed writing it.

ABOUT THE AUTHOR

Bella Matthews is a Jersey girl at heart. She is married to her very own Alpha Male and raising three little ones. You can typically find her running from one sporting event to another. When she is home, she is usually hiding in her home office with the only other female in her house, her rescue dog Tinker Bell by her side. She likes to write swoon-worthy heroes and sassy, smart heroines with a healthy dose of laughter and all the feels.

Stay Connected

Amazon Author Page
Facebook Page
Reader Group
Instagram
Bookbub
Goodreads
TikTok
Newsletter

Made in United States
Orlando, FL
08 January 2025

57043208R00190